# A SKIRL OF SORCERY

## THE CAT LADY CHRONICLES
### BOOK THREE

HELEN HARPER

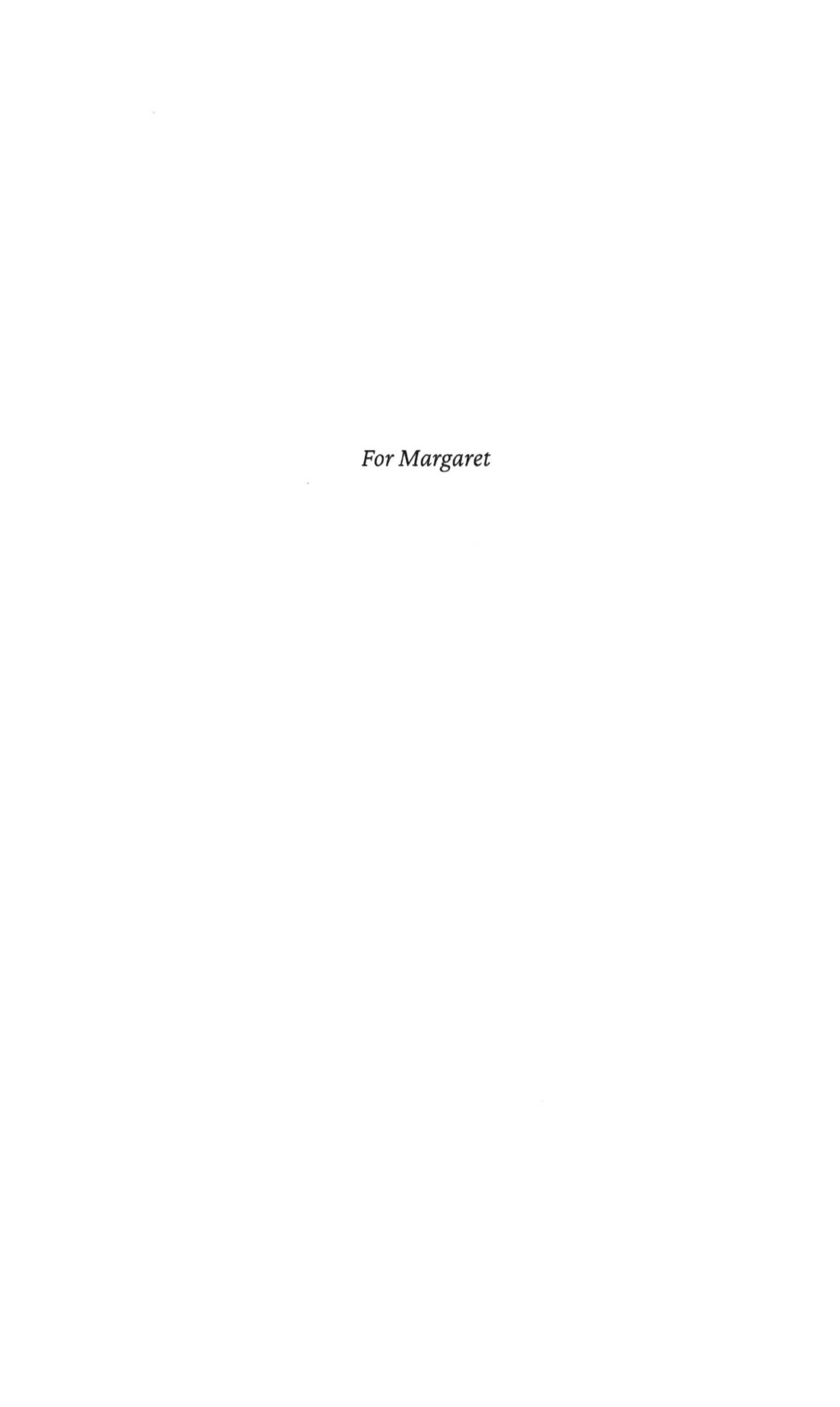

*For Margaret*

CHAPTER

# ONE

I blamed Trilby. For the past three years, I'd tucked myself up in bed at a reasonable hour and enjoyed eight decent hours of uninterrupted kip almost every single night. It was what a cat lady was supposed to do; it was what *normal* people were supposed to do when they weren't creatures of the night. Or hard-working, conscientious, well-prepared assassins.

Although I was neither vampire nor ban sith, nor any sort of darkness-dwelling denizen – and I was certainly no longer an assassin – I wasn't normal, and it was Trilby who kept reminding me of that fact. Their repeated suggestion that I was responsible for the waifs and strays of Coldstream, and in particular my own small suburb of Danksville, was the reason why I was perched on top of Mrs Jones's roof at half-past two in the morning. That, and the fact that there had been a recent spate of late-night robberies.

If I were being honest, I didn't usually spend my time railing against thieves or trying to halt their actions. Given my own past, I wasn't in a position to judge them. Most of the time they

1

didn't physically hurt anyone; in fact, most of the time they performed their burglaries and home invasions when their targets were out at work and the houses were empty. It was far safer and more sensible to steal when you weren't likely to be caught by an irate homeowner with an explosive magical spell in their dressing-gown pocket.

However, the thief currently terrorising my neighbours had decided to throw logic and reason out of the proverbial window. For the past five nights, someone had broken into twelve separate occupied properties – three of which were on my street. Their actions were causing angst in my community and I was curious why our less-than-salubrious neighbourhood was garnering such unpleasant attention.

I also wanted to know why any thief would take such obvious risks. Sooner or later somebody would end up dead, and it was likely to be the burglar. I reckoned I could forestall any bloodshed if I found them first.

A warm breeze swirled up from below, making my sleek fur ripple. Although my feline eyes could pierce the darkness and fix on any twitch or jerk from a living or undead creature prowling the night, I had yet to locate my target.

There had been two strolling vamps an hour earlier, their heads bowed together in deep conversation, and around midnight I'd spotted a boggart shuffling towards the river. I'd noted several scurrying rats and I was fairly certain the slinking figure of my old buddy She Who Hisses had been padding behind them. But there hadn't been any sign of my thief.

I turned my head left and right, then raised my front paw and gave it a vigorous lick before starting to wash my face. I might be in a temporary body, but that was no reason not to maintain standards of cleanliness. Once I was satisfied, I flexed my claws and stretched my back. Everything was in working order.

I shook out my fur and jumped to the next roof. I'd patrolled this way three times already so I'd give it another hour then call it a night. It was late April, after all, and although the summer solstice was still two months away, dawn came early at this time of year. I was determined to get at least some sleep before the business of the day began. A woman could only do so much.

I pattered along the tiles, leaping across the chimneys that stood in my way, until I reached the end of the terrace of houses. I was tempted to drop to the ground and do a swift sweep of the surrounding streets – but as soon as that thought popped into my head there was a flicker of movement to my right.

I turned. At first I couldn't see much though I could hear an odd snuffling sound. My ears twitched and I looked in the direction of the noise. A small, stout figure was shuffling through the shadows.

Interesting. From their stuttering steps and hunched shoulders, this was someone who didn't want to be seen. If it was my thief, they possessed little in the way of confidence and they didn't look as if they were someone to be feared. Quite the opposite.

Their head was bowed, making it impossible to tell what manner of Preternatural they were until they were almost directly below me. It was only when they turned to check over their shoulder that I realised: it was a male trow, likely middle aged. Huh. Trows were nocturnal creatures and if this was the thief it explained why all the burglaries took place during the night.

Unless I was mistaken, this particular trow was from the hills rather than water. Water trows were skinnier than their land-dwelling counterparts and they had gills on either side of their neck. It was odd, though: hill trows preferred the countryside and rarely ventured into the city, so there were few reasons why one would come to Coldstream.

I watched him wend his way along the road. Although my cat eyes could only decipher a narrow range of colours, I could tell that his cloak was moss green and his knee-high boots were made from supple dark leather. He was holding a drawstring bag in one hand, which likely contained the ill-gotten gains he'd garnered that night. All I had to do was establish that he was the thief who'd been skulking through Danksville for the better part of a week and my task was halfway complete.

I purred, then skittered down the roof and jumped down to the ground so I could follow him more easily. With luck, he was planning another burglary and I would catch him in the act, though if he was already heading home for the night it might complicate matters.

The trow was muttering to himself, ragged, angry words escaping his mouth with every fourth step. *Bastards. Fools. City scum*: there was a definite theme. I prowled after him, leaving enough distance not to alert him to my presence, but he seemed to be fixated on his destination and he didn't turn around again. This was too easy.

We passed house after house, some ablaze with lights as if the occupants were worried that they would be targeted next. The trow didn't pause at any of them. He shuffled past the small witchery store that contained mostly stale, useless spells that were for sale at inflated prices. He didn't glance at any of the blocks of flats that would surely have offered ripe pickings but would have made a hasty getaway difficult. He ignored the crossroads that led towards the riverside and the empty market stalls. In fact, he kept going until he reached one of the larger houses in Danksville: a detached sandstone monstrosity decorated with gargoyles and grotesques.

Once upon a time it had been occupied by a powerful coven,

but these days a commune of peripheral characters who lived on the fringes of polite society inhabited it. They were the sort of people who didn't quite fit in with the local Danksville community but still enjoyed the company of others rather than wanting hermit-like solitude. They shared clothes, meals and often beds.

It was a strange place to target for a robbery since the residents eschewed all but the most essential items for day-to-day living and certainly didn't have much money or many items of value. Perhaps the trow had chosen it because they were mostly harmless and unlikely to hurt an intruder, even if they caught one in the act; they'd be more inclined to offer him some nettle soup and a comfy chair than tie him up and call the MET to arrest him.

I hung back while he opened the garden gate and plodded towards the house. The commune grew most of their own produce and used every scrap of useable outdoor space so the trow had to pick his way carefully through foliage. He was incredibly careful for a thief and didn't once tread on anything that might be harvested. His respect made me doubt my suspicions; maybe he wasn't a burglar at all but simply an innocent visitor.

When he reached the door, however, he delved into his pocket and pulled out a small box. He took out a pinch of powder and sprinkled it on his hand before crouching down and blowing it towards the lock. Alrighty. He was definitely breaking in.

I bounded forward, leapt onto the stone wall that surrounded the house and down into the garden, then ran forward until I was directly behind the trow. When my claws scraped on a pile of broken eggshells that had been saved for compost, he finally registered my presence. Turning around, he blinked owlishly down at me then placed a finger to his lips and crouched down to scratch my ears.

I hissed and backed up before he could touch me. The trow shrugged. 'Suit yourself, kitty,' he whispered.

I usually did.

My whiskers quivered and I started to cough until I'd hacked up the magicked furball from my stomach. I had to be quick: I was vulnerable during the brief moments of transformation. Thankfully, the trow was too astonished to do more than stare; it was only when I was back on two feet and pulling back my lips to offer him a human snarl that he roused himself to action.

He threw himself forward and his short but powerful body smacked into mine. He shoved me so hard that I staggered, then he swerved around me and ran, his feet slapping against the earth. He wasn't worried about stepping on the plants now; all the trow was thinking about was escape.

He vaulted the garden gate and sprinted left but he only covered about five metres before I launched myself at his back and sent both of us sprawling to the cobbles. He struggled and writhed but it was clear he wouldn't get away.

'You're mine now,' I whispered in his ear with enough of a menacing chill that he went rigid with fear. Good: this would be easier if he was scared of me.

I hauled him up, making sure to keep one hand tight on the scruff of his neck, spun him around until we were face to face and bared my teeth again. 'You've been a very naughty boy.'

The trow was visibly shaking. 'I've done nothing!'

I raised an eyebrow. 'Oh, really?' I wrested the drawstring bag from him with my free hand and jiggled it. Something clanked. 'So what's in here?'

'It's my stuff! You cannae take it! It's mine!'

My gaze hardened; I'd always been able to conjure up an

effective death stare and this occasion was no different. The trow squeaked and his dark eyes widened. Before I could say anything more, he started to babble. 'Alright! I nicked it all! I'm sorry! I was desperate. I'm not a bad person. I don't have a choice! I have to do this!'

I hadn't expected such a quick confession. Whatever was going on with him, he certainly wasn't a hardened criminal. I didn't soften my expression, though; I was a cat lady and I couldn't demean my own kind by acting like a pushover.

'There is always a choice,' I growled. 'You have been terrorising my neighbours, stealing from my friends. There must be a reckoning.'

The trow yanked himself hard enough to escape my grip, but instead of turning to flee he fell to his knees. 'I had to do it,' he mumbled, more to himself than to me. 'I *had* to.'

His guilty routine felt genuine. I nibbled on my bottom lip then crouched down to join him. 'What's your name?'

He was scared enough to tell me. 'Bin,' he said. 'I'm called Bin.'

'Well, Bin,' I drawled, 'why don't you tell me exactly what's going on here? Why don't you have any choice?'

The trow's thin mouth turned down at the corners and something dark flickered in his eyes. I waited another beat; when no answer was forthcoming, I reached down and shook him. 'Hey!' I said sharply. 'I asked you a question.'

'My name is Bin. I live in Green Humbleton.' He wrapped his arms around himself. 'I don't mean anyone any harm.'

I eyed him. Either he wasn't willing to speak openly – or he wasn't able to. 'Name, rank and serial number, huh?' He blinked up at me, obviously confused. 'Why are you targeting Danksville?'

'My name is Bin.'

'Why are you stealing from the good citizens here?'

'I live in Green Humbleton.'

'Why did you have to do this?'

'I don't mean anyone any harm.'

I sighed: this was getting me nowhere. I stepped back and folded my arms. 'I can make things very unpleasant for you, Bin.' I spoke clearly so that he fully understood.

The trow flinched. 'I'm sorry,' he mumbled. He dropped his head and his shoulders sagged; the small man was simply waiting for his punishment, regardless of what it might be.

I gazed at him for a long moment then said in a gentler tone, 'Has somebody made you do this?' I asked. 'Have you been coerced into thieving?' He flinched again. 'Bin,' I began.

'My name is Bin. I live in Green Humbleton. I don't mean anyone any harm.'

Hmm. 'I can help you.' I meant it. Something was going on with this poor trow and it certainly wasn't greed or pure evil.

He lifted his head and met my eyes. 'I don't want your help.' He snatched the drawstring bag from me.

I made a decision: it might damn me – and damn Bin – but it was what it was. Bearing in mind my past career it didn't seem fair to judge the poor trow.

'The people around here don't own much,' I said. 'And you shouldn't keep returning to the same area night after night. Try Broughton over to the west side of the city, and Fallie beyond Crackendon Square. Those people are richer, though not so well-off that they have a lot of home security.'

The trow stared at me.

'But,' I added, 'no matter where you go, your luck will only last for so long. Keep this up and you'll end up dead.' The answering flicker in his eyes was one of resignation. 'My offer of help remains open. No matter what mess you've got yourself into, I have the skills to make your life better.'

I told him where I lived and added a stern warning that it

wasn't an invitation to steal from me. In response he sniffed wetly and rubbed his glistening nose with the back of his hand. 'Can I go now?'

I grimaced. I couldn't force him to accept my help.

I gestured to the empty street behind me and a second later the trow sprinted away into the darkness as fast as his short legs would carry him.

CHAPTER

# TWO

S everal hours later, as I made myself a late breakfast – or perhaps an early lunch – I was still pondering the conundrum of Bin the trow. Should I have dealt with him differently?

When I was a child, I'd never imagined that being an upstanding member of society who made good decisions would be so complicated. Sometimes there wasn't a correct road to take; sometimes there was a fork to the left and a fork to the right and nobody to advise you which one to take. But I was only forty-two, and at some point surely I'd grow up sufficiently to make the right decisions, the decisions that proved I was a serious person with responsibilities, who cared for others and always made good choices.

I wasn't sure that allowing a thief to continue stealing from the inhabitants of Coldstream would count as a good choice.

I opened the fridge and gazed at the contents. There were the makings of a decent salad in there, or I could eat leftover pizza. I shrugged: there was no contest. I could be a sensible adult with healthy eating habits tomorrow.

I took my plate out to the garden and settled in the

deckchair next to the fence that adjoined my neighbour's garden. On cue, Dave's front door opened and the man himself strolled out. I could swear that he always waited until he saw me before he left his own house.

He leaned over the fence and eyed my food. 'Cold pizza? You ought to be careful. You're not eighteen with the constitution of an ox anymore.'

There was a loud purr of agreement from a corner of my own scrap of garden: Dave wasn't the only one who seemed to think I needed dietary advice. He Who Crunches Bird Bones was equally disapproving.

I glared at them both. 'In that case,' I said pointedly, 'I will stop bringing cake around when I do a batch of baking. Too much sugar isn't good for you.' I took another mouthful and turned to the cat. 'And I'll be sure not to give you any more treats between meals.'

He Who Crunches Bird Bones immediately stopped purring. Dave snorted loudly.

I held up the pizza. 'There are vegetables on this. Tomatoes. Onions – and at least one whole basil leaf.' He clicked his tongue. 'You don't want a slice then?'

Dave clambered over the fence with surprising ease for a druid of his girth and age and I grinned as I held out the plate. He nodded, tried not to look pleased by offering me his characteristic scowl, and took the last slice. 'Thank you.'

He was nothing if not polite. 'You're welcome.' As he munched, he cast a critical eye around my garden. I preened: it was looking good. The careful flicker of a few appropriate spells meant that the rose bushes were already starting to bloom, there were shades of verdant green in every direction and a pleasing number of buzzing insects.

Dave swallowed a mouthful of pizza. 'Why don't you have any weeds like I do?'

The 'weeds' on Dave's patch of land were actually priceless silphium plants that could enhance the magic of any Preternatural being, but I wasn't planning to tell him that unless it was absolutely necessary.

'Because I weed,' I told him.

Dave grunted at the bizarre vagaries of plant life and took another bite. 'I heard,' he said, once he'd finished chewing, 'that Jimmy Leighton over on Sitwell Road was burgled last night.'

'Uh-huh.'

'If that damned thieving burglar comes around here, he'll get a surprise.' He curled his hands into tight fists. 'If he tries to break into my place, I'll show him what's what.'

'Uh-huh.'

'You ought to invite that wolfie friend of yours to stay,' he suggested. 'It's the full moon tonight. He'll keep you safe, especially when he turns furry.'

There were several responses I could have made to that. I decided to settle for a quiet life and plumped for the obvious one. 'Uh-huh.'

'And you could clearly do with a decent leg over.'

I gave him a flat look and he grinned. 'You know it's true.'

Yeah, yeah. It wasn't worth arguing about. Besides, he was right: I wanted to get my legs over Thane, and my legs between his legs. And, more to the point, his legs between mine...

We'd been dancing around the issue for weeks now but I suspected that both of us knew it was only a matter of time. Hell, even *Dave* knew it was only a matter of time. I decided it was a good thing I'd promised Thane I'd see him that afternoon.

'You need a good man about the place,' Dave went on, clearly unwilling to drop the subject.

I raised an eyebrow. 'Just like you need a good woman?'

He looked only mildly horrified at the thought and I smirked. 'In any case,' I said, dusting off the last few pizza crumbs, 'I wouldn't worry about any more thieves. I reckon whoever was behind those burglaries has moved on to pastures new.'

Dave's eyes narrowed in suspicion. 'What do you know that I don't?'

He Who Must Sleep appeared from around the corner and made a determined beeline for my lap, jumping up and curling into a tight ball before closing his eyes. 'I'm a middle-aged cat lady who's not getting her leg over. What on earth could I possibly know?'

I stroked the top of He Who Must Sleep's head and smiled to myself – but I still couldn't shake the image of the troubled trow out of my head.

I DIDN'T KNOW why Thane was currently living in a swanky penthouse apartment in one of the best areas in Coldstream. He wasn't short of a bob or two, so it was possible he owned the place, but given what else I knew about him it was equally possible that he was squatting there.

Thane never stayed in the same place for long; he moved around on an almost monthly basis, as if he were afraid of putting down roots somewhere and then being disappointed when he was forced to leave. I suspected there would always be a scared boy inside that taut, muscular body, a boy who was afraid that he didn't belong anywhere. We all had our demons; some were simply more obvious than others.

Just in case, he wasn't supposed to be in residence, I avoided the concierge at the front desk and took the stairs rather than the lift to the top floor. Better safe than sorry.

'Thanks for dropping by, Kit,' Thane said, when he opened the front door. 'And thanks for doing this.' I stared at him.

'You've not changed your mind, have you?' I opened my mouth but no words came out. 'If there's a problem,' he began, 'tell me what it is.'

I gestured wordlessly towards his body. He'd clearly just stepped out of the shower, and he was topless, his chest beaded with droplets of water. A white towel was slung around his hips. One tug and it would pool on the floor around his feet, exposing him fully to my gaze. My eyes caught one particular shining drop of water as it trickled down from Thane's collar-bone, creating a mesmerising trail on his faintly tanned skin. The droplet curved around his exposed nipple before tracking lower. And lower. And lower...

Thane glanced down at himself and looked surprised. 'Oh, I'm sorry.'

'Don't apologise.' I finally managed to speak with at least a little coherence.

A slow, lazy smile lit up his face as he flexed his arms and leaned casually against the door frame. It was an open invitation to jump his bones. *What the hell*, I figured. Dave was right; it was about time we did this.

I took a step back, licked my lips very, very slowly, and allowed my eyes to travel all the way down his body then back up again to linger at the towel. 'You're very wet,' I murmured.

His answer was instantaneous. 'Are you?'

I drew in a breath. *Come on, Kit. You like Thane. Don't be afraid of this.* 'It's time that you found out,' I whispered.

Thane's nostrils flared: he hadn't been expecting that response. 'This could complicate our friendship.'

Sure it could, but I'd already considered the ramifications, many times, and I knew Thane had done the same. 'We're both adults. We can deal with the fallout. I want sex, Thane. With you.' Thane flushed. 'And we both know you've done this delib-erately.'

His blush faded away and he frowned. 'Done what?'

'The towel. The wet, half-naked body. You saw me coming from your window and prepared yourself for my arrival.'

He flashed me a tight, knowing grin. 'You know me too well.'

I swallowed. 'Not well enough. Not yet, anyway.'

His emerald eyes glittered and he extended a hand. I reached out to take it.

Then I froze.

'What?' he asked. 'What's wrong?'

I pointed wordlessly to his stomach. He glanced down and registered the large patch of thick, glossy fur that had appeared. 'Fucking full moon,' he muttered.

In theory there were several hours to go until Thane was supposed to transform. Once the sun went down and the moon's effect took force, Coldstream would be filled with baying furry hounds; by midnight, Thane would be on four furry paws and roaming through Coldstream with his tail in the air whether he wanted to or not. But I knew that werewolves often partially transformed in the hours – and sometimes days – before the moon was full, especially when they were under a lot of stress. Or excitement. That was why I was picking up Tiddles this morning rather than later in the day.

'Can you control it?' I asked.

Thane grimaced. 'Sure.' No sooner had the word left his mouth than more patches of fur appeared on his arms. There was a cracking sound and his face began to change shape.

I crossed my arms over my chest. 'I'm somewhat vanilla when it comes to my preferences,' I said.

'No wolf?'

Definitely no wolf. I nodded.

He exhaled. 'Me too. I guess this will have to wait for another day.' His voice was hoarse with the effects of his semi-transformation. 'Anticipation will only make the actual event more delicious.'

At this rate, it would be the best sex of my life given how long I'd been anticipating it. 'I can wait if you can.'

Relief flashed in his eyes as he realised I wasn't blowing him off. 'I'll fetch Tiddles.'

I made no attempt to disguise my disappointment. 'That's probably a good idea, then I'll get out of your ... fur.'

He huffed slightly and vanished from the doorway, reappearing a moment later with his small ginger cat in his arms.

'Have you chosen a name for yourself yet?' I asked her.

She stared at me unblinking so I guessed not. She was more than old enough to have sorted out her own moniker; it appeared that Tiddles was a late bloomer.

'I think she likes being called Tiddles,' Thane said with an air of misplaced authority,

I snorted. 'If you say so.' I took the cat from him. At only about seven months old, she wasn't yet fully grown though she certainly wasn't the tiny kitten I had first met. Quite the opposite. I suspected that when she was done growing, Tiddles would be a very large cat indeed.

I scratched between her ears and let her clamber onto my shoulder. It wasn't particularly comfortable for me, but Tiddles seemed to like it and she'd be safe up there during the journey to Danksville. 'Shall I drop her off again after the full moon?' I asked.

Thane nodded, his eyes darkening with smoky, heated promise. 'Tomorrow morning.'

I raised an eyebrow. 'You won't need more time to recover?'

'No. I want you here before noon tomorrow.' He gazed at me. 'I *need* you here.'

My heart rate ratcheted up a notch. 'Okay.'

Thane ran his tongue across his lips. 'Give me your word, Kit.'

'My, my. That is serious.'

'Where you and I are concerned,' he said, 'I'm *very* serious.'

'In that case you have my word,' I whispered. 'I'll be here,' I glanced at my watch, 'in twenty-six hours' time at the very latest.'

'Good. Don't forget about me in the meantime.'

Fat chance of that. I adjusted Tiddles slightly, nudging her to the right so that her tail wasn't obscuring my vision. Then, still feeling somewhat deflated at the turn of events albeit excited about what was to come, I left.

# THREE

The nearest tram stop was quite a distance away and the streets were surprisingly busy. Normally that wouldn't be an issue but Tiddles took umbrage at the stares she garnered from various passersby. I didn't blame her; she didn't want to be touched by strangers and that was definitely a desire I could get behind.

'Wow!' exclaimed a tall witch who crossed the street to get closer to us. 'Nice cat!' He stretched out his fingers to stroke her then recoiled when Tiddles hissed. He looked at me askance, as if I'd somehow commanded her to react negatively. I shrugged and swerved around him, keen to get on my way.

Things got worse when three teenage dryads tripped towards us. 'Oh my gosh!' The nearest one reached out with her arms extended, determined to move Tiddles from my shoulder to her own. Naturally Tiddles responded with a swipe – and she had no qualms about extending her claws.

When beads of scarlet blood appeared across the dryad's pale green skin, she looked as if she might cry. 'Your cat attacked me!' she complained.

'You should have asked for permission before you got too close,' I said.

Her lip curled and her two friends opened their mouths, keen to spring to her defence. I stepped to the side to continue walking; I was happy to get into an argument with most people but I knew I was no match for a group of teenage girls who wouldn't take any prisoners once they got going. It was safer for us all if I extracted myself from the situation.

'You old bitch!' one shouted after me.

Tiddles growled and tensed, clearly prepared to defend my honour. 'It's not necessary,' I told her quickly. 'And you have to learn to choose your battles.'

I turned my head and called, 'You're right! I *am* an old bitch and I'm fucking proud of it, too!'

The girls exchanged looks. 'Damn straight,' the third one muttered. 'I hope I'm like that when I'm older.'

I grinned, waved and moved on.

When I rounded a corner less than a hundred metres from the tram stop, yet another figure approached us. My irritation was beginning to get the better of me and I gritted my teeth in annoyance. Then I realised who it was and my eyes widened.

'Good day, Ms McCafferty.'

I sighed at the spriggan. 'Hello, Boris,' I said. 'I'd say that it's good to see you again but I can only imagine you're talking to me because Mallory wants to call in that favour I owe her.'

I'd signed a contract with the squib a few months earlier: in exchange for information about the witches' council, I'd agreed to do a favour for her. Even if I'd wanted to back out of the deal, which wasn't my style, I couldn't because it was fully binding. I'd signed on the dotted line with my own blood.

The spriggan bowed slightly to acknowledge my words. 'I am glad that you understand. She is waiting for you at her flat.'

He indicated in the vague direction of Crackendon Square where Mallory lived.

Tiddles glared malevolently; apparently a blood contract didn't impress her and she didn't care whether I fulfilled the terms or not. I gestured to her. 'Let me take this one home, then I'll go straight to Mallory.'

The spriggan's lips thinned. 'Not possible, I'm afraid. She is very busy with another client and doesn't have much time to spare. She has to see you now.' His tone brooked no argument. I could have pushed the matter because nothing in the contract said that I couldn't take a couple of hours to respond to the summons, but curiosity got the better of me.

I had no idea what favour Mallory was about to demand of me and I was fascinated to find out, so I ignored Tiddles' brief growl and changed direction. Boris immediately disappearing down the street, his errand complete. He clearly wasn't concerned that I'd refuse the order – but, of course, blood contracts were powerful things.

I AFFECTED A GRIM, haughty expression, which was enough to deter further advances from well-meaning members of the public who were keen to make Tiddles' acquaintance. That didn't mean the ginger cat was pleased with me; unimpressed by my detour, she huffed and hissed at regular intervals. I ignored her adolescent bristling and made a beeline for the pub above which Mallory had made her home.

The entrance was the same as I remembered from my first visit: narrow, with an old creaking wooden staircase, There was a map of Coldstream on the wall by the front door with various coloured dots and pins placed at seemingly random points. Last time I hadn't known what the dots were supposed to indicate but now I noted that one of them marked the location of my house. Ah. The dots showed the locations of Mallory's clients. My dot was blue, so I figured that colour indicated those owing favours.

There were as many red dots as blue ones, but only two yellow dots. I peered at them and raised an eyebrow when I recognised one of the properties which was marked; it appeared that Mallory had taken on an interesting new client. Maybe that was why she was so busy.

It wasn't any of my business but I hoped she knew what she was doing. That particular Coldstream resident, while devastatingly handsome and often kind, had teeth.

As soon as I started to climb the staircase, Tiddles dug her claws into my flesh. I reached up a hand to stroke her and realised that her hackles were raised. 'It's fine,' I murmured. 'Mallory is a nice person and I know that she likes cats. Besides, this won't take long.'

Either Tiddles didn't believe my reassurances or she didn't care, because she doubled down, whipping her tail from side to side to indicate her displeasure. 'You can wait down there if this bothers you so much,' I said.

She didn't need telling twice. She sprang from my shoulder, ripping both my skin and my T-shirt, and bounded back down the stairs. Her eyes were wide, her pupils elongated and fearful, and I felt a sudden prickle of apprehension. There was no reason for Mallory to provoke that reaction in any cat; maybe it was time to be less curious and more wary about what I was about to confront.

I climbed the rest of the stairs more slowly, listening hard, but all I could hear was chatter and faint music from the pub beneath. I didn't relax, though: if there was one thing I trusted, it was a cat's instincts.

I reached the tiny landing and knocked tentatively on the door.

When Mallory appeared she looked different, though I couldn't put my finger exactly on what had changed. Her hair was the same mess of frizzy curls and her clothes were the same colourful boho patchwork that would have looked ridiculous on anyone else, but the brightness in her eyes and pinkness in her cheeks were definitely new. I tilted my head, more fascinated by her than ever.

'Kit!' she exclaimed warmly. 'Thank you for coming at such short notice.' She didn't sound stressed or unhappy.

'I don't believe I had much choice in the matter,' I said, not unkindly.

She offered me a rueful grin. 'Yes, I'm somewhat busy with a new client at the moment. I don't have a lot of time to spare.'

I considered mentioning that I probably knew who her new client was but she didn't give me the chance. As she ushered me inside, she was talking so quickly that I couldn't get a word in edgeways.

'I have the perfect favour to request of you,' she said cheerfully. 'It's not too onerous – in fact, you'll probably find it very easy. I know you have rooms to let at your house so I immediately thought of you when this matter arose.'

I only had one room – or rather only one small flat – available in my house because the others were uninhabitable. One of these days I'd get around to doing them up, but I was in no rush to let them out and my ground-floor flat was more than spacious enough to cover my needs. The last time I'd rented a room to someone had been to Alexander MacTire's nephew, and I wasn't convinced that being a landlady was an attractive proposition after that particular experience.

'Let me guess,' I said, with an audible lack of enthusiasm. 'You'd like me to welcome a guest into my home.'

If Mallory noticed my attitude, she didn't show it. 'Yep!' She beamed brightly. 'You'll like Keres and I'm sure she'll be no bother. You won't notice she's there.'

I put my hands in my pockets. I was starting to understand why Tiddles had been so bristly. 'Keres,' I said.

'Yes.' Mallory was still smiling.

'That's a Greek name.'

She shrugged. 'Is it? Keres is Scottish. I doubt she speaks any Greek.'

'It means death spirit.'

Mallory blinked innocently. 'Does it?' I growled at her deliberate obfuscation and she pulled a face. 'Alright,' she said. 'Alright. Keres is a ban sith.'

I didn't move a muscle.

'She's a lovely lady.'

I found my voice. 'A ban sith,' I said slowly.

'Yep.'

'As in a woman who stands outside somebody's home and shrieks at them to tell them they're about to die.'

'Yes.'

'And then they do actually die.' Sometimes it was possible to avoid the impending doom that a ban sith advertised by taking appropriate safety measures, but statistically 74% of a ban sith's predictions came true.

'Ban siths don't kill people, Kit. They're not *evil*. There's no such thing as pure evil.'

'You say that like someone who's never experienced microwaved tea.'

'Kit—'

Irritated, I interrupted her. 'I know, I know. Ban siths perform a useful service and give people time to wrap up their affairs and say their goodbyes. They give some people who play their cards right a chance to avoid whatever doom is coming their way. But that doesn't change the fact that most people hate them.'

Mallory looked disappointed. 'I didn't think you'd be so prejudiced.'

'I'm not, but I have several neighbours who are garden-variety bigots and they won't take kindly to a ban sith in their midst. They will cause problems for this poor woman.'

She relaxed. 'I'm sure you can put out any fires – you're more than capable of dealing with uneducated arseholes. And it will be a good opportunity for members of your community to realise that ban siths are to be respected, not feared.'

That would be easier said than done. I wasn't a politician and my usual solution to problems – unlike a ban sith's – was to kill people.

From behind Mallory I heard somebody clear their throat. 'I won't be doing any shrieking. I've lost my ban-sith voice and my power.'

I stared at the diminutive woman who had appeared in the hallway. Yeah, she was definitely a ban sith.

Great.

CHAPTER

# FOUR

It was obvious as soon as we left Mallory's flat and descended the staircase to the outside world that Tiddles' earlier reaction was because of Keres. The cat arched her back and hissed as if her life depended on it. I'd never seen any of my cats react so violently towards a ban sith before, quite the opposite in fact, but Tiddles was highly unimpressed by Keres' existence and determined to make sure as many people as possible were aware of her feelings.

'Deal with it,' I told her flatly, ignoring her histrionics. She growled at me. 'Do you normally provoke this sort of reaction with cats?' I asked Keres.

'I couldn't say,' she replied. 'I don't tend to get close to them.' That was a reason to mistrust her if ever I'd heard one.

Tiddles' body language changed and I knew she was about to launch herself at Keres and attack. I grimaced and scooped up the cat before any blood was shed.

'Sheathe those claws,' I commanded. I glanced at Keres. 'I have five more cats at home,' I told her. 'Plus a collection of ferals that I feed every day. If they all have a problem with you, this is going to be difficult.'

'I'll keep out of their way.' Keres' eyes flickered, not with defiance or anger but resignation.

I'd never seen a defeated looking ban sith before; hell, I'd never seen such a *young* ban sith before. Everything about Keres was unusual. She was in her early thirties and, as far as I was aware, ban siths didn't usually attain their power until they were at least forty. She was dressed casually in jeans and a T-shirt rather than a long flowing dress that was more typical of her kind, and her brown hair was tied up in a messy ponytail. She was painfully thin and there were dark shadows beneath her eyes, but I couldn't see any signs of physical injury.

The black curl along her right cheekbone marked her out as a ban sith. People often mistook those markings for tattoos but they occurred naturally, and Keres would possess that dark stain until the day she died. It broadcast what she was to the entire world, it couldn't be removed by surgery and no make-up would ever conceal it. Short of wearing a balaclava, she couldn't hide her identity. Tiddles ought to have been pleased by her presence; with Keres by our side, no random passersby would dare to approach us.

Keres flinched at the bright sunshine as we stepped outside and shielded her eyes as if the light pained her. Curious. 'I haven't been outside in daylight for several days,' she muttered before I could ask.

I wasn't sure if she was telling the truth and I was equally unsure if it mattered, but I asked anyway. 'Why not?'

Keres touched her neck with one hand and her magicked mark with the other. 'I don't have my powers anymore,' she said, as if that were more than enough explanation. She took a breath. 'You're only helping me out because you owe Mallory a favour, but *I* don't owe *you* anything – not even an explanation.' Her tone wasn't antagonistic – and she was right. She didn't owe me anything.

I told myself to leave her to her secrets, but I couldn't prevent the niggle of doubt growing inside me.

It was a long journey to my home in Danksville because Keres flatly refused to take the tram, despite the bulging bag on her back that presumably contained her most important possessions. When I tried to persuade her that the tram was the easiest way to travel, she clammed up and there was complete silence for almost two hours as we trudged south. Even Tiddles chose to stay silent.

I hadn't been lying to Mallory when I'd told her that some of my neighbours were prejudiced people who would judge Keres because of what she was. There had always been stories swirling around about ban siths, and their proximity to death didn't endear them to those who found it easy to despise what they feared. You couldn't avoid death, but you could avoid ban siths – unless, of course, they chose to target you with their nightly shrieks.

Word about Keres' presence would whip around my neighbourhood within an hour, and before night fell the likes of Trilby would sell out of magicked silver clovers to protect against a ban sith's predictions. The amulets were especially popular with the young and healthy. I ought to drop by Trilby's stall later and demand some commission.

The first person to spot Keres was Arthur Dinsbury, who lived on the corner close to the Danksville tram stop. The half-leprechaun half-troll was in his front garden chewing on a betel nut, his red-stained gums and teeth visible from a distance. He started to raise a hand in greeting, then stopped in mid-wave when he registered my companion. His jaw slackened and his eyes widened.

I waited for some sort of verbal explosion but instead he spun on his heel and sprinted up the path into his house. He slammed the door shut behind him as if the stained oak would protect him from a ban sith's caterwauls, though any reasonable Preternatural would know that their shrieks only started when the sun went down. It was barely noon and dusk was a long way off.

I sneaked a glance at Keres. If she'd seen his reaction, she didn't show it: shoulders pulled back, she was looking straight ahead.

Being a ban sith was far from easy and I couldn't help wondering if she'd deliberately lost her predictive powers. 'Your ban sith voice,' I began. 'You said you've lost it. Does that mean—?'

'I told you that I don't want to talk about it.' Her tone brooked no argument.

I had the distinct impression that she had already decided I wasn't to be trusted but I could hardly complain given that I had similar misgivings about her. I stopped walking and turned to face her.

Keres also stopped. 'What?'

'I think that we got off on the wrong foot,' I said, choosing my words carefully. She eyed me warily. 'I don't care what you get up to at night.' I shrugged. 'People die.' *Sometimes because of me*, I added silently to myself. 'If you want to tell them that their days are numbered, that's up to you.'

'I told you that I've lost my ban sith voice. I no longer have that power.' She sounded irritated.

I held up my hands to indicate that I believed her. 'I wasn't expecting to repay Mallory today and I wasn't expecting her to ask me to let somebody stay in my home. And I certainly wasn't expecting Tiddles' reaction.'

Keres frowned. 'Tiddles? That's the cat's name? Really?'

I smiled. 'I know, it's a terrible name but I didn't give it to her and I keep waiting for her to choose an alternative.'

From her position on my shoulder, Tiddles emitted a tiny hiss. Yeah, yeah.

'My point is,' I said, trying to explain myself more clearly, 'that I was thrown off guard when Boris came to me. And,' I admitted, because I somehow had the feeling that Keres would understand, 'I thought I'd get some fabulous sex this morning and I didn't. But none of those things mean I shouldn't welcome you. I've discovered lately that I quite like helping people, and I'd quite like to help you. Whether you want anything from me besides a roof over your head is up to you – but I don't want to be your enemy.'

She blinked rapidly. Over her shoulder I could see Arthur Dinsbury, whose wife had now joined him, staring at us fearfully from his kitchen window. I waved and smiled.

'Thank you,' Keres said eventually in a small voice. 'I appreciate that. Ban sith or not, I'm not a bad person.' She hesitated. 'I mean, I don't *think* I'm a bad person – I try not to be. But maybe bad people don't know that they're bad. I guess villains don't wake up in the morning and think, "Hey, today I'm going to be evil." Ban siths are usually good. We don't hurt people, we only warn them. I know the thought of death can be terrifying, but it's the most natural thing in the world.' She bit her lip. 'Shit. Does saying that aloud make me a bad person?'

For somebody who'd been silent for the past two hours, Keres could certainly talk when she chose to. I grinned. 'No, of course it doesn't.' I ignored Tiddles' sudden growl.

Keres glanced nervously towards the ginger cat. 'As soon as I said I didn't get close to cats I knew it was the wrong thing to say. I don't dislike them, I just haven't met many of them. That's all.'

'Well, that's great because you're about to meet loads,' I promised.

She didn't look thrilled at the prospect but neither did she look horrified. I stretched out my hand. 'Hi,' I said brightly. 'Nice to meet you. I'm Kit McCafferty.'

She managed a smile and carefully shook my hand. 'Hi. I'm Keres Johnson.'

'There, that's better.' I beamed at her and pointed down the street. 'My house is only a few minutes' walk away. We can get the kettle on and I'll show you the spare flat. It's small but I think you'll be comfortable.'

I'd barely finished speaking when a group of young children barrelled out from a house in front of us followed by their mother. The woman glanced at the children then at us, stiffened and raised her voice. 'Sam, Kate, Lewis! Inside!'

All three of them turned towards their mother, their disappointment and confusion palpable. 'But, Mum...'

'Now!' Her voice was high-pitched and tight with anxiety; she was clearly expecting an imminent attack.

As with Arthur Dinsbury, there was no visible reaction from Keres but I felt irritated on her behalf. She was only walking down the street.

'Don't,' she said in a low voice. 'You'll only make things worse.'

I twisted on my heel and headed straight for the woman. I recognised her, although I didn't know her name; she was a shop assistant in one of the larger witchery stores in the centre of Coldstream. I'd watched her deliver shopping to Mrs Miller when the elderly lady had broken her ankle and couldn't get out. All the neighbourhood kids came round to her house to play. Her husband wasn't there much, but I knew him as an affable druid who always had a kind word for my cats when he passed by. None of that mattered right now.

'Hello!' I said with a brash cheeriness that demanded her attention.

Her mouth tightened, making her red lipstick look less like a perfect pout and more like a slash of thin colour across her face. I silently christened her Slasher; it seemed to suit her.

She flicked her eyes at me then at her children, who were still in her front garden. 'I told you to get inside.' She raised her voice another notch. 'I'll not tell you a third time!'

The two boys, Sam and Lewis, dropped their heads and trudged indoors looking defeated, but Kate was less compliant. She turned away from her mother and approached me. 'Hi.'

I smiled at her. 'Hi.'

She grinned shyly. 'Your cat is very pretty.'

Tiddles relaxed for the first time since we'd left Mallory's flat. She preened herself and blinked wide-eyed at Kate before emitting a chirruping miaow. Bless her white-tipped tail: every action was designed to show herself off at her best, as if she were a kitten straight out of an old Disney film rather than a demon from the netherworld.

'Can I pet her?' Tiddles leapt off my shoulder before she'd finished the question.

'Catherine Alison McGrath!' Slasher shouted. 'Get inside now!'

'You should do what your mum says,' I told her.

Kate sniffed and reached out a hand to Tiddles. 'I will. In a minute.' She angled her head up towards Keres. 'You're a ban sith.'

Keres nodded reluctantly. 'I am.'

'Are you going to shriek outside our house? Are we all going to die?' There wasn't a trace of fear in her voice; she was simply curious.

'No,' Keres said. 'And no. Not yet, anyway.'

Slasher sucked in a sharp breath. 'Get away from my child!'

I continued to smile, though it was through gritted teeth. 'I'm Kit,' I called. 'This is my friend Keres. We're out enjoying the sunshine. It's a beautiful day.'

Slasher responded by yelling at her daughter again. 'Kate, either get inside now or you'll go to bed early tonight!'

That was the magical threat that finally worked. Kate sighed heavily and stroked Tiddles for a final time. 'I have to go now,' she said to the cat. 'But it was wonderful to meet you.' She straightened up and skipped into her house.

As soon as she'd gone, I addressed Slasher. 'You shouldn't be afraid of a ban sith. They're not bad people, they're just people. Keres won't hurt anyone. She predicts certain events but—'

'Fuck off.' Slasher spoke quietly but there was no denying the steel in her tone. 'Stay away from my house and stay away from my children. I don't want that *thing* anywhere near us.'

'She's not a thing,' I bit out. 'She's a person.'

'Come within ten feet of my property again and I'm calling the MET,' Slasher hissed at Keres, who was standing at least twenty feet away. She whirled around and stomped up her path and into her house.

'The MET won't do anything,' I called after her. 'They don't lock people up for simply existing!'

If Slasher heard my words, she didn't respond and simply slammed her front door closed. It was ridiculous.

'You've only made things worse,' Keres said mildly. 'She's all riled up and scared now. You've not helped at all.'

Unfortunately, I knew that she was right.

# FIVE

We returned to our earlier silence. I didn't know what Keres was thinking but, for my part, I was musing on different ways I could have approached Slasher to make her see that her reaction to the ban sith was unmerited. Thus far, I was coming up short.

As soon as my garden gate came into view, I spotted She Who Loves Sunbeams. My old darling was stretched out on the top of the wall and living up to her name. Dave, meanwhile, was standing in his garden with a mug of tea, scowling up at the blue cloudless sky as if its very existence offended him.

I glanced at Keres' stoic face. Uh-oh. There was no way Dave would manage to keep his mouth shut about my latest house guest. This could get ugly.

Tiddles scampered ahead and vaulted over the gate into the garden. She Who Loves Sunbeams lifted up her head and yawned. Her nose twitched and she glanced at me, then her gaze landed on Keres. Her whiskers quivered and, in an instant, she was on all four paws and arching her back.

I stiffened. My old cat was laid back: she didn't react to werewolves, she could rarely be bothered to bat a paw at passing wildlife, and she enjoyed a placid, carefree life. I had never seen her arch her back like this, and I had to do a double take to ensure I wasn't seeing things. There was no doubting it: She Who Loves Sunbeams was terrified of Keres.

'Wait here,' I muttered to the ban sith and hurried forward. 'Darling,' I said, 'there's nothing to be afraid of.'

I wasn't sure She Who Loves Sunbeams heard me. Her pupils were enlarged, wide black circles that indicated every ounce of the fear that was currently attacking her. I stroked her, trying to smooth her hackles but it didn't work.

In the end, I scooped her up and carried her through the garden and into the house. Once Keres was settled in the empty flat upstairs, I'd let She Who Loves Sunbeams outside again. It seemed safest for everyone if she was contained, but I couldn't deny how much her reaction worried me.

I dropped her onto her favourite cushion, repositioning it slightly so that a shaft of sunlight fell in from the window. She gave me a long, baleful look of reproach and curled up into a ball, still huffing.

'I don't understand,' I said softly, trying not to allow my concern get the better of me. 'You've been close to ban siths before and you understand what they're about. You know they're not to be feared, so why did you react to this one?'

She Who Loves Sunbeams buried her head in her paws and refused to look at me. I frowned at her for a moment then left her in peace. Perhaps she'd feel up to communicating more later.

I checked on the other cats, who were all asleep. I was beginning to suspect that their reaction to Keres would be similar. Next I cast around until I located Tiddles, who had already found her own spot underneath the kitchen table. 'Alright,' I said. 'What's the deal with Keres? Why don't you like her?'

Tiddles wasn't feeling any more inclined to answer me than She Who Loves Sunbeams.

'I know I didn't listen to you before,' I told her. 'But I'm listening now.'

From Tiddles' sigh, it was far too little too late. I gave up and left her alone. I would have to warn Keres again to stay as far away from the cats as possible. If She Who Loves Sunbeams reacted so badly, I couldn't begin to imagine what She Without An Ear might do. She was a war-mongering moggy who rarely allowed an opportunity for a cat fight to pass her by.

I headed outside and my stomach dropped when I saw that Keres had engaged Dave in conversation. My grumpy neighbour would give her short shrift; if the likes of Arthur Dinsbury and Slasher hated Keres on sight, Dave would certainly be no different.

I prepared yet again to defend the ban sith as I strode towards them.

'You know Barton Road?' Keres was asking.

Dave nodded vigorously. 'Know it? Once upon a time, I could have told you the names of every single resident on that street.'

My mouth dropped open.

'Number thirty-two?' Keres said, arching an eyebrow.

'Agnes Johnson,' Dave told her without missing a beat.

'That's my nan.'

'Old Nessie is your grandmother?'

She nodded. 'Great-gran. Yep.'

'It's a small world. How is she doing?'

The smile that had finally lit up Keres' face vanished. 'She passed away last year.'

Dave's shoulders dropped. 'Oh. I'm sorry.'

'She had a good innings,' Keres said. 'She was a hundred and two.'

'Good for her,' he murmured. He doffed an imaginary cap in her direction. 'You ever want to reminisce about old times, you knock on my door, you hear? Don't hesitate. I've always got a cup of tea for Nessie Johnson's great-granddaughter.'

Keres blinked rapidly. 'Thank you,' she whispered.

'Any time.' He turned away and went inside his house, leaving me staring after him.

'Your neighbour is friendly,' Keres said to me.

My jaw was working soundlessly.

'He's very chatty and he has kind eyes.'

I found my voice. 'Yes,' I managed. 'Dave's a real sweetheart.' I pointed to the set of stone steps leading upstairs. 'Come on. The flat is this way.'

It didn't take long to show Keres around. The flat was a small one-bedroom affair with basic furniture but it was comfortable enough. The front door had been repaired since the last tenant, Nick, had departed and I'd paid extra to ensure it was reinforced against further intrusions by nasty people. It wasn't the Ritz, but Keres would be safe there.

'If you need anything,' I told her, 'let me know.'

'Thank you,' she whispered. She seemed to mean it. She was more relaxed after her chat with Dave and was gratifyingly pleased with her surroundings.

Whatever had brought her to Mallory and then to me, she was clearly in need of a long rest so I left her to it, promising to check on her later. I suspected that Keres was the sort of person who wouldn't ask for water if she were on fire; it would be a fine balance to ensure she had everything she needed without appearing intrusive.

As soon as I returned to my garden I went straight to Dave,

who was still in his garden scowling at a particularly gnarly patch of silphium. I folded my arms and waited. After several beats had passed, he spoke. 'You'll have to tell me what you want,' he grunted. 'I can't read your mind so I don't know what's wrong.'

'Nothing's wrong,' I replied. 'But you know what I want from you.'

'I thought that ginger wolf of yours was ready to satisfy your physical needs but I can oblige, if you insist.' He wiggled his eyebrows in vigorous amusement.

Under any other circumstances, I'd have smirked and offered a snarky comment but I wasn't feeling particularly inclined to humour. Thankfully, he sensed that. He sighed and met my gaze. 'You want to know about the ban siths.'

I nodded. 'I do. I didn't realise you knew any of them.'

Dave drew his brows together in his familiar grimace. 'I didn't always live in this glorious manor.' He waved a hand at the ramshackle house behind him. 'When I was a lot younger, I lived on Barton Road.'

I watched him carefully. 'Where the ban sith community is located.'

'Yep.' He shrugged. 'It was all I could afford at the time – if I'd had a choice, I would have gone elsewhere.' He scowled deeply. 'In the end it was the best thing I ever did.'

I tried – and failed – to picture what a younger version of Dave would have looked like. 'Why?' I asked. 'Why was it the best thing?'

'They welcomed me and looked out for me, Old Nessie most of all.'

Keres' great-grandmother. I tilted my head and waited for him to continue.

'She was a good woman and she worked hard, too. She had the longest ban sith success record of anyone I've ever known. If

Nessie turned up at your door and started shrieking, you paid attention.' His mouth turned down. 'She looked after me – the whole community did. They still check in on me from time to time.'

My surprise must have shown because he went on with an uncharacteristic flash of amusement, 'They're discreet.'

Hmm; they would have to be very discreet to visit Dave without me noticing. But I wasn't infallible, and unless I was in feline form I didn't have the nocturnal skills of a ban sith. 'They're a tight-knit community?' I asked.

'They look after their own and anyone else who needs it. I owe them a lot.' His voice was deep and reflective. I'd never heard him talk like this before.

'How long did you live on Barton Road?'

'Long enough to know that they're amongst the most decent people you'll find in Coldstream.'

All of which begged the question why Keres had chosen to leave them. 'Have you ever heard of a ban sith losing their powers?'

Dave took a long moment before answering. 'No,' he said finally. 'I haven't.'

'If one *did* lose their powers, what do you think the other ban siths would do?'

This time, he replied instantly. 'They'd close ranks and look after that person whether they recovered or not.'

'They wouldn't kick them out? Make them leave because they no longer belong?'

His response was unequivocal. 'Not a chance.'

I turned and gazed up at the windows of the upper flat. Despite my initial misgivings Keres seemed like a decent sort, but the cats' reaction to her and the fact that she'd left the safety of her own community sent prickles of apprehension rippling through me.

All Mallory had asked was that I provide the young ban sith with a place to stay, but I'd already decided that I couldn't leave it at that. Keres was in my home and I had a duty of care to both my cats and my neighbours to make sure they were safe, especially if I was defending Keres' presence.

My blood contract with Mallory meant that I had to allow Keres to stay but I couldn't take her on blind faith, even though I was beginning to like her and I wanted to help her. She wouldn't answer any of my questions or satisfy my anxious curiosity – but I had more avenues to explore.

I CONSIDERED MAKING another attempt to discuss Keres with my furry family but discarded the thought quickly; cats were stubborn wee bastards when they wanted to be. Instead I told all five of them to stay inside then grabbed my bag, checked that Keres was still upstairs in the flat and went out again.

There were several places I could go to gain answers without demanding them from the ban sith herself. It was unlikely I'd find many ban siths out and about at this time of day, so I didn't head straight for Barton Road; instead I jumped off the tram at the closest stop to Migden, a well-heeled suburb of Coldstream.

This was a neighbourhood I knew far better than the one where the ban siths resided. I'd never had cause to visit the Barton Road neighbourhood when I was working as an assassin for EEL; in fact, when I'd started as a baby assassin at least two of my more experienced colleagues had told me to avoid ban siths if I could. I'd always assumed that was because having a woman shrieking for hours outside the house of a person who'd been placed under contract to be killed could cause no end of problems for the killer. I hadn't questioned that advice at the time, an oversight that I now intended to remedy.

I marched down the street and into a wide, tree-lined cul-de-sac. The house I was heading for was far grander than my own; its occupant had done well with the stock market and made a series of canny investments that had allowed her to purchase it. Well, that was what she told everyone; the truth was somewhat more complicated and involved an aptitude for wielding lethal poisons.

The window boxes contained several varieties of deadly nightshade, laburnum and hemlock. I knocked on the front door and waited. It didn't take long for Louise to answer.

It was eight years since I'd last seen her. Socialising with other ex-assassins wasn't a particularly wise move so we tended to leave each other alone once we'd left the business Once upon a time she and I had been close, and we'd worked together on at least three contracts that had required our combined skills. We'd always been friendly.

I felt a flicker of warmth when I saw her familiar face. Apart from a few extra grey hairs and faint wrinkles around her eyes, she looked the same as always.

Pleasingly, she didn't appear remotely surprised at my unannounced arrival. 'Kit! It's so wonderful to see you!' She stretched out her arms and pulled me into a tight hug.

She smelled of cinnamon and warmth, and I was immediately transported back to a time when my younger self had relied on her. Louise had been there when I'd sobbed after completing my first assassination contract; she'd understood that my tears were both celebratory and tragic all at the same time. She'd supported me when I'd refused to complete a contract on a local politician who was being targeted by one of his political rivals. She'd guided me through the ups and downs of my previous life and I'd missed her when she'd retired. I hadn't realised how much.

'It's good to see you too,' I mumbled into her shoulder. Although I was a middle-aged woman, for a moment I felt like a kid again.

She pulled back and examined me. 'You look good,' she said finally. 'Healthy. Happy.' She raised an eyebrow. 'I'm assuming this is a social call. You retired – what? Three years ago?'

'Closer to four years now,' I admitted.

'Are you finding much to occupy your time?'

I smiled. 'I'm keeping busy. That's why this isn't entirely a social call. I was hoping to pick your brains about something.'

Louise smiled back at me. 'Then you'd better come inside.'

CHAPTER

# SIX

I'd never been inside another assassin's home. If I hadn't already known Louise I might have expected a stark interior with various weapons on display, but she'd never placed importance on the tools of her trade – beyond the plants outside. Despite her profession, she was a warm person with a surprisingly caring nature. She'd told me at her retirement party that the thing she was looking forward to most was the opportunity to ditch every black item of clothing she owned because she wanted colour in her life. It was a sentiment I understood; in fact, it was part of the reason my hair was now dyed purple.

So I wasn't surprised that Louise's house was welcoming, with its colourful artwork, bohemian fabrics and comforting clutter. Light beamed in through every window, illuminating corners that were free of dust balls. I wished that my house could be this clean but alas, that was next to impossible with five cats shedding fur on a minute-by-minute basis.

A glass-fronted display contained an astonishing collection of thimbles: small thimbles; big thimbles; whimsical thimbles; magicked thimbles. There were thimbles shaped liked bears and castles and knights and, I noted approvingly, cats. 'You do a lot of sewing these days?' I asked.

Louise grinned. 'Nah. I just like collecting them. Call it a bad case of nostalgia or a source of relaxation, a psychological buffer against past trauma or the enjoyable pursuit of rare items. Collecting thimbles fills a need in me that can't easily be explained.'

I shrugged. 'Everyone needs a hobby, I suppose. There are far worse things you could do.'

'I could be spending my retirement talking to cats.'

I cocked my finger and thumb at her like a gun. 'Watch it.' She smirked.

She directed me to a small, well-appointed lounge then disappeared to make tea. In less than five minutes she was back with a tray laden with mismatched china, a steaming teapot and home-made cakes.

I eyed her baked offerings with envy. 'I keep trying to bake but I rarely have much success.'

Louise snorted. 'I remember your lack of skill in making poisons so I'm not surprised that you struggle with baking. The measurements need to be precise and you have to follow the recipes exactly.'

'When was the last time *you* followed a recipe exactly?' I asked.

'I'm so good that I don't have to,' she replied serenely. 'Tea?'

I allowed her to pour me a cup, picked it up with both hands and leaned back in my chair. 'I'm here because I want to ask you about ban siths.'

She looked surprised. 'Ban siths? Why on earth would you be interested in them?'

'It's a long story,' I explained, 'but essentially I've rented one of the spare flats in my house to a ban sith and I have a few concerns about her.'

'If you have concerns then why not kick her out?' Louise asked mildly.

'It's not quite that straightforward.'

Her clever eyes were watching me. 'It rarely is.' She folded her hands in her lap. 'Ban siths tend to remain amongst their own kind – safety in numbers, that sort of thing. It's unusual for one of them to leave their people.'

'So I've heard.' I licked my lips. 'Once upon a time you warned me away from ban siths.'

'I did.' She paused for a beat. 'You know what a ban sith does?'

Everyone knew, but I nodded anyway.

'I bet that you don't know all of it.'

I returned my full cup of tea to the tray and leaned forward. 'Go on.'

'Not all ban siths are created equal. Some are more sensitive and more accurate with their powers than others. And there's more to their skill than predicting impending death. They are *in tune* with death, it's as much a part of a ban sith's life as breathing might be to you or me. They can sense death approaching and they can sense when it has passed.'

I was slightly puzzled. 'What do you mean?'

'In my twenties, soon after I joined EEL, I was contracted to kill a druid. He was a nasty sort and deserved what was coming to him. I don't need to go into details – you know the sort of man I'm talking about.'

Unfortunately I did.

Louise continued. 'The contract required some complicated body removal because he couldn't be found at the scene of his death. I had to transfer his corpse to the steps of Tweed Hall, near Crackendon Square.'

I raised an eyebrow but she waved a hand dismissively. 'The person who'd taken out the contract wanted to send a message to the druid's cronies that they'd be next if they didn't stop what they were doing. It didn't work, and they ended up as dead as their friend. It was a long time ago and it's not relevant to this story. What *is* important is that twelve hours after the contract had been completed, a ban sith walked over the spot where the druid had died and knew what had happened.'

'She knew someone had died on that spot without any physical evidence to indicate it?'

'Yes.'

'Was there a chance any blood had been spilled?'

Louise pulled a face. 'Please! I was a professional, Kit, and I was good at my job. As good as you were.'

I couldn't argue with that.

'Besides,' she went on, 'the ban sith didn't just know that someone had been killed, she knew who it was.'

I blinked. 'Seriously?'

Louise nodded. 'Seriously. And in case you still doubt me, I completed the contract with a poison-tipped umbrella that only required contact with the skin to work. No blood was spilled, not a drop.'

Hmmm. I didn't doubt Louise's words but nonetheless I was shocked. I chewed on the inside of my mouth as I considered her revelation. As a cat sith, I possessed the ability to see spirits re-enact the moments before their death. It only worked if I effected my transformation with fur from a cat who themselves possessed that ability. Many cats couldn't see the dead in that way, and I'd never heard of any other creatures who could do it, but there were many different Preternaturals in Coldstream and not all their abilities were documented.

'Can every ban sith do this?' I asked.

'I don't think so. Only the more powerful ones.'

A trickle of unease dripped through my veins. 'Do you know which particular ban sith felt that death?'

Louise nodded. 'An older woman by the name of Agnes Johnson.' She gazed at me. 'You've gone pale, Kit.'

'Mmm.' I swallowed.

She was still watching my face carefully. 'There's more.'

'Go on.'

'I sought out Agnes Johnson – I was curious about her and I wanted to know the extent of her powers.' She grimaced. 'That was a mistake.'

As I waited to hear the words, I had a horrible feeling that I knew what she was going to say.

'Agnes could also sense that death followed me.' Louise's expression was sombre. 'Not because I was about to die, you understand, but because I had *caused* death. She told me that death enveloped me like a cloud.'

'Because you were an assassin,' I whispered.

'Exactly so.' She sighed. 'Despite EEL's views about unsanctioned kills, I made it clear what would happen if she spoke about the matter. I didn't want to threaten her but it was an uneasy time for me. There were plenty of other EEL assassins who would have killed her immediately to remove the problem.'

She was correct, but that didn't make it right.

'Agnes Johnson said nothing and I avoided ban siths afterwards,' she continued. 'Even if most of them don't possess the skill to sense that someone is a killer, it's wise to steer clear of them.'

I drew breath. 'The ban sith staying in my house is Agnes Johnson's grand-daughter.'

'Ah.' Louise's mouth flattened. 'That does put an interesting spin on matters.'

And then some. I dug my fingernails into the fleshy part of my palms. Keres' kinship to such a powerful ban sith might mean nothing – but it might also mean everything.

Louise stood and picked up the tray. 'I'll make a fresh pot of tea,' she said. 'You've not touched this one.'

I'd picked the cup up but I certainly hadn't been stupid enough to drink from it. 'Neither have you,' I pointed out.

She smiled. 'This time, I won't add poison. I should have known that you weren't here to harm me and that you wouldn't drink it. You're too careful.'

I inclined my head to acknowledge her faint praise. I wasn't offended that Louise had tried to kill me; if she'd shown up unannounced at my door, I'd probably have reacted in a similar fashion. For the most part ex-assassins were left in peace but, given our past careers, it paid to be cautious.

'You can watch me brew the pot if you wish,' she offered.

'I'll trust you,' I said.

She laughed slightly. 'You shouldn't.' Then she sobered. 'You used to work for EEL, Kit. You were one of their best. You shouldn't trust anyone.'

I stayed for another hour chatting about more pleasant matters, and yes, I drank a cup of tea, but I was pre-occupied by Louise's revelations. Maybe it wasn't coincidence that had brought Keres to me via Mallory; maybe she was after me because of my time as a contract killer. If she possessed the same level of skill as her grandmother, she'd know what I used to do for a living. Was this a strange, convoluted revenge for my life choices or for Louise's threats to her grandmother? It seemed unlikely that Mallory would set her onto me if that were true, but I couldn't ignore the possibility.

For that reason I headed back to Mallory's after I left Louise's house. My suspicions that had been triggered by the cats' reaction to Keres were growing and I wouldn't be able to relax until I had some answers,

I passed the door to the pub beneath Mallory's flat and headed up the creaking staircase. The marker on the framed map that indicated my house had been removed, suggesting that Mallory believed I had fulfilled the terms of our agreement. Would she still believe that if I kicked Keres out less than a day after taking her in?

There wasn't an immediate answer when I knocked on Mallory's front door so I knocked harder. I heard footsteps and exhaled, relieved that she was in and I could talk to her – but it wasn't Mallory who opened the door.

Boris was wearing a silk robe that perfectly matched the colour of his skin. He glowered at me, his eyes flashing with irritation. 'What do you want?'

I smiled pleasantly; I wouldn't get anywhere with the spriggan unless I was polite. 'I need to speak to Mallory.'

'She's not here.' He started to close the door but I blocked it with my foot.

'When will she be back?'

'I don't know.'

'Can I wait inside?'

He snorted derisively. 'No.'

'I'll wait on the stairs, then.' I could be patient; it was one of my more useful skills.

'You'll be waiting a long time. She won't be back today or tomorrow. In fact, I'm not sure if she'll ever return here.'

Something tightened inside my belly. 'I saw her here only hours ago. Is she okay?'

'Depends on your point of view.' I stared at him hard and he sighed and appeared to relent. 'She's fine.'

Strictly speaking spriggans weren't Fae, but they worked for the Fae and it was documented that the Fae didn't lie. In fact, they *couldn't* lie. Although it wasn't guaranteed that Boris was telling the truth, I had no reason to suspect otherwise.

'I really, *really* need to speak to her.'

'Well you can't.' He glanced down. 'Now please remove your foot.'

Not a chance. 'The ban sith – Keres. Did she ask Mallory to contact me? Did she ask to stay with me in particular?'

'I don't have to answer your questions,' Boris said.

'No, you don't,' I replied softly. 'But I'd like to know if I've let someone into my home who is planning to kill me.'

Boris sucked in air through the large gap in his front teeth. 'No. The ban sith had never heard of you until Mallory suggested your name.'

'Are you sure?' I pressed.

'Can anyone ever be sure?' he returned.

True. I sighed. 'Alright. Thank you.' I pulled back my foot and Boris immediately slammed the door in my face. 'Tell Mallory I'd still like to talk to her!' I called, but if he heard me he didn't respond.

I HAD one final port of call before I returned home. The riverside market in Danksville would be closing up for the day and I couldn't visit Trilby's home without a prior invitation, so I had to catch them before they finished for the day. At least the late timing meant that I wouldn't be interrupted by any other customers; it was always helpful to talk to Trilby without anyone eavesdropping.

Head bowed, they were packing away the last few items when I jogged up. They smoothed over a skein of fabric, checked the contents of three small glass vials, and sealed a larger wooden box with a magical flourish. Then, without looking up, they spoke. 'Hello, Kit.'

The more time I spent around Trilby, the more I learned that their powers were deep and mysterious. I didn't know what manner of Preternatural they were, but knowledge could be dangerous and sometimes it was better to live in ignorance. Even so, curiosity scratched at me whenever the black-market seller was involved.

'Hello, Trilby.'

'I was hoping I'd see you today. I'll be getting a fresh supply of magicked catnip at the end of the week. I shudder to think how you'd react if it sold out before you could get your grubby paws on some.'

I doubted Trilby had used the word *paws* by accident. I might not have actually told them that I was a cat sith, but somehow they had learned what few others knew. I allowed their remark to pass without comment; only a true fool with no self-control draws notice to that which they want to hide.

'Brilliant,' I said. The cats would be pleased, and happy cats equalled happy Kit.

'But you're not here to buy anything, are you?' Trilby lifted their head and gazed at me with their dark, enigmatic eyes. 'I know that expression. You want information.'

'Actually, it's more advice that I'm after.'

Interest flashed across Trilby's face. 'I'm flattered that you would come to me. The answer is yes.'

I frowned. 'Yes?'

'Yes to Thane – yes to spending more time with him, yes to kissing, yes to sex. Yes to allowing yourself to fall in love with him.'

Whoa: hold up a minute. That wasn't the advice I wanted. 'I'm not falling in love with Thane.'

Trilby grinned. 'Okay.'

'I'm not! I like him. He likes me. We will embark upon a lot of … fun … together once the full moon is over and he's past his wolf phase. We'll be friends with benefits. That's all.'

'If you say so.'

'I do!'

'Cat ladies are allowed to fall in love, you know.'

'I didn't say otherwise,' I huffed. 'But I'm *not* falling in love.'

'Sure thing, Kit.' Trilby shrugged. Then they leaned forward and lowered their voice. 'Because only a true fool with no self-control draws notice to that which they want to hide.'

My mouth dropped open. What the fuck? That was word for word the same sentence that had passed through my mind only moments before. 'Trilby?' I growled, in a tone that suggested violence.

They blinked innocently. 'What?'

I folded my arms and gave my best death stare but they didn't flinch. I stared harder, making a mental note to guard my thoughts more carefully whenever I was in Trilby's presence. *Are you Fae?* I projected silently.

Trilby didn't say anything and their expression didn't alter. Next I filled my head with the opening strains of 'The Lion Sleeps Tonight', silently humming the song to myself to block Trilby from reading any more of my thoughts.

Trilby looked at me; I looked at Trilby.

Eventually they cleared their throat. 'So if you're not looking for advice about your love life, how can I help you?'

I flicked a mental switch and quietened the earworm tune. 'Ban siths,' I said, trying to push away the feeling that I'd made a fatal error by ever trusting the market seller but sensing that it was too late to backtrack now.

'You've been targeted by one? A midnight skirl predicting your death?' Trilby reached for the wooden box in front of them. 'I have some charged-silver four-leaf clover available. It can be effective.'

I shook my head. 'No, my situation isn't like that.' Trilby probably already knew exactly what my situation was like but I told them anyway. 'I have a ban sith staying with me. She's left her family, friends and community and she's lost her ban sith powers.' I hesitated. 'Or so she says.'

'You think she's lying?'

I shrugged uncomfortably. 'I don't know.'

'You think she's dangerous?'

I shrugged again. 'Maybe. Or maybe she's in danger and hasn't told me. She's already unsettled several of my neighbours through no fault of her own, and she's only been in my house for a couple of hours.'

Trilby scratched their chin thoughtfully. 'You can handle your neighbours, Kit, and you're more than capable of dealing with any danger that comes to your doorstep. A ban sith, even a sick ban sith without her powers, would realise that. I don't think you're in any danger from her. Neither are your cats,' they added.

'So what should I do? Leave her alone and trust that everything will be fine?'

Trilby smiled. 'I expect the answer will present itself to you very soon.'

CHAPTER

# SEVEN

I was annoyed with myself for feeling wary when I turned the corner onto my street, but there weren't any baying neighbours at my gate and there were no signs of carnage, ban-sith related or otherwise. All the same, I quickly went inside to check on all five of my cats, plus Tiddles.

As soon as I opened the front door, they emerged from different doorways with the same insistent miaows that told me they wanted their dinner. I gave in to the inevitable and obliged. Anything for a quiet life.

As soon as they were fed and watered, I climbed the steps to the flat upstairs. The door was closed; if Keres was inside, there was no sign of her. I hesitated before knocking quietly. There was no answer.

I pursed my lips, reminding myself how tired and drawn she had looked. She needed to rest and I couldn't allow my uneasy suspicions to get the better of me because I had no hard evidence that she was up to no good. Although it was wise to be cautious, Trilby's words and Boris's grunts had gone some way towards reassuring me and I shouldn't invent scenarios that hadn't happened.

I decided to sleep on the matter then speak to Keres the following day. Nevertheless, I'd be keeping my favourite curved dagger close at hand. If she tried anything during the night, I'd be ready for her.

I pushed the matter out of my head and made myself a salad to compensate for the unhealthy pizza I'd eaten earlier, then settled down in my comfiest chair to read. As three of the cats vied for prime position on my lap, I tried not to wonder what Thane was up to.

The cats eventually came to a compromise with She Who Loves Sunbeams curled up on one side and He Who Crunches Bird Bones and He Who Must Sleep on the other side. She Without An Ear was on guard duty, sitting by the window and blinking out at the darkening sky.

Tiddles and He Who Roams Wide had ventured outside. I'd watched them until they left the garden to make sure they weren't slinking towards Keres' flat, but they were too smart for that. They didn't once look up in that direction, and He Who Roams Wide only twitched his tail when I told him to keep Tiddles out of trouble.

With every passing purr, feline snore and chapter of my book, I relaxed. I had been jumping at shadows. Keres wasn't here through nefarious means; I'd never crossed the ban-sith community and, threats or no, Louise was living proof that they didn't interfere with assassins no matter what they might sense about us. I was fulfilling the terms of my favour to Mallory and helping out a woman in need at the same time. There wasn't a problem.

Or at least there wasn't until I heard a sudden thud reverberate through the ceiling above.

My house was old and sturdily built. The soundproofing might not be modern but it was surprisingly effective, and it was rare to hear any but the loudest of noises from the flat upstairs even without magical muffling intervention. I wouldn't have rented the place out otherwise. But I had certainly heard that particular noisy thump. Whatever Keres had done up there, it had been dramatic.

All four cats with me were now standing and staring upwards with various degrees of raised hackles and wide eyes. 'Everything is fine,' I soothed.

She Without An Ear swung her head towards me, sending me a look that told me I was a complete idiot; to be fair, she might have been right. I stood up, walked out of my door and up to Keres' flat.

As far as I could see, nothing had changed in the past few hours. I knocked loudly and, when there was no answer, called, 'Keres? Are you there? Is everything alright?'

There was no immediate response so I knocked again. I'd break the door down if I had to, but it had only just been repaired after the trouble with Nick MacTire and it was a rigma-role I didn't want to go through again. Besides, Keres deserved her space; for all I knew she was a fan of breakdancing and was having a mini ban-sith rave.

I knocked again, more sharply and insistently. 'Keres!' I called. 'Let me know that you're okay and I'll leave you in peace.'

For a few moments, I heard nothing but eventually I was rewarded with the sound of heavy shuffling footsteps. The door creaked open and Keres appeared, swaying alarmingly from side to side. Her skin was ash grey and her eyes were feverishly bright. Shit.

Any lingering doubts that this was a strange ploy to attack me disappeared: Keres was in real trouble. Suddenly Trilby's words echoed through my mind. They'd called her a *sick* ban sith. Damn it. I should always pay close attention to Trilby's choice of words.

'What's wrong? What's happened?'

Keres' voice was weak and strained, as if she were dragging the words out of her own mouth. 'I'm fine,' she whispered. 'I had a nap and I was a bit woozy when I got up. My legs gave out for a few moments and I fell down. I'll be fine in a few minutes.'

I doubted that because she looked seriously unwell. 'Let me get you some water,' I said. 'You need to sit down and—'

I didn't get the chance to finish my sentence. Keres stopped swaying, stared at me unblinkingly then her eyes rolled back in her head and she collapsed into my arms.

Caught unawares I staggered backwards, though it certainly wasn't her weight that made me unsteady. Although she was a grown woman, she was little more than skin and bones. I hissed under my breath then picked her up, carried her to the bedroom and laid her on the bed.

She was taking shallow, ragged gasps that sounded unhealthy but at least were regular. Her skin felt clammy, and when I pressed my hand to her forehead her eyelids fluttered open then closed again.

I got to work. First I loosened her shirt buttons to make sure her chest wasn't constricted in any way. Thinking of Louise, I tilted back her head and checked the inside of her mouth in case she'd been poisoned. There was no discolouration around her gums; without a blood test I wouldn't be able to tell if she'd ingested anything lethal.

'I'm going to check your body for wounds, Keres,' I said aloud. I had no way of knowing whether she could hear me or not, but I wanted her to know what I was doing. 'You might have a cut that's gone septic.'

I ran my hands along her arms and her hands, then unfastened more of her shirt buttons to check her torso and her back. There was nothing but a graze on her knee that appeared to be healing well. Whatever was happening to the ban sith was happening internally. That was not good at all.

I covered her with a blanket and darted out of the flat. Downstairs, four baleful sets of feline eyes watched me as I ran through my front door and into my spare room to retrieve my small magic chest. My skills were limited to first aid and field surgery but it would take a while to get Keres proper medical help; I had to have something that would help her until I could find a real doctor.

I flicked through the small packets of old magics and reserved spells until I found some feverfew, a general cure-all that was used by Preternaturals in lieu of aspirin or paracetamol. It was stronger than either of those, though it certainly wouldn't cure anything serious. Unfortunately it was all I had, so I scooped it up and prepared to return to Keres.

The cats were in the doorway, bristling with uncharacteristic malevolence. 'What?' I asked. 'You don't want me to help her? She's ill – very ill.'

They continued to stare.

I drew in a breath. 'I know you have a problem with her but none of you will tell me what it is. Right now *my* biggest problem is that Keres is seriously ill.'

The cats continued to glower, then He Who Crunches Bird Bones reluctantly padded forward and butted my lower leg with his head before presenting me with his left flank. His whiskers twitched and he glanced up at me. 'I'm not sure there's time,' I said. 'She's passed out upstairs.' I waved the small packet of magicked herbs. 'I have to give her this first.'

He Who Crunches Bird Bones hissed softly but I stood my ground. 'It's not that I don't trust you, but none of us need the decaying corpse of a ban sith upstairs. I'll give her this medicine,' I promised, 'and then I'll do it.'

The cat sighed heavily but moved aside to let me pass. The other three also gave me space. 'Five minutes,' I told them. 'Tops.'

I took the stairs two at a time. Keres was still unconscious, still in the same position. 'I've got some medicine,' I said aloud. 'It's nothing special, only witched feverfew, but it might bring your temperature down to normal and keep you stable for a few hours. I'll tip it into your mouth. It tastes nasty, but that's only temporary.'

There was no response. I ripped open the packet, gently opened her lips and scattered the contents into her mouth, following it with a drop of water. Thankfully, Keres' instincts kicked in and she swallowed.

My shoulders sagged with relief when her breathing eased. 'I'll be back shortly,' I promised her before I returned to the cats.

He Who Crunches Bird Bones was already waiting by the front door. 'Will this give me answers?' I asked.

He didn't respond, just presented his left flank again. Fair enough.

I plucked some fur from his body and pinched it between my finger and thumb before dropping it onto my tongue and swallowing. The twisting spasms began shortly afterwards.

When I returned to Keres, it was on four legs rather than two. I was too amped up to wait for the tingling from my transformation to stop and I bounded up the stairs, my temporary tail waving behind me.

I'd barely taken two steps inside the flat when I sensed the shift in atmosphere. There was nothing specific to put a finger –

or claw – on, but there was a deep sense of wrongness, of something evil and nasty taking root and curling its dark ways into every corner of the small flat. My fur rose and I felt my lips pull back over my teeth. I had to fight against the snarl that threatened to escape.

It took me a while to compose myself but, when I was calm, I started forward again, my claws scraping faintly against the wooden floorboards. The closer I got to the bedroom, the greater my sense of foreboding. Every part of my body was screaming at me to turn tail and flee. I couldn't do that, though; I had to see what the cats were seeing.

I entered the bedroom and my whiskers quivered as the faint scent from the feverfew tickled my nostrils. The ban sith's breathing was more audible through these cat ears and I was aware of every scrape and gurgle from her lungs.

I jumped onto the foot of the bed and stared at her. That was when I knew.

Her arms and legs were just as I'd left them and her eyes were still closed. To all intents and purposes she looked exactly the same as she had a few minutes earlier, but my feline eyes could see far more than my human ones. Now I could see what the cats could, it was impossible to look away.

Keres was enveloped in a dark miasmic cloud, the core of which appeared to be the centre of her chest. At first it was hard to see beyond the malevolent aura that surrounded her, but when I focused on her body I saw more.

Evil had taken hold of her and was growing within her like an invasive tree root. Gnarly black tendrils were stretching out from her heart, pulsating with every heartbeat. They started to quiver and bend towards me as if they were sentient and wanted to capture me in the way they'd captured Keres, to insinuate themselves beneath my skin and take root within my veins.

My limbs were rigid with terror. This wasn't an enemy I could defeat no matter what weapons or skills I used. It would take everything – it would take *me*. I hissed and then I did the only thing I could do. I ran out of that room as fast as my legs could carry me.

# EIGHT

My heart rate eventually returned to a normal steady beat and my thoughts coalesced into a more rational form, but I didn't fully calm down until several minutes after I'd choked up the hairball and transformed into the two-legged version of myself.

Something was attacking Keres from within. It wasn't the ban sith herself that the cats were afraid of, it was whatever was inside her that had put the fear of God into them. It was some sort of parasitic evil, but whether it had been placed there by a curse or whether it was a contagious magical virus, I didn't know. Whatever, it was definitely the reason my cats were terrified of her – and it might also be the reason she'd lost her ban sith powers.

Had Mallory been aware of what was happening to Keres? I doubted it. Skilled as Mallory was, she was a squib and didn't possess any magical power of her own. If Keres had looked ill, Mallory would have put it down to a bug.

At that moment, my concern wasn't where the black weed inside Keres had come from but how to stop it because I felt certain that she would be dead by the end of the week if it remained unchecked.

Tension clawed at me. I suddenly wished that Thane was with me and I wasn't dealing with this on my own, but he was out for the count and turning furry. He wouldn't be capable of much other than monosyllabic grunts and shuffling footsteps until late tomorrow morning. Werewolves were nothing if not predictable in their transformations.

You've dealt with worse than this, Kit, I told myself sternly. You've always coped on your own before and you can cope on your own now. An invisible enemy was harder to fight, but I wasn't powerless. There would be a solution.

I glanced down at the assembly of cats. 'We need a doctor.' She Without An Ear miaowed. 'No.' I rolled my eyes. 'Absolutely *not* for euthanasia.'

She Who Loves Sunbeams flicked her ears and blinked. 'No,' I told her. 'Not that sort of doctor either. We need the sort of doctor who...' My voice trailed away and then I smiled. 'We need the sort of doctor who isn't a doctor.'

I grinned and sprang up: I knew exactly who could help Keres. I grabbed my bag and headed straight for the door.

She Without An Ear and He Who Crunches Bird Bones came with me, determined to wait outside until I returned so they could protect the house from the monster upstairs. Whether she was unconscious or not, they wouldn't take any chances with Keres and nothing I could say would appease them.

The sky was darkening as I reached my garden gate and stepped onto the street but I could still see Mr and Mrs Dinsbury marching towards me. No prizes for guessing what they wanted, but at least they weren't carrying pitchforks. Not yet, anyway.

The unhappy couple strode towards me, their expressions

set and their shoulders pulled back; they wanted me to know that they meant business. My gaze travelled down as I assessed them for weapons but their hands were empty, although Arthur Dinsbury had curled his fingers into tight fists.

His wife had a slight bulge by her right hip, suggesting there was something in her pocket, but it wasn't gun or knife shaped. It was probably nothing more than a crumpled bag of mint humbugs – I'd seen Mrs Dinsbury sucking them on many occasions after she'd weaned herself off betel nuts. I supposed that mint humbugs were a healthier replacement.

Despite their lack of obvious weaponry, I wasn't daft enough to let my guard down. This was Coldstream; plenty of inhabitants didn't need a sharp object to cause bloody havoc. Then I ran through what they might say and how I should best respond.

From the garden, She Without An Ear growled, sensing the impending confrontation. 'It's fine,' I murmured. She sent me a narrow-eyed glance to emphasise her belief in my absolute stupidity but at least she stopped growling.

He Who Crunches Bird Bones quivered then jumped onto the low wall that marked the boundary of my property. 'Sheathe those claws,' I told him. Naturally, he ignored me.

Mrs Dinsbury – Muriel to her friends, of whom I was not one – cleared her throat. 'Ms McCafferty.' Her voice was thin and reedy but she still managed to convey an air of command.

I smiled. I didn't want to waste a lot of time on this pair. Polite but firm was the way to win the day. 'Good evening.' I side-stepped, turned my back on them and moved towards Dave's gate. Perhaps I'd get lucky and they'd walk away.

'We want to talk to you!' she called after me.

Damn it. 'I'm afraid I'm very busy,' I replied.

Dave was peering out of his window and I held up two

fingers. I needed to talk to him but the confrontation with the Dinsburys would be easier without his interference. He scowled but nodded; he was a better neighbour than I deserved.

'This will only take a minute,' Arthur Dinsbury said, deepening his voice in a bid to sound like a tough guy.

I sighed and turned to face them. Although their timing sucked, this might be a good thing because a confrontation would be easier to handle than a long-drawn-out campaign of neighbourly passive aggression. 'Go on.' I smiled again, to show that I was still the friendly harmless neighbour with too many cats and too little in the way of protection.

Unfortunately, He Who Crunches Bird Bones compromised my attempt to establish a peaceful tone by snapping out a paw towards Arthur Dinsbury. It was only a warning shot but Arthur jumped backwards and gave an inarticulate yell. This wasn't going as well as I'd hoped and we'd not even got to the crux of the matter yet.

Muriel Dinsbury's eyes spat hatred. 'You've been living on this street long enough to know what's expected of you, Ms McCafferty.'

'Did I miss the last bin collection day?' I asked sweetly. 'Maggie the wirry cow still comes on Fridays, doesn't she? I don't think I put my bins out late.'

Arthur bared his teeth. 'This isn't about the bins,' he spat.

'Oh good!' I beamed relief. 'I'd hate to leave rubbish lying out on the street. Nobody wants to attract rats, especially when the rats attract bigger creatures that cause all sorts of problems.' My tone was innocent but I was well aware that the Dinsburys had received several complaints from other households about leaving their bins out at the wrong times.

Muriel clearly wasn't in the mood for prevarication or implied criticism. She put her hands on her hips and snarled, a surprisingly impressive sound from such a small woman. I flinched and looked alarmed. 'Goodness, are you feeling alright? That sounded nasty.'

Her cheeks turned scarlet. 'I am *not* feeling alright!' She jabbed a finger in the direction of the upstairs flat. 'You have a ban sith in there!'

There was no point in denying it or explaining that Keres had lost her ban-sith powers. Even if they believed me, they would only distrust her more. 'I do,' I said calmly. 'Keres is a good friend of mine.' I didn't think she'd mind that lie.

'Friend?' Muriel shrieked. 'You're friends with one of those … things?'

'She's a person. She's not a thing.'

'She brings death!'

'No, she doesn't.'

'She's a fucking ban sith! That's what they do! She can't stay here! We all have a responsibility to keep this neighbourhood safe!'

'Ban siths *predict* death, they don't bring it,' I said. 'In fact, that's why she's here. I asked her to stay for a few weeks to ensure that everyone is safe.'

'*What?*' Arthur Dinsbury was baffled – and very, very loud.

I waved my arms expansively and hoped that the Dinsburys were too irate to notice my outlandish lie. 'I love this neighbourhood. I want to be sure that everyone is fit, healthy and nowhere near death's door. Having a ban sith around is the best way to guarantee everyone's safety.'

Muriel's face scrunched up. 'That makes no sense! She'll kill us all!'

'She's in my house so if anyone is likely to die, it'll be me. But I won't die because Keres told me that there's no death anywhere near me and there never has been. I am a death-free zone.'

That was a bald-faced lie and if the Dinsburys hadn't been

so full of self-righteousness, they'd have realised it. I warmed to my topic. 'In fact, Keres has told me that nobody on this street is in any danger of dying – not me, not you, not anyone.'

The couple stared at me. If anyone did pass away in the next few weeks, I'd be screwed so I mentally crossed my fingers that all my neighbours would remain hale and hearty.

I produced an earnest smile. 'I was concerned about all those recent burglaries. I thought the thief might end up hurting someone, so I asked Keres to check and make sure that nobody was in mortal danger. I thought having her stay around would be a good idea because it'll keep that burglar away.' I blinked a few times and silently congratulated myself on my quick thinking, though that damned thieving trow had better stay away or there would be a lot of explaining to do.

Arthur nudged his wife. 'That makes sense,' he muttered.

Muriel wasn't so sure. 'How long is she staying?' she barked.

Good question. 'Until the danger has passed,' I replied smoothly.

Her eyes narrowed. 'There are other ways to keep Danksville safe. A ban sith is extreme.'

'You know that Jimmy Leighton was targeted the other night?' I said.

'I heard that,' Arthur said.

His wife's expression turned mutinous. 'If anybody on this street dies...'

'They won't,' I replied. They'd better not.

'She can't stay for long.'

Keres was in no state to harm me, so as far as I was concerned she could stay as long as she wanted to – although given her current condition that might not be long at all. 'She's here as a favour to me and to Danksville,' I said. 'She's not here to harm us. Once she's confident we're all safe, I'm sure she'll leave.'

'She'd better!' Muriel grabbed her husband's hand and they marched back in the direction of their own house. I exhaled. That could have gone worse.

'Was any of that true?' Dave called from his porch. I glanced over my shoulder at him. 'You know that Sitwell on the corner is ninety-six years old?'

'I'm aware,' I replied.

'And that Alicia Timmings at number forty-eight has stage three cancer?'

'I know that, too.'

'All hell will break loose if either of them croak while Keres is here.'

'I took a calculated risk. Given enough time, everyone will realise that there's no reason to be afraid of a ban sith living in this street.'

'Hmm.' He scratched the whiskers on his chin and looked at me dubiously. 'People like the Dinsburys have deep-seated beliefs. It will take more than time to change their minds. Obviously I don't mind her staying with you, but it might be better for her if she didn't stay too long.'

Easier said than done; at the moment Keres couldn't leave even if she wanted to. 'She's not well,' I told him. 'I don't know what's wrong. I need to get a doctor to come and see her. She's unconscious, Dave – I think she's very sick.'

He stiffened. 'She's ill?'

'Really ill.'

Dave straightened his shoulders. 'I'll sit with her until you get back.'

It was what I'd hoped he'd say. 'You're sure?'

'Of course I'm sure,' he snapped. 'But if I catch a nasty disease and die, you'll be the one who has to deal with the fall-out,' he added, with a deep scowl.

He Who Crunches Bird Bones hissed but Dave only

shrugged at him. 'I'm telling the truth. Which is more than she did to the damned Dinsburys.'

True. But as long as nobody died in the near future, it would be fine. I hoped.

# NINE

There were a lot of doctors, nurses and wellness practitioners in Coldstream because Preternaturals often required medical attention. Magic didn't always go hand in hand with good health; quite the opposite, in fact. I could have found plenty of medics nearby to help Keres but I wanted the right sort of person. And he lived some distance away.

I'd come across Fergus a few months earlier when I'd dragged the semi-conscious body of a pompous witch called Quentin Hightower through the streets. Fergus wasn't exactly a doctor but he ran a tiny clinic and possessed exactly the sort of skill that I reckoned Keres needed. If anyone could work out what was wrong with her – and help her – he could.

Fergus wasn't a cat sith so he couldn't transform into a cat and see the black weeds growing inside her body, but he did have the magical ability to sniff out ailments. It would be worth travelling to the other side of the city to fetch him, although going from one end of Coldstream to the other would be more complicated during the full moon.

I waited patiently at the end of the road for the next purple-spark-laden tram to stop in front of me. The on-board guard inspected me briefly before allowing me to pass through the wolfsbane barrier.

Werewolves wouldn't be allowed on public transport until Monday when the full moon had passed. Although they were generally able to control their more violent urges when they were in public, there were exceptions to every rule. It was twenty-two years since a werewolf had boarded a tram during the full moon and killed everyone on board, and painful memories like that took a long time to subside. Besides, no transformed wolf needed to take the tram because their four legs would carry them much further and faster than any vehicle, even a magical one such as this.

I changed trams at Crackendon Square and underwent the same checks. There was a group of seven werewolves, all furry, hovering in the far corner of the public square. Even though Thane was a lone wolf who was usually ignored by his own kind, I checked the small posse to see if he was among them. He wasn't. By the time we pulled away, the werewolves were leaving, doubtless heading for the outskirts of the city where there was more space for them to expend their lupine energy.

I disembarked outside Bruggens, a well-appointed witchery store with marked-up prices, and walked the few hundred metres to the grubby clinic. The Caring Touch Institution looked like the sort of place that would scam you out of every last penny you owned then kick you while you were down, but appearances were deceptive. Anyone who crossed me always found that out very quickly.

I pushed open the front door, pleased to discover that the waiting room was devoid of patients. To be fair, it was late in the evening so I was lucky that the clinic was open. although the welcome desk – which wasn't welcoming in the slightest –

was as empty as it had been during my first visit. Fergus clearly hadn't paid any attention to my advice to hire a receptionist.

Rather than take a seat and wait, I marched to the inner door, opened it and drew breath to call out. I didn't get the chance, though, because Fergus appeared with his arm hooked through that of an elderly witch. He was clearly escorting her to the exit.

'Hi, Fergus,' I called brightly.

Both he and the old witch ignored me. 'Mind your step, Mrs Davidson,' he murmured.

She responded with a breathy expression of gratitude, and I stepped back to let her get past. That didn't stop the older woman from jabbing me with her bony elbow, which I was certain was no accident. I smiled; I looked forward to the day when I was old enough to carry out minor assaults without comment from my victims.

'Remember to take the pills with every meal.'

'Yes, doctor.'

'Just Fergus,' he answered smoothly.

'Yes, doctor.'

Fergus gave up and helped her outside. 'Mind how you go.'

I didn't hear what she said in return but whatever it was made Fergus appear less blearily beleaguered for a long moment. He closed the door after her.

Now he was all mine. 'I need your help,' I said loudly.

He glanced at me, nostrils flaring. There was no sign of recognition. 'You're fine,' he said dismissively.

'It's not me who's ill. It's a friend of mine.'

He raised a thin eyebrow. 'Another friend? Is this one another highly placed witch that you've kidnapped?'

So he *did* remember me. 'A ban sith.'

I didn't miss the flare of interest in his eyes though he masked it quickly. 'Ban siths have their own clinic.'

That was news to me. I wondered if Keres had gone there when she'd lost her powers and, if she had, what they'd told her. 'I think your particular medical skills will be more appropriate in this scenario,' I said smoothly.

Fergus spun round slowly. 'I don't see any ban siths here.'

Ha. Ha. I held my patience. 'She's too sick to travel. She's resting at my place.'

'Where's that?'

'Danksville.'

He pulled a face. 'That's almost an hour away.'

Hardly. 'Forty minutes,' I said. 'Tops.'

'I don't make house calls. Anyway, it's late. I'm clocking off for the night.'

'I can make it worth your while.'

Fergus gave me a long look. 'I'm not so desperate for money that I'll travel to the worst suburb in Coldstream during the full moon.' He inclined his head. 'Good day to you.' He trudged off behind the desk towards the rooms beyond.

'Something is inside her,' I called after him. 'Something dark that's eating away at her. I don't know what it is, but it feels evil.' He stopped moving. It was almost imperceptible but there was a definite stiffening to his shoulders. I doubled down. 'I think it'll kill her if we don't find a way to get rid of it.'

There was another long silence then Fergus gave a heavy sigh. 'Very well. Give me a few minutes to get my bag and some supplies.'

I allowed myself a small smile of triumph. 'No problem.'

THE TRAM RIDE to Crackendon Square passed without incident. I tried to engage Fergus in small talk by mentioning the full moon and the price of witched saffron powder but he ignored me. He gripped his black-leather medical bag tightly in one hand and stared out of the window as the tram wended its way through the streets.

When we boarded the second tram, things were different. Fergus submitted to the wolfsbane check then clumped towards its centre while I dropped two tokens at the front to pay for us both. Instead of gazing out of the window again, he sniffed the air and his eyes widened in alarm. He swung his head from side to side to examine the other passengers then fixed on a teenage dryad sitting quietly in the far corner.

Her head was bowed, her long hair draped across her shoulders, and she was giving off more stay-away vibes than the most anxious of feral cats. Fergus didn't appear to care that she wanted to be left alone. He strode towards her, pushing past a troll and an exhausted looking druid, until he was standing over the teenager, breathing heavily.

I watched with interest. On the first occasion we'd met I'd worked out that although Fergus might not be a trained doctor, he possessed the magical ability to sniff out health problems – literally sniff them out, judging by the way his nose was hovering over the dryad's head. After several seconds twitching his nostrils, he crouched beside her and began to speak.

He kept his voice low so that even though I strained to listen, I couldn't hear what he was saying above the trundle of the tram. At first the dryad didn't move her head or look at him but he didn't appear bothered by her lack of interest; he continued talking to her until she finally reached out, grabbed his hands and squeezed them tight.

When she lifted her head, I caught a glimpse of tear-filled eyes – but she was smiling.

Fergus waited until she released her hold on him, nodded, patted her shoulder and stood up. He joined me by the tram window. 'Problem?' I asked.

He smiled serenely. 'No. No problem.'

I glanced at the dryad. She was no longer staring at her lap. Although I could still see the glint of unshed tears in her wide violet eyes, she looked at peace with herself.

'You're a good man, Fergus.'

He snorted in response.

I couldn't know what had bothered the young dryad or what Fergus had said to reassure her, but his actions made me think of my own insignificant issues. 'Is reading minds one of your skills?' I asked quietly.

He snorted again. 'Nobody can read minds but anyone can read facial expressions and concealed cues. Some people can see auras or recognise emotions, and there are a few like me who can sense illness. But nobody can actually read another living being's mind.'

'Are you sure?' I pressed.

His derisive expression melted away as he glanced at me. 'No,' he said. 'I can never be completely sure. But I'm *mostly* sure.'

I thought about Trilby. It might have been a coincidence that the enigmatic black-market seller had voiced the same words that had passed through my head only moments before. I'd known Trilby for some time; if they could read my mind, I was certain it was a new development.

'There are many skilled con artists living in Coldstream,' Fergus said. 'You don't strike me as someone who is easily fooled, but nobody is immune. Sometimes it's the more educated and experienced people who are susceptible to scammers.'

I was well aware that self-confidence and the belief that you weren't a typical fraud victim could make you fall into a con-artist's trap, but I didn't believe that Trilby was a scammer. Not for a second. All the same, my new wariness of them wouldn't dissipate any time soon.

'I'm careful,' I said aloud.

Fergus nodded. 'You should be.'

I looked again at the dryad and then at Fergus. At least I was certain of one thing: he was definitely the right person to help Keres.

CHAPTER

# TEN

I could feel my neighbours glaring at me from behind their net curtains as we completed the last of our journey on foot. It was late spring; the sun was still shining and the air was warm; at this time in the evening there would usually be people outside. In Scotland, you have to make the most of the good weather while you can, but every front garden was empty and nobody was in the cobbled street. It bothered me that they were afraid to step outside their houses but, to be honest, my neighbours' concerns were far less worrying than Keres' condition.

She Without An Ear greeted us, miaowing from her position on top of a wall before we reached my garden gate. I saw Fergus flinch out of the corner of my eye. 'Not a cat fan?' I asked in a deceptively casual tone.

'I won't admit to a preference for dogs when I'm in the company of a cat sith,' Fergus said, reminding me that his abilities extended to more than sensing illness.

'I like dogs,' I said. She Without An Ear miaowed plaintively. 'But,' I added quickly, 'I like cats more.' The grumpy moggy relaxed. 'You know that cats can sense when someone is ill,' I told him.

'Sure. But can they do anything about that illness?'

Not really.

Fergus examined my face and nodded. 'In that case, I win.' I wasn't going to argue with him – not until he'd helped Keres.

I directed him to the flight of stairs that led to the upper flat. Fergus knocked lightly on the front door and entered while I followed on his heels. Dave immediately appeared and glared at us. 'This is Fergus,' I said quickly. 'He has considerable medical skills. I think he can help Keres.'

Dave's expression didn't soften. 'She's not doing well. She's running a high temperature and she seems to be delirious.'

Fergus nodded and hefted his bag. 'She's in there?' He pointed to the bedroom.

Dave didn't answer him; instead he looked at me. 'He doesn't look like a doctor.'

'That's because I'm not a doctor,' Fergus responded. He pushed past the druid. 'Word of advice,' he said cheerfully. 'Cut down on sugar. You're about three months away from a diagnosis of diabetes.'

Dave went pale. 'Druids are susceptible to diabetes,' he muttered. 'Everyone knows that.'

'Perhaps,' I said gently, 'that's a good reason to eat less sweet stuff.'

'Says the pizza lady.'

Fergus called, '*You* should cut down on that, too.' My face fell. More salad for dinner, then.

He strode into the bedroom and I followed while Dave hovered by the door, his suspicious eyes watching Fergus's every move. It was clear that Keres had deteriorated, despite the minor herbal concoction I'd poured down her throat. Her skin was flushed and her limbs were twitching. Her pale lips were moving, whispering feverish words that made little sense.

'Is she—?' I began.

'Hush,' Fergus ordered. I fell silent; the best thing I could do was keep out of his way.

He knelt by the bedside and took Keres' hand. She moaned slightly. 'Don't you worry now,' he said. 'My name is Fergus Boneward and I'm here to help you. I'm a witch who specialises in sickness and injury. I'll take a quick look and see if I can find out what's wrong.' He leaned across her bed and inhaled deeply.

Dave stared, his expression growing more incredulous. 'This is too strange,' he muttered.

I waved my hand to tell him to stay quiet, but even I felt uncertain when Fergus spent the next five minutes sniffing every part of Keres' body. At one point his face was so close to her skin that he could have licked her. Strange didn't begin to cover it.

Eventually he pulled away and stood up. 'Okay,' he said to Dave and me. 'Pay attention. There are several ingredients you need. Three tablespoons of dandelion essence. A teaspoon of sprigglewort – the powdered stuff, not the root. Spanish mistletoe, three and a half grams, no more, no less. You can buy the good stuff at the Pickover Witchery store. Simmer the ingredients for four minutes and stir them together using the bark from an alder tree that's been harvested at midnight. *Exactly* midnight. You'll have to collect that ingredient yourself because it's got to be fresh.' He gave me a long, flat look. 'I'd do that tonight, if I were you. Much longer and your friend here won't make it.'

I nodded. 'Will that cure her of whatever this is? Will she be okay?'

Fergus's expression didn't alter. 'She won't be cured and she won't be okay.'

'Then what's the point?' Dave demanded.

'It'll buy you some time. That's the best I can do.'

'That's not good enough!'

I agreed. 'What's wrong with her? There must be other medicine we can use or somewhere we can take her.'

'You can drag that poor ban sith all over Coldstream and shove as much medicine into her as you like but it won't help. There's only one person who can cure her now, and I doubt you'll be able to find them in time.'

My eyes narrowed. 'Who? Who do we need to find?'

Fergus sighed. 'The person who stole her voice,' he said reluctantly.

'*Stole* her voice?' I repeated.

'Her magical voice has gone – that's why she's sick and that's why you can sense something evil inside her,' Fergus explained. 'Somebody has used magic to steal the essence of what makes that woman a ban sith, and the emptiness that remains is destroying her.'

'Why would someone steal her magical essence?'

'I can't answer that.' He shook his head sadly. 'All I can tell you is that somebody has taken her power and now she's being attacked by her own body. Unless you can retrieve her ban sith voice and return it to her, you can't save her.' He met my eyes. 'Any medicine will be a temporary salve. Without her voice, she'll die.'

I swallowed. 'How long does she have?'

'With the medicine?' Fergus considered. 'Two weeks, maybe a bit longer. Without it, less than three days. I'm sorry.'

Dave and I stared at him and, from her bed, Keres moaned again.

My ANGER GETTING the better of me, I stomped around my kitchen. What was happening to Keres seemed like a cruel and unusual punishment. Stealing someone's life was one thing but ripping out the essence of who they were was far worse. My cat-sith powers made me who I was and I couldn't begin to imagine the horror I'd feel if I could no longer access that part of my soul.

Keres was adrift in an ocean without a raft, a paddle or even a lifejacket. I tried to picture the thieving bastard who'd stolen her powers and failed. Even to me, such villainy was beyond the pale.

One problem at a time, I told myself. Focus on what you can change *now*, not what you can't.

I had sprigglewort and dandelion essence in my box of supplies and Dave went to buy some Spanish mistletoe from Pickover at the same time as Fergus left. Thankfully, the large witchery store was open 24/7.

The problem was the alder bark: in this part of the country, alder trees only grew in one of the dryads' groves on the west side of the city and they controlled the supply of bark and essence. To harvest some fresh bark at midnight I would have to petition the dryad leaders for access, which would take more time than Keres had left. It would be far quicker to steal it.

Unfortunately, with the advent of the full moon, security around the groves would be heightened because some groups of fully transformed werewolves didn't always pay attention to the niceties of normal society. Left unchecked, they had a nasty habit of trampling over the carefully cultivated plants and seedlings when they were under the moon's control. It wouldn't be easy to collect a section of bark without being noticed – I could do it, but I'd have to plan carefully.

All five of my cats had assembled in the kitchen, including He Who Roams Wide who was back from wherever he'd been. Tiddles, curious at the turn of events and no doubt affected by my angry mood, had joined them.

'Yes, of course I'll help her,' I told them all. 'I will find the bastard who's stolen her magic and make them pay, but first I need to buy her some time.'

He Who Crunches Bird Bones and She Without An Ear looked dubious, He Who Must Sleep yawned, and She Who Loves Sunbeams began to groom herself nervously. He Who Roams Wide was already on all four paws, ready to go at a moment's notice.

I nodded at him. 'Yes,' I said. 'That would be helpful indeed.' He purred as Tiddles emitted a small questing miaow.

'No,' I told her. 'You stay here.' She was a young cat, little more than a kitten really. She was high in feline confidence but low in experience, and she'd be a liability. Besides, Thane would kill me if anything happened to her.

I ignored her narrow-eyed response and jerked open one of my cupboards, rummaging around for everything I would need. Taking weapons wouldn't be a good idea; dryads were more capable than they were given credit for, especially when it came to the sanctity of their groves. Although it was unlikely they'd catch me, if they did I'd be hard pressed to explain carrying lethal weapons. Neither did I want to harm any dryads.

It would be far safer to take some minor sleeping potions. I was aiming for stealth, not violence, despite the desire for vengeance that was tugging at my soul. Even the sleeping powders were only to be used as a last resort.

I extracted three sachets and taped them to the right and left sides of my ribcage. Only that which touched my bare skin could endure the transformation process from human to cat and back again. My hand hovered over my favourite curved dagger but I resisted the urge to strap it to my thigh. Its presence would cause problems, not solve them.

In my bedroom I abandoned my fuzzy cat-lady attire for tight black clothing that would allow me to sneak around in the shadows undetected. The only faint glint of colour came from my watch face, but I couldn't leave it behind because I had to harvest the alder bark at the stroke of midnight or all this would be for nothing. I double-checked that its timing was accurate, though I needn't have worried; it was an expensive piece of kit from my EEL days when every second on the job had counted. It kept perfect time.

She Who Loves Sunbeams swished her tail from side to side. 'Don't worry,' I told her. 'Everything will be fine. I'll be back by two am.' I patted her head, then turned to each of the other cats in turn. Once all their needs had been satisfied, I nodded to He Who Roams Wide. 'Come on then,' I told him. 'We've got quite a distance to cover and it's already getting late. '

His eyes glinted with adventurous anticipation. Half a minute later, both of us were out of the door and away.

# ELEVEN

I avoided the tram. Word on the street was the tram witches and the dryads had grown particularly close in recent months and in the unlikely event that my theft was noticed, I didn't want anyone to be able to track my movements. It was rare for anyone who wasn't a dryad or a dignitary from another of the main Preternatural groups to travel to the groves, especially at this time of night. Going there on foot was by far the most sensible option, even if I wasn't as fit or as fast as I used to be.

I offered He Who Roams Wide the option of perching on my shoulder like Tiddles had done but he refused with a derisive sniff. 'Very well,' I told him. 'But we have to move fast. We can't spare any time sniffing interesting patches of darkness or investigating random sounds.' He blinked once: that was the most I would get from him.

I set off at a steady jog. Fortunately my sleek black cat heeded my words and didn't dally, even when a plump rat with far more bravado than sense crossed the street a few metres in front of us.

We moved fast, and little more than an hour later the dark

perimeter of the first grove came into sight. There were still thirty-nine minutes until midnight. Go me.

'I've still got it,' I whispered to the cat. 'I'm still good at this.'

If he heard me, he didn't react. I'd have to save any further boasting for She Who Loves Sunbeams; she'd be far more appreciative of my accomplishment.

I wasn't foolish enough to stroll through the main gates of the grove; the dryads would be wary of any unknown creatures, human or cat, passing that way. I could already see a large group of them at the entrance keeping an eye out for roaming werewolves. Although that entrance would be lined with wolfsbane, there wasn't enough of it in the country to ring such a vast grove on a monthly basis. The dryads, like most other big estate owners, relied on manned security during the full moon. They'd be alert and ready for anything and I knew I had to avoid them.

I beckoned to the cat and we skirted the high wooden fence until we reached a quieter corner where a towering oak tree was standing helpfully outside the perimeter. He Who Roams Wide emitted a questioning chirrup and I nodded; it was perfect, especially with those high, overhanging branches.

'Twenty minutes,' I said quietly. 'I don't want to spend any more time than necessary in the grove. We'll wait out here until the right moment.'

I pressed my spine against the trunk of the old oak where the shadows were deepest; it would take very keen eyes to spot me. I shivered slightly, though not from the cold, while the cat at my feet pawed at a section of the ground with vague disinterest.

He stopped and drew closer to my feet when the night air was suddenly filled with the sound of approaching howls. He Who Roams Wide was both brave and adventurous but he was cautious when large groups of marauding werewolves were involved. One wolf on its own wasn't too dangerous, but they tended to move in packs when the moon was full and pack mentality was never a good thing even at the best of times.

The first werewolf to appear was a brash young mutt, little more than a teenager, but he slunk out from the buildings on the other side of the grove with the puffed-up arrogance that only the full moon could provide. I didn't know which pack this kid was from, or why he'd separated from other elder and more experienced members of his extended family. I didn't particularly care as long as he kept out of my way.

His coat was silver and it was shining brightly despite the darkness, making him more visible than he realised. When his buddies appeared, I saw why he was so confident: six werewolves were trailing him with lolling tongues and bright eyes, knocking into each other, giddy from their transformation. They stopped behind the youngster and simultaneously raised their heads and howled to the glowing round moon that was barely visible behind the clouds.

Shit: seven werewolves spoiling for a fight was the last thing I needed. They weren't trying to hide and they were less than fifty metres from my oak tree; there was no chance that the dryads on guard at the main gate wouldn't be drawn towards them.

If I left the relative safety of the oak tree, somebody would see me. I silently cursed the pack alpha who had allowed these idiots to roam unchecked; at least three of them looked old enough to know far better.

It was a small number of dickish wolves that forced the majority of Coldstream's residents to hunker down indoors during the official full moon nights. Werewolves could generally control their baser urges regardless of the time of the month, but the inclination of less-disciplined wolves to whoop, holler and occasionally riot their way through the city's streets could be off-putting. Usually they grew out of such behaviour; more mature werewolves simply enjoyed a night of furry transformation and the freedom to run. But there were exceptions to every rule.

It didn't take long for the dryads to appear, seven suited-and-booted figures striding down the street towards the howling wolves, one dryad for each werewolf. Grove security knew what they were doing: any more would be seen by the wolves as an act of aggression, any less and the dryads might be viewed as weak. I didn't have to check their expressions or read their minds to know that the dryads would want to move the wolves on without any bloodshed.

I double-checked the time, hoping this matter would be dealt with swiftly because I couldn't afford a delay. That alder bark had to be stripped at midnight exactly if it was to be of any help to Keres. My plan was to enter the grove in cat form, but both groups would notice me swallowing a clump of fur from He Who Roams Wide and effecting my painful transformation so I needed them to leave as soon as possible.

The tallest dryad pulled slightly ahead and stopped. One by one, the werewolves ceased their howling and glanced in his direction. I noted with a sinking heart that the youngest wolf, who'd been leading the way, was baring his teeth. He was hoping for a fight.

The lead dryad didn't smile, but when he spoke his tone was pleasant. 'Good evening.'

A small female werewolf lunged towards him and snapped at the air. It was little more than a warning shot and the dryad didn't flinch. He was far more experienced with this sort of confrontation than most of the werewolves who were now growling at him.

His voice rang through the night. 'This is not a suitable place for you to be. I strongly suggest you turn and leave.'

The female werewolf lunged again and drew closer; she was growing bolder and so were her buddies. The silver wolf was pawing at the ground, snarling more loudly; even from my concealed position by the oak tree, I could see that his hackles were raised. If young Silver had been a feral cat I'd already have been backing away, but the dryad had to hold his ground.

Although the three older werewolves were making no move to draw their compatriots away, they were smart enough to hold back and watch rather than try any moves of their own. It was difficult to tell from this angle but at least one of them seemed to have old battle scars and that didn't bode well. The younger wolves would likely covet similar badges of honour.

One of the skinnier werewolves padded forward and circled around the cluster of dryads. He was joined by another, then another, until the three wolves were parading around the dryads in ever-decreasing circles. A knot of tension tightened in my belly.

Then I saw one of the younger dryads reach into the folds of her robe and turn her head towards her companions with a questioning glance. They nodded. Something was about to go down.

'You must leave now,' the tall dryad said calmly, though now it was an order rather than a suggestion.

Silver responded with a snarl and the circling werewolves joined in. The three older werewolves stalked towards the dryads, their heads lowered not in an act of submission but as a prelude to aggression. I held my breath. Perhaps that would have been a good time to grab He Who Roams Wide and get out of there, but if I ran I'd be labelled as prey by the werewolves and as a security threat by the dryads.

I checked the time again. There wasn't long to go until midnight. *Make this quick*, I prayed silently. *Please.*

A second later, it was as if the dryads had heard me. When

the young dryad pulled her hand out of her pocket, she was holding a small linen pouch. I scooped up He Who Roams Wide, who had the sense not to protest, covered his face with one hand and squeezed my eyes shut. A beat later there was a bright, white flash of light that pierced my eyelids, and the night sky was rent with anguished howls.

It was the magical equivalent of a military-grade flash bang, although this particular version was soundless – all flash and no bang. The dryads didn't need noise because the searing light incapacitated all seven werewolves.

When I opened one eye to peek, it was clear that even the three more experienced werewolves had been taken unawares: two of them had collapsed. Silver was swaying off-balance, barely managing to stay on all four paws, and the three who'd been circling the dryads were crawling away on their bellies. It was over as quickly as it had begun.

The older dryad raised his voice. 'This is your final warning. Leave this place and do not return or there will be consequences.'

He might not have regained his sight yet, but Silver wasn't in the mood for backing down. He growled, a rumbling sound that grew in intensity. His nearest companion whined while the one of the older werewolves who'd stayed upright slunk forward and nudged Silver's flank. The meaning was clear: *Not tonight. We've been outsmarted and we have to go.*

One by one, they picked themselves up and returned in the direction from which they'd come. Eventually only Silver remained. He shook out his fur and snarled one last time then, in a last-ditch effort, lifted his head and howled. This time his companions didn't answer. His broad shoulders dropped and he turned and padded away, his tail between his legs.

I smiled. I hadn't doubted the dryads' capabilities but I was impressed they'd dispatched the werewolves so quickly.

The young dryad who'd thrown the magical concoction was beaming. 'That was brilliant – it worked even better than you said it would! Those bastards will know better than to come back here again.' She pumped the air with her clenched fists and performed a triumphant pirouette.

'Don't get too excited,' one of the others said drily. 'That young silver wolf will doubtless return next month.'

Her face fell. 'But we defeated him!'

'That's why he'll be back. He was humiliated and he didn't strike me as the sort of werewolf who appreciates that.' The dryad was right: Silver was trouble. He clearly had a chip on his shoulder and a lot to prove.

'We'll double the patrols next month and change our defensive spells. That blinding trick won't work a second time.' The older dryad didn't sound afraid; he was merely considering his next move. I suspected it would be a long, long time – if ever – before Silver gained the upper hand.

I crouched down and released He Who Roams Wide then watched while the dryads turn back to their posts by the main gate.

CHAPTER

# TWELVE

The remainder of my grove heist went smoothly. As soon as the dryads were out of sight and far enough away not to sense a burst of cat-sith magic, I checked the time on my trusty EEL watch. It was 11.51. Obviously I couldn't wear the watch when I was in cat form so I'd have to rely on my body clock, but that wasn't a problem. Although I tended to lose count beyond the twelve-minute mark, I could time myself effectively enough to snag the alder bark at the right moment – if I could find the right tree.

I plucked a small tuft of black fur from He Who Roams Wide and swallowed it. Unfortunately I banged my forehead on one of the oak's branches as my body rose, spun and spasmed into transformation; I'd have a duck-egg sized lump come tomorrow.

Once I was safely on four paws, I shook off the pain and dipped my head in gratitude towards He Who Roams Wide. He knew better than to follow me into the dryads' grove and I could trust him to wait close to the oak tree until I returned.

I touched my nose briefly to his then performed an unnecessary – but very satisfying – air spin so I was facing the high

90

fence. I checked its length for inconsistencies or weak points but, as I'd already thought, the easiest way into the grove was via the oak tree where I'd been hiding. I purred deeply, unsheathed my claws and sprang up the trunk to the first broad branch.

He Who Roams Wide was hovering at the foot of the tree, watching my progress with his judgmental gaze. I knew better than to show off; I was a cat sith, not a cat, and my joints often reminded me of that. As a result, it took me a while to choose the best branch to access the grove. I wanted to get as close to the top of the fence as possible so that it would be easier to jump over, but the nearest branch was rotten and wouldn't hold my feline weight. Instead, I opted for a higher one which, although narrower, appeared to be sturdier.

My claws dug into the soft bark and I swayed for a moment or two as I fought to maintain my balance, but I relaxed as my feline instincts kicked in. I sauntered the length of the branch towards the other side of the grove wall. I was less than a foot away when the branch started to shiver from my weight. I paused, but it seemed strong enough to let me inch a few more steps. I kept going.

I eyed the jump ahead. The top of the fence was wide enough for me to land on it without too much trouble but I suspected that would trigger some sort of magical warning system. The dryads weren't stupid; they could enforce a simple perimeter spell that wouldn't activate if a mere bird landed on the fence but which would screech an alarm if anything bigger did the same. My smartest move would be to leap over the fence and land on the ground on the other side of it. In theory that was easy, though I couldn't see what lay directly below it so I'd have to be careful.

I moved forward another inch and the branch swayed alarmingly. I moved back an inch: I'd have to jump from where I was. My eyes pierced the darkness, scanning as much of the grove as I could; it looked safe enough and my time was running out. I had to make my move.

I stopped prevaricating and focused on a spot at least a foot away from where I thought I could reach, bunched up my muscles and went for it.

Leaping through the air in a feline's body is vastly different to jumping in human form. As a cat, I had five hundred muscles, all of which engaged when I leapt – it was closer to a bird's flight than a human's jump. In mid-air, I could make micro-adjustments and switch direction so that I landed where I wanted, and I would hit the ground like a coiled spring rather than a lump of concrete. If I were a full-time feline, I'd jump all the time. It was brilliant.

I landed exactly six inches from the spot I'd aimed for, straightened up and waited to see if my landing had activated an alarm. There were no shouts and no vibrations of running feet: my entry had gone unnoticed. Pleased with myself, I licked my paws clean of loose dirt and cast around for an alder tree.

The nearest trees were willows, which had their uses both magically and medicinally but weren't what I was looking for. My whiskers twitched as I swivelled to my left and looked for anything that was alder sized. There appeared to be at least twenty of them only about thirty metres away to the east of the willows. I moved towards them.

I estimated I had five minutes until the stroke of midnight; if I was wrong, it would only be by about ten seconds or so and I reckoned that fell comfortably within the margin of error. I had about a minute to strip the bark I needed. It would be more than enough.

As soon as I passed the last of the willows, I knew that my cat eyes hadn't failed me. I was so taken aback at the ease with which I'd located the alders that I hesitated and double-checked that I wasn't padding into a strange dryad trap. No: it appeared that sometimes things really were straightforward.

I battened down my concerns and approached the trees. Now all I had to do was find one that would let me strip a section of its bark with my teeth.

The first alders were young so their healthy, supple bark would have to be harvested by a sharp knife. The next line looked easier to work with, but I passed them by and headed for the innermost trees. They were the oldest so their bark would be gnarlier and easier to pull off. With about a minute to spare, I found the perfect specimen.

Somebody had already carefully stripped several sections of bark away from its trunk, doubtless a dryad harvesting produce for the markets or witchery stores, so I felt easier about taking some for myself. The tree could clearly withstand the assault. Even so, I paused in front of it with my head bowed respectfully for several seconds, thanking it for its sacrifice. It was what a dryad would have done, and I hoped it was also what Keres would want me to do.

The clouds shifted, temporarily obscuring the moon, and I heard the distant howls of more of the Coldstream werewolves. I ignored them. It was time: I had to harvest the alder bark now or never.

I tipped my head forward, snagged a loose section with my feline fangs, and pulled. Thanks to some dryad's earlier efforts, it came away easily. I didn't need a lot; as long as I had enough to make the concoction for Keres, I'd be happy. I yanked hard and peeled away a good four inches. I twitched in satisfaction then, holding it carefully in my jaws, I set off back. I wouldn't celebrate until I was home safe and sound but, thus far, I was smugly pleased with my progress.

I returned to the spot where I'd entered the grove. There were no overhanging branches to clamber up so I had no choice but to use the fence. Yes, it might set off any in-built magical defences but I was leaving now, not arriving. I had a plan. Unless the situation were truly dire, I always had a plan.

I tensed my muscles and sprang upwards, scrabbling up the final foot. As I passed over the top, I felt the ripple of barrier magic: I'd been right that the dryads had other security measures in place.

I darted to the same oak tree as before, dropped the alder bark and miaowed at He Who Roams Wide. His ears twitched in response. He scampered up the fence then stopped on top of the nearest post and planted his cute furry arse in place while I pressed myself against the trunk of the oak tree.

Three seconds later, four dryad guards came sprinting over from the front gate of the grove.

They might have been dryads but they were highly trained dryads: their gaze was focused and they didn't waste time chatting. The one at the front was the older dryad who'd confronted the werewolves. I'd already seen that he knew what he was doing.

He ran to the fence, craned his neck upwards and immediately spotted He Who Roams Wide. He gestured to a tall woman beside him who fixed my sleek black cat with a long look and murmured several words under her breath. A breeze rippled He Who Roams Wide's fur before it receded again.

'A cat,' she said.

'Just a cat?'

'Definitely just a cat.'

If it had been me on that post, they'd have sensed something else. They might not have thought cat sith but they'd have known I was dangerous. It was a good job I'd planned ahead.

'Shoo!' The male dryad waved his hands. When He Who Roams Wide blinked lazily down at him, he gently shook the fence. 'It's not a good idea for you to stay up there, Kitcat – in fact, you shouldn't be out tonight. It's dangerous.' He jiggled the fence again.

He Who Roams Wide took pity on him and jumped down. He wove around the dryad's ankles and purred loudly.

'Maybe we should grab him and keep him until dawn,' one of the others said. 'He might get eaten.'

As the older dryad nodded and reached down, He Who Roams Wide darted away, running for the dubious safety of the city streets.

'So much for that idea. It looks like that kitty can look after himself.' The dryad's head jerked up and his nostrils flared. 'Another alert has been triggered on the north side.' He nodded at his companions and all four of them sprinted away.

# THIRTEEN

I found He Who Roams Wide eyeing an open drain in the narrow street that led away from the grove. With our business concluded for the night, he doubtless considered it his right to spend the next hour or so hunting rodents. I wouldn't stop him; he'd served me well and his inner demon deserved satisfaction.

I touched my nose to his, indicating that I'd see him at home in the morning when his adventures were over. I didn't need to warn him about the packs of werewolves he might encounter; He Who Roams Wide would take care of himself and stay out of their way.

The smart move would have been to return to my human form for the journey home. It was never wise to spend too much time in a cat's body, and there was every chance I'd have to be human for at least part of the return journey. But I'd enjoyed my foray into the grove and I wanted to stay cat for a while longer, jumping around rooftops and walls and breathing in the perfumed night air.

I decided to carry the strip of alder bark in my mouth and

allow myself thirty minutes of feline freedom before I returned to my human body. It was about time I had some kitty fun; it had been far too long since I'd been a cat for no other reason than pure enjoyment.

Alas, less than ten minutes later I was regretting my impulse.

The first strains of an impending werewolf fight reached my ears as I was sauntering along the top of a brick wall and eyeing up the rooftops to my right. At first I ignored them; werewolf packs often came across each other during the full moon and fur flew as a result. Minor pack brawls were considered unimportant, and once all the parties were back in human form there was rarely any political fallout unless there'd been serious injury or a death. But something about these howls and excited yelps was different; there was an edge to the noise that spoke of genuine bloodlust.

I stopped briefly – and that was when I heard the chillingly familiar, high-pitched caterwaul. My initial flash of fear was for He Who Roams Wide, although my instincts told me the screech hadn't belonged to him. But it was definitely familiar...

I didn't complete the thought. Out of nowhere He Who Roams Wide barrelled past, racing along the street below with his black fur raised. He wasn't running away from danger – he was running towards it. Cats weren't stupid; they avoided fights whenever they could, and my sleek, adventurous moggy was far too experienced to involve himself in any danger unless it was absolutely necessary.

My mental traffic lights flicked from lazy green to bright flashing scarlet and I leapt after him, quickly abandoning the narrow wall for the ground below.

He turned right at the far end of the cobbled street. I gained several metres on him, powering forward with all of my energy, and did the same. I jumped over a wide puddle and swerved to avoid a row of pretty plant pots. I could feel my heartbeat thudding through my chest. My stamina was already weakening, but I maintained my speed as best as I could and less than sixty seconds later I caught up with him. Then I realised what the problem was.

Eight werewolves had gathered in the centre of a narrow street and a bloody fight was definitely brewing. This was not an evenly matched situation, however: it was seven against one.

My stomach dropped. There were few reasons why any werewolf would be alone during the full moon.

I squinted at the group of seven and recognised the same bastards who'd caused problems for the dryads at the grove. Silver's distinctive fur was gleaming in the moonlight; frustrated by the dryads' magic, he'd obviously decided to aim for a different target.

I switched my attention to the lone wolf facing them – and the small ginger cat at his side. I'd not seen Thane in wolf form before but I knew instinctively it was him – and he'd got himself into a ridiculous situation. I would give him an earful the next time I spoke to him, but the tongue lashing he'd receive was nothing compared to what I'd say to Tiddles who should have been curled up asleep on my bed on the other side of the city. She must have sneaked out after I'd left.

If there'd been time, I'd have hawked up my furball and approached on two legs because, even without weapons, it would have been easier that way. But I could tell from Silver's stance that he was about to attack and transforming would cost precious seconds that I couldn't spare.

I spat out the alder bark and growled at He Who Roams Wide to stay back. Then, as Silver jumped forward with his sharp teeth bared, I ran.

Thane and Silver became a blur of fur, rolling together on the ground, vicious snarls ripping through the night air. This was no play fight: Silver was out for blood and Thane had no choice but to match his thirst for violence. At least the other six werewolves were hanging back. They could have chosen to surge forward as a pack and rip Thane to pieces but they were holding themselves in formation, their narrowed lupine eyes tracking every move of the fight. None of them noticed my approach.

I prioritised. While Tiddles remained in play, Thane's concern would be for her and not for himself. Her back was arched and she was spitting angry hisses at Silver; in another heartbeat she would throw herself at him and get herself killed.

I lunged for her from behind and sank my teeth into the scruff of her neck. She screeched with pain, which made Thane lose focus and give Silver the upper hand. While the younger wolf bit Thane on his shoulder and blood spurted, I dragged Tiddles away. She fought me every step of the way, but I'd taken her unawares and I had the upper hand. Growling warnings, I hauled her into the nearest corner and a moment later He Who Roams Wide joined me.

Tiddles stopped struggling and went limp. I released my hold on her and she slowly turned and gazed first at He Who Roams Wide then at me. Her annoyance was obvious but she dropped her head to tell me that, albeit reluctantly, she would stay out of the fight. I nodded and turned back to Silver and Thane.

With Tiddles no longer by his side, Thane clearly felt that he could give his full attention to the fight. Although blood continued to drip from the wound in his shoulder, he had turned the tables on Silver. The younger wolf was still on all fours but he'd pulled back to allow space between himself and

Thane. I silently applauded when I saw that his right ear was ragged. Thane had stood up for himself. Perhaps we'd get lucky and Silver would make the smart choice to slink away.

Silver was quivering but Thane was as still as a marble statue; there was barely a sign that he was breathing as he towered over the younger wolf. Without baring his teeth or making a noise, he was proving his superior status. In most werewolf fights that would have been enough but, just as I thought Silver would twist away with his tail literally between his legs, the young female werewolf behind him gave a yip of encouragement. Goddamnit.

Silver raised his head, his tail and his shoulders. A rumble started in his chest, growing in intensity until his growls were loud enough to wake the neighbourhood. Thane tensed, then Silver flung himself forward and the fight resumed again with even more tumbling and gnashing of pearly fangs.

I couldn't intervene because it would diminish Thane's standing even as a lone wolf; he had to maintain appearances or he could expect any number of attacks during the next full moon. Besides, my small furry cat body stood no chance between these two predators. But I wasn't powerless and I could still engage the remaining werewolves. Sometimes attitude was far more intimidating than strength.

I puffed up my fur so that my small black body appeared much larger than it actually was, then arched my back, dropped my forehead and advanced on the six remaining werewolves. It was their presence that was encouraging Silver to continue his attack; take out the rest of the pack and he would back down.

The young female was the first to notice me and the look in her yellow eyes was pure amused derision. She was ten times my size and she had five buddies to back her up. She raised a heavy paw and swiped at the air to suggest she'd easily bat me away if I drew any closer.

I didn't blink as I swerved around Thane and Silver and continued to advance. One by one, the other wolves spotted me.

Obviously, in a real fight between one cat and six massive wolves, the cat would be destroyed in seconds so I was aiming to avoid a real fight. I would win this encounter through my brazen attitude, not through my claws.

As I eyeballed each werewolf in turn, one of the other young males flinched slightly. Excellent: he was their weak point. Wolves were pack animals; if I could force one of them to retreat, the rest of them would probably follow.

The young male, whose tail was slightly bushier than the others and streaked with flashes of ink-black fur, had no visible scars; not only was he young, he lacked experience. The three older werewolves would swipe me dead with a forceful paw but hopefully this youngling would give in to his instincts and run.

Adjusting my trajectory, I fixed my eyes on his and continued to place one paw in front of the other as I moved steadily in his direction. His tail was already beginning to droop.

Behind me, Thane and Silver's snarls were growing more vicious. I resisted the urge to turn and look, and kept my gaze on the young werewolf. *I'm coming for you*, I promised. *I'm going to eat you alive.* In my mind's eye, I was a large, sleek jaguar prowling through a jungle rather than a furry housecat padding along a city street.

It worked. Bushy Tail gave a tiny whine, showing that he was far more scared of me than I was of him. He backed up one step. Then another.

The other werewolves started to react. The two older males growled a warning in his direction and the older female nudged him with her muzzle, but his fear was infecting them. In my peripheral vision I saw the second young female look away from me in favour of the cobblestones before she also started to back away. One more, and I reckoned I'd win.

I was only two feet away from the group. I drew my lips over my teeth. *I mean business*, I projected. *You should run while you still can.*

I was within a whisker of succeeding when there was a sudden, high-pitched yelp of pain from behind me, too shrill for me to decipher whether it came from Silver or from Thane. It pierced the night – and it spurred the more antagonistic female werewolf to act. She moved so swiftly I scarcely glimpsed her body as she flew at me.

Although I managed to twist and avoid her sharp teeth, she still managed to knock me to the ground. I righted myself in a flash. My situation was suddenly more dangerous but it was far from desperate. As long as I avoided her jaws, I could still fight.

Flickering images of ways that I might beat her raced through my head. If I could skate underneath her, I'd be perfectly placed to rake my claws across her belly. She wouldn't like that very much. Before I could tense my muscles and move, however, there was another blur of movement – ginger movement.

*For fuck's sake, Tiddles.*

I hissed loudly to admonish her in the vain hope that she'd re-join He Who Roams Wide in the shadows but she didn't even acknowledge me; her green-eyed focus was wholly on the female werewolf. She arched her back, spat ferociously and landed with perfect precision on the female's back. She dug in her claws, dipped her head and took a bite.

Like pure wolves, werewolves have thick skin and even thicker fur so I knew that Tiddles hadn't come close to drawing blood, but that didn't matter. The shock of being attacked and ridden like a pony by a kitten sent the female wolf into panic.

She swung first to her left then to her right as she tried to shake Tiddles off.

Tiddles simply bit her again.

I turned my head to the other werewolves and we stared at each other. The older, more battle-scarred wolf took a step forward but I knew he wasn't planning to fight me; from the way his yellow eyes were flickering, it was clear that he'd recognised there was more magic to this situation than he could comprehend. That meant there was more danger, too. He didn't exactly submit to me but he did drop his head briefly and turn away. The four werewolves beside him followed his lead.

I returned my attention to Tiddles and miaowed at her with high-pitched insistence. She blinked at me; she was weighing up whether to listen or to continue baiting the female werewolf. Thankfully she extracted her claws and leapt away. Part of me expected the wolf to lunge after her in retaliation but she was too glad to be relieved of her clawed, fanged, feline burden. Without another glance she bounded after her departing companions.

Now there was only Silver.

The young werewolf was focused on Thane and I was certain that he'd not yet noticed the departure of his furry buddies. Blood was dripping from his ragged ear and there were bloody, matted patches across his body. I knew Thane; he would only have inflicted flesh wounds – but they would hurt.

Thane was bleeding in several places. His thick fur was obscuring the worst of the damage but I reckoned that most of his wounds were superficial. No doubt Silver had intended mortal damage but Thane had more than held his own.

The young werewolf was obviously tiring: his movements were growing sluggish. All I needed to do was make him realise his companions had abandoned him then this brawl would be over for good. I lifted my head, pricked my ears and emitted a shrill, ugly caterwaul. It was impressive – even Tiddles glanced at me in admiration.

Silver backed away from Thane and turned to assess if I posed a new threat. His eyes flicked to me then to the empty street beyond. He blinked.

*Yeah, buster. You're alone now.*

His furred mouth dropped slightly.

*So much for pack loyalty.*

His gaze shifted left.

*Not so much fun now you're on your own, right?*

His gaze flicked right.

*This is where bullying gets you. Now you're the one who's outnumbered and in mortal danger.*

I was prepared to wait for Silver to make the right decision by himself and I knew enough of Thane to believe he would do the same – but Tiddles wasn't so patient. She wanted vengeance. She hissed loudly and sprang at Silver, raking his muzzle and drawing a few beads of blood. For Silver, that was enough. A second later he bounded away.

As soon as he vanished into the darkness, I coughed up my furball. Enough already.

It took me a moment or two to recover my equilibrium and for the tremors to subside. Then I straightened, ran a hand through my hair, placed my hands on my hips and glared at Thane. 'What the hell? What were you thinking of wandering into a pack of werewolves?' My irritation was genuine and he knew it.

He raised his nose and sniffed loudly then lifted a paw, pointed to me and then to his nose. Oh. 'You scented me?' I asked. 'My smell distracted you, you came to find me and instead you found those dicks?'

He made a lupine attempt at a sheepish shrug and I rolled

my eyes. At least that explained why he'd made such a schoolboy error, though it didn't mean I approved.

I turned to Tiddles. 'What about you?' I demanded. 'What's your excuse?'

Obviously believing that I didn't deserve an explanation, she ignored me. He Who Roams Wide strolled up to her and she ignored him too.

Something wet touched my hand and I glanced down. Thane was licking my fingers. He huffed slightly and performed a slow spin so I could see all of him. 'Your wounds are minor,' I told him. 'You'll be fine.'

He spun again.

'There's hardly any blood.'

He tossed his head and turned yet again, this time more slowly. He added a butt wiggle for good measure. I yielded. Alright. 'Yes, you're very handsome. You make a good-looking wolf.'

Looking pleased with himself, he sat on his haunches and licked his lips. 'Don't push your luck,' I warned him.

I stalked over to the piece of alder bark and picked it up. My fingers were shaking; I was well aware that this could have gone very differently for Thane. He'd been lucky – and that meant I had been, too.

'I can see you home,' I said in a clear voice. Thane shook his shaggy head. 'You're not badly hurt and I'm not trying to offend your sense of male superiority...' His eyes narrowed. 'But you might need me,' I finished.

He didn't react. 'Suit yourself.' I pocketed the bark and picked up Tiddles. '*You're* definitely coming with me.' She nipped my finger.

'Enough.' I checked on He Who Roams Wide. 'What about you?' He answered immediately by headbutting my shin. Good:

he was coming home too. There was a time and place for roaming and adventures and my lovely black cat knew it.

'I'll check in with you tomorrow morning, Thane, as I promised.' I moved closer to his ears and whispered. 'You are a *very* good-looking wolf. Don't get into any more damned fights.' Then I turned away and finally headed for home. At the corner, when I glanced over my shoulder to check on him, he was in the exact same spot. He wasn't watching my departure, however. He was staring off into the distance in the direction of the now departed Silver and his bitter pack of antsy werewolves.

# FOURTEEN

By dawn the next morning Keres' condition hadn't changed. I should have been pleased that she hadn't deteriorated but I'd hoped the concoction would achieve faster results. I'd brewed it as soon as I'd reached home and made sure she drank every last drop. After that, I'd crashed out for three hours; it wasn't much of a sleep but it would see me through the day. I'd survived on far less in the past.

'How long did that fool doctor reckon it would take before she started to improve?' Dave demanded.

'He didn't say.'

My druid neighbour's mouth flattened. Dave's default expression was a scowl but it usually implied warmth and general bonhomie; now there was a despairing quality to his expression that indicated his unhappiness. He delved into his back pocket and yanked out a bulging leather wallet. 'I have savings,' he declared gruffly.

I didn't immediately understand what he was telling me. 'Uh, okay.'

Dave waved the wallet in my face. 'I'll hire a private investigator – I know a few druids who do that sort of thing. I'll hire one of them to find out what happened to Keres and find the bastard who ripped her powers from her.'

'Don't do that,' I said softly.

He bristled with anger. 'It's my money.'

'Yes, but—'

'I owe ban sith community far more than money.'

'Okay, Dave, but the thing is—'

'That young woman doesn't deserve to die like this!'

I reached out and gripped his hands as he drew in a shuddering breath. 'Put your money away, Dave.'

'I have to try and help her.'

'I will search for whoever is responsible for this,' I told him.

'Kit,' he whispered, 'we need to find someone who knows what they're doing.'

I didn't look away. '*I* know what I'm doing – and I won't flinch from what needs to be done.'

He grimaced. 'You're a good neighbour, but you're just a cat lady.' He said the words gently as if he didn't want to offend me. Bless him; I'd always known Dave was a softie but I hadn't fully appreciated how kind he could be.

I lifted my chin. 'I can do this.' Then I added, 'I'm a true resident of Coldstream, Dave.' In other words, I won't tell you what I can do but I'm more capable than you know.

I continued. 'Keres is under my roof and that makes her my responsibility. And you'd be surprised at some of my abilities.' That was an understatement. 'But I do need your help. Watch her while I'm gone, make sure she's hydrated, give her food if she wants some. Can you do that?'

Dave sniffed. 'You don't have to ask.' He continued to eye me. 'Are you sure that you—?'

'Yes.'

He licked his lips. 'Okay, Kit. But please don't let me down. Don't let Keres down.'

He knew that I couldn't promise anything, and he wasn't going to force me into a lie. Instead he went off to the upstairs flat without another word. His footsteps were very, very heavy.

Leaving nothing to chance, I checked I had everything I would need: dagger, poison, several different potions and my most sensible footwear. My final port of call was the back room where Tiddles had been shut in since we'd returned last night.

She didn't attack me when I opened the door, which I took as a positive, but if cat looks could kill I'd have been on the floor and writhing my way to a quick death. I pointed. 'Comfy blankets and cushions. Fresh water bowl. Tasty treats. You've got everything you need.'

Tiddles hissed.

'No, you don't have your freedom but that's your own fault. You shouldn't have sneaked out last night.'

She extended her claws pointedly but I wasn't going to be intimidated by a teenage cat even if she'd come straight from the demon netherworld.

I shrugged. 'Either you stay grounded in here until I return, or you can come with me—' Tiddles skittered towards me in her rush to join me '—but,' I added firmly, 'you stay with me at all times and you do exactly what I tell you to.'

She purred loudly.

'*Exactly* what I tell you,' I reiterated. I crouched down and held out my arms. Tiddles gave my fingers a lick then let me pick her up and put her on my shoulder. I'd probably regret this but it would forestall my guilt at locking her up. I stood up, adjusted my weight until she was comfortable and walked out of my front door.

A tall man was standing at the garden gate and I recognised him instantly as Slasher's husband. Well, that was just peachy. I wasn't in the mood for any prolonged confrontations and, frankly, Keres deserved far better. I strode towards him.

He didn't smile. 'Hello,' he said. 'I live down the street.'

I was prepared to offer him a grunt and nothing else, but She Without An Ear was perched on the wall beside him and she gave me a long look to remind me that I was supposed to be fostering good relations with my neighbours. Even the shitty ones. 'I know,' I said. 'You have a beautiful family.'

My compliment took him by surprise. 'Uh, thank you.'

'Your daughter Kate is very friendly. It's wonderful that we can all get along – we're fortunate to live in a community that's so welcoming. It's one of the many things I love about Danksville.'

His cheeks were turning red. 'Well, yes, that's good.'

'I mean, look at you,' I said, unlatching the gate. 'You know what people in other parts of Coldstream say about druids, but here you're welcomed with open arms.'

He frowned. 'Huh? What do people say about druids?'

Obviously, I didn't answer. 'I'd love to stay and chat – in fact, I'd love to invite you in for some tea but I'm on my way out. I have several appointments to keep.' I gazed off into the distance. 'Perimenopausal symptoms have to be taken seriously when you're a woman of my age.'

Mr Slasher blanched. There were likely several years to go before I experienced the dubious pleasure of the peri-menopause, but sometimes people could be pleasingly predictable.

I went on. 'The cramps are horrendous. And there's so much blood...'

Mr Slasher was already backing away. 'I can see you're busy,' he said hastily. 'I'll let you get on your own way.'

'That's very kind of you. If you're looking for a chat,' I told him, 'Mrs Miller is home.'

As if on cue, the older woman who lived across from me – and who possessed enough Fae blood to entrap almost anyone

– opened her front door. She was beaming. 'Would you like to come in, dear?' she asked him. 'I've just made some scones. They're still hot from the oven.'

I smiled, patted Tiddles and went on my way.

IT WAS STILL EARLY, so there was little point finding Thane until later. I knew enough about werewolves to wait until late morning to try to talk to him; in fact, I wasn't sure if he'd be able to speak coherently until the following day.

Keres was also in no state to talk but I could still learn more about what had happened when her ban sith powers were stolen. If I visited the probable scene of the crime, I'd be bound to locate a few early risers who could be persuaded to chat.

Given that I'd avoided the ban sith community for decades, I'd only passed through Barton Road on my way to somewhere else. I'd certainly never spent any time there, though in a way that wasn't a bad thing because at least I'd never killed anyone in that neighbourhood. But after hearing Louise's story, I was wary that the ban siths would recognise what I used to be. That wasn't reason enough to avoid them though, not if I wanted to help Keres.

Anyone who didn't know that Barton Road was home to the ban siths would certainly get an inkling as they strolled down it. Death was celebrated, and it was visible in every nook and cranny. Western sensibilities lean towards pretending that death doesn't happen; I could understand why some would be discomfited by such obvious awareness of life's one absolute truth, that death was coming for us all, sooner or later.

Funereal black was the colour choice for every front door, window sill and lamppost, and I suspected that if I peered into the houses I would see black wallpaper. There were plenty of hanging baskets full of flowers, though there were no sunny daffodils or blushing roses on display; they all contained lilies.

I frowned and tapped Tiddles. 'You see those flowers?' She nibbled on my ear. 'As far as you're concerned, they are poisonous. Stay on my shoulder and stay away from them.' She chirruped. 'I mean it,' I warned her.

We passed a shop selling gravestones and another displaying coffins. On the other side of the street, there was an arresting window display of cremation urns. There was even a store that proudly advertised death powder, a substance that supposedly sent someone to their death through skin-to-skin contact. If you believed that, you'd believe anything because death powder didn't work; if it did, it would hardly be openly for sale. Its presence did, however, prove that the shop owners here had thought of everything.

If you'd come across a similar scene almost anywhere else in the world, it would have seemed cheesy, like a clichéd film set or a theme park, but instead of feeling like a gratuitous celebration of death Barton Road felt normal.

I couldn't see any ban siths, though; their work was nocturnal and most of them would be fast asleep. Even so, I hoped to find someone who knew Keres.

'Good morning.' I turned my head to see not a ban sith but a robed deacon from the Church of the Masked God.

He was standing in the doorway of a small building with a plaque on it. Having a Masked God office here made sense because they benefited enormously from bequests and legacies; I had no doubt that the church leaders were fans of death.

I smiled. 'Morning.'

'You look a little lost. Is there something I can help you with?' The man knew what he was doing; in matters of impending death – unless you were a doctor or an assassin – the gentler the approach and the softer the sell, the better.

I twitched anxiously. It was only partly an act. 'Uh…'

His eyes were kind. 'There are many different reasons why people visit Barton Road. Sometimes it's morbid curiosity, sometimes it's to make a purchase.' He waved a hand at the row of shops behind us. 'Sometimes it's because of timing – you look like that is your reason. Either you or someone you know is sick, and you want to know if a ban sith can tell you how long you or they have left in this world.'

It wasn't what I'd been expecting but I'd roll with it. I giggled nervously. 'I guess I'm more obvious than I realised.'

As he reached for my hands and gently squeezed them, the faintest brush of magic tickled my skin. It was some sort of reassurance spell designed to help me relax, a mild version that would put me at ease without twisting my mind or my emotions so I couldn't be annoyed by its use.

'I use lavender lotion,' he told me, interpreting my thoughts correctly. 'Enhanced with a sprinkling of witched St John's Wort.' He released my hands. 'I can assure you that it's harmless. It will help you. Nothing more, nothing less.'

I believed him – but that might have been because of the effect of the magic.

'I'm Martin,' he said, bowing his head. 'As you might have gathered, I'm not a ban sith though I stay in this community. I know everyone here and they accept me, although I'm here primarily as a church outreach worker.' He raised his palms. 'I'm not here to evangelise, I'm here to help.'

Definitely soft sell. 'I'm looking for a ban sith,' I admitted. 'Not for me but for my friend.' In a sense that was true.

'Your friend is ill?'

I nodded.

'Very ill?'

I bit my lip and nodded again.

'The reason I ask,' Martin said, 'is that the ban siths' power is immense but even the most skilled can only predict death up to five days before the event. They can't tell a healthy person when they'll die – they often can't tell a terminally ill person when they'll die. A lot of people in Coldstream are scared of what ban siths can do but the truth is that their predictive magic is quite limited.'

'But they're drawn to death, aren't they? They can feel when it's approaching?'

'They are *overwhelmed* when it is approaching,' he corrected gently. 'That's why they shriek. They have no control over the skirl of the ban sith. Think of it like the tide or the moon. When a ban sith spots death, they have to sing.'

I wouldn't have called a ban sith's bone-juddering shrieks singing, but each to their own. I twitched again, doing my best to appear nothing more than a cat lady trying to help a friend. 'Who is the most skilled ban sith? Who should I approach for a … consultation?'

Martin sucked air in through his teeth. 'There's a young one who's very good. She lives at number thirty-four.'

I brightened. 'Brilliant.'

'Her name is Keres. She's a friendly sort.'

I had to work hard not to lose my smile. 'Keres?'

'Yes. She's the best of her generation. I can call her if you like and see if she's available? Put in a good word for you?'

I doubted that very much. 'That's very kind of you,' I said.

Martin smiled in an avuncular fashion. 'You can wait inside while I get in touch with her. Then we can have a cup of tea while you tell me some more about your friend.'

'Mmm.' I twitched again. 'Maybe I'll wander around a bit first instead and think about it. I want to be sure I'm doing the right thing.'

'You can trust ban siths. They're not the scary monsters

some people think they are.' He folded his hands. 'You can trust me too.'

'I appreciate that.' I inclined my head and stepped away before he tried even harder to pressgang me into tea and sympathy. Martin didn't know as much as he pretended to; Keres had told me she'd left this community days ago. He'd already outlived his usefulness.

Tiddles adjusted her weight on my shoulder and we continued down the street. At least I now had an address and I might find some clues in Keres' home. I doubted that the bastard who'd stolen her powers could have done it from a distance; they must have approached her in person, possibly without her noticing. Maybe they'd broken in and ripped her powers from her as she slept. If they had, there would be signs of forced entry.

The front door of number thirty-four was a glossy black, like every other door on Barton Street. Ignoring Tiddles' yowl of protest, I crouched down. She dug her claws into the flesh of my shoulder while I examined the lock. There were no obvious scratches on the paintwork and nothing to suggest magical tampering.

Tiddles screeched again; she seemed to have perfected the art of vocalising her displeasure at the most annoying pitch possible. 'Alright,' I muttered. 'Alright. I'll stand up.' I held her with one hand to steady her as I rose. 'If you don't want to be here, I can always take you to the house. You won't be alone. All the other cats are there, as well as Dave and Keres.'

She miaowed a loud, huffy protest – and that was when Keres' glossy front door swung open to reveal a thin man with heavy bags under his eyes and a taut, worried expression. 'Did you say Keres?' he demanded. I stared at him. 'Do you know where she is? Do you know where my wife has gone?'

My mouth dropped open and, from her position on my shoulder, Tiddles miaowed once more.

CHAPTER

# FIFTEEN

Mr Keres – or Harvey Johnson, as he was actually called – was a nervous man. There could have been any number of reasons for his visible anxiety, but something about his demeanour suggested that edgy apprehension was his default approach to life regardless of what his wife was doing or where she was.

'Keres has never mentioned you before,' he said from his perch on his leather sofa. 'I thought I knew all her friends.'

I waved a vague hand. 'I've not seen her for years. I was in the area and I thought I'd drop by and see how she is.' I smiled pleasantly though my thoughts were far from sweet.

*Why did Keres run away from you?*

Harvey twisted his fingers together. He was wearing a simple gold wedding band but I was almost certain I'd seen no ring on Keres' finger. 'She's away at the moment.'

*Did she abandon her entire community because of you?*

'That's a real shame,' I said aloud. 'When will she be back?'

'I'm not sure. It, uh, depends.'

*Are you a violent man?*

'Perhaps I can call her?' I suggested. 'Leave her a message?'

Mobile phones rarely worked in Coldstream but landlines were stable enough, and it was a reasonable sounding request.

He stared into the distance. 'I can pass on your message to her.'

Tiddles, who had abandoned my shoulder as soon as we'd entered the house in favour of circling the room and sniffing, padded to the centre of the rug that lay between Harvey and me and gave him a long look. Harvey flinched and looked away.

'Are you unwell?' I asked solicitously. 'You look quite ill.'

A flush rose up his neck from beneath his wrinkled shirt. 'I'm fine. I didn't sleep well last night, that's all.'

Uh-huh. I offered him a sympathetic look.

Obviously I wouldn't tell him where Keres was; if she'd wanted her husband to know, she would have told him herself. My silence on the matter would be deafening, but I was still going to do whatever I could to winkle information from him. I took a leaf from the church deacon's book. Martin used a soft-sell approach because it worked.

'I'm very sorry to hear that,' I said. 'Lack of sleep is no joke. I can recommend some excellent witchery stores and sleep potions. Do you suffer from nightmares? Is your insomnia related to a physical complaint or is it more psychological?' I managed to sound neighbourly rather than prying. Go me.

'I don't need a potion,' Harvey replied. 'I have a lot on my mind, that's all.'

'I'm a good listener,' I said. 'Sometimes it can be easier to talk to strangers than people you know well. And I don't judge.' Not much, anyway.

As he heaved in a shuddering breath, Tiddles got to her feet and ambled towards him. For a painful moment I thought she was planning to use the leather sofa to sharpen her claws, which wouldn't have helped in the slightest, but instead she leapt onto Harvey's lap and rubbed her head against his folded hands. Almost immediately he untwisted his fingers and stroked her. *Clever girl, Tiddles.*

'She's cute.'

I smiled. 'She is. And she knows it.'

'I've always thought we should get a pet. Keres wanted a dog but I like cats. I admire their independence.' On cue, Tiddles started to purr.

It is well documented that petting a cat can decrease cortisol, though since I'd learned that cats were demons I'd suspected that was a deliberate move on their part: be kind to me and I'll help your stress levels. Then I'll suck you into my vortex and you'll be my happy slave for life. It was a feline version of a strong contentment spell, only far less dangerous. Depending, of course, on your point of view.

Whether it was a deliberate ploy on Tiddles' part or simply because she wanted some attention, it was smart because Harvey was visibly relaxing. Thirty seconds later, he opened his mouth and spilled the beans. 'She's gone.'

I played dumb. 'Who?'

'Keres.' He swallowed. 'She packed a bag last week and left. I've been searching but there's no sign of her. I've checked with all her friends – or at least the friends I know about.' He looked pointedly at me. 'Nobody knows where she is. It's as if she's vanished into thin air.'

I chose my next words carefully. 'Were you having problems? Is that why she left?'

Harvey continued to stroke Tiddles. 'Things have been tense lately. Not,' he amended hastily, 'because of our relationship, but because of what's happened to her.' His eyes filled with tears. 'She's lost her ban sith powers and it's all been too much for her.'

I evinced surprise. I didn't do a particularly good job, but fortunately Harvey was distracted enough by Tiddles and his confession to notice. 'She's lost her powers?'

He nodded. 'It happened overnight. She was at a property in Danksville, singing for a man who was about to die. Everything started out fine but on the third night, right before the man passed, she lost her voice.' He grimaced. 'I mean, she could still speak – she still had her physical voice but not her magical one. And she'd lost her thread to death.'

'Just like that?'

Harvey sighed. 'Just like that. One minute it was there, the next it was gone.' His eyes reflected deep, miserable resignation. 'We tried everything we could to bring it back – spoke to the community elders, visited the local doctor. We tried so many different spells but nothing worked and Keres grew more and more depressed. After a month, she gave up. She said there was nothing more to try and it was making her sick. Staying here with all the other ban siths wasn't helping.'

'The community wasn't supportive?'

Harvey's eyes widened a fraction. 'Everyone has been hugely supportive! Nobody has said a mean word. But Keres has always felt so much pressure to perform. Her great- grand- mother Nessie was a very powerful ban sith, and Keres came into her powers so young that everyone thought she would become stronger than her great-gran. The expectations were so high that they were a lot to deal with even before all this happened. Keres felt like she'd let everyone down – and people were getting scared, too.'

'Because if Keres could lose her powers, they could lose theirs?'

Harvey nodded sadly and a single tear escaped down his cheek. Tiddles immediately responded by licking his hand vigorously, but unfortunately a spot of feline grooming wouldn't be enough to heal this particular hurt.

'She'd already said she wanted to leave. I…' He hiccupped. 'I argued with her, told her to stay and her voice might come back. This is our home – these are our people. She told me I didn't understand. Eventually she calmed down and said she'd wait a bit longer and maybe try a few more things. Then, when I was out at work, she packed a bag and she left.'

His gaze dropped to his shoes. 'She wrote a note: *I'm sorry. I can't stay here.* Eight years of marriage and all she could leave me were six words. I don't know where she's gone or if she's alright. I just want her home with me so I can take care of her. Keres is my everything. Without her I'm lost.'

And without her ban sith voice Keres was lost, too. Man. What a mess.

I believed Harvey loved her with all his heart and was prepared to do anything to get her back, but that didn't alter my stance. Keres didn't want him to know where she was and I had no choice but to respect her wishes, but if she died as a result of her loss and without Harvey by her side, it would destroy him body and soul. Now I wasn't only fighting for Keres, I was fighting for him.

'The man in Danksville,' I said. 'The one she was singing for when she lost her voice. Do you know who he was?'

'His details will be logged in her work journal.' He nodded to a small oak desk by the window and I spotted a leather-bound notebook on top of it.

'Could I have a look at it?'

Harvey looked confused. 'Why?'

'I know Danksville. Maybe there's something about the part she was in that triggered what happened to her.'

'I checked out the area myself. There's nothing out of the ordinary.'

I persisted. 'I want to help, Harvey. Let me at least have a look.'

He sighed. 'The man died and his family have taken over the property. There's nothing to see. But fine, take a look. Maybe you'll see something I didn't.'

I certainly hoped so. There had to be a reason why Keres had agreed to stay in Danksville when that was the very place where all her problems had started.

ONCE I'D MADE a note of the address and bade farewell to Harvey, Tiddles and I headed for Thane's swanky penthouse. As we walked, I considered the different versions of Keres I'd encountered so far.

There was taciturn Keres, who'd told me that her problems were none of my business, and there was chatty Keres who'd babbled about villainy. I'd met placid Keres, who hadn't appeared to care a jot about what others thought of her being a ban sith. I'd also seen grieving Keres mourning the loss of her powers, and patient Keres who had spoken amiably to young Kate. I hadn't officially met wifey Keres, although she obviously existed, too.

'People are complicated,' I told Tiddles.

She snorted derisively in response.

I shrugged. 'It's true. We present different sides of ourselves all the time. We're different people at different times. I can be a cat lady and a killer and a conscientious neighbour and the person who locks you up in the back room for your own good. We're not one-dimensional. Cats are no different. You can be furry demons one moment and purring puddles of contentment the next.'

She extended her claws and scraped them against the skin of my exposed neck. She didn't draw blood but the scratch was enough to make her point.

'Alright,' I grumbled. 'Alright. Here endeth my TED talk.' Honestly; He Who Roams Wide was much better at listening to my philosophical rambling than Tiddles.

We slipped into the building, bypassing the concierge once again. As soon as we reached the staircase, I felt a surge of irritation: there were splatters of blood in several different places. I nudged Tiddles from my shoulder and she immediately went to the nearest bloody splodge, sniffed it and narrowed her eyes. It didn't happen often, but we were on the same page. We exchanged glances then climbed to the top of the stairs.

I knocked hard on the door, crossing my fingers that Thane was conscious and alert enough to answer.

There was no answer. Tiddles growled faintly as I knocked again. If I'd been hoping that he would appear semi-naked, dripping with water and smiling at me lazily with come-to-bed-now-and-let-me-ravage-you eyes, I was disappointed. The door didn't open and there was no sound from behind it.

'This is a posh building – it's bound to have excellent soundproofing,' I told Tiddles. 'He might be taking his time. Just because we can't hear anything and he's not come to the door doesn't mean he's not there. He'll still be recovering from the full moon. Thane knew I was coming – he made me give him my word that I'd be here.'

She arched her spine and her hackles rose. I sighed.

'Yeah,' I said. 'That's what I was thinking too.' I reached into my pocket and took out my keyring, flipping through until I found my trusty old lockpick.

The lock on Thane's door wasn't bound by magic and would be easy enough to pick, but I was well aware that he was a fan of booby traps. I didn't doubt that there would be some sort of cunning set-up inside that could render me unconscious if I weren't careful.

'Lucky you're here,' I murmured to Tiddles before I leaned in and got to work.

The lock was fiddly and it was a good two minutes before I heard the satisfying snick that told me I'd been successful. I rocked back on my heels and nudged the door open. It didn't squeak; it didn't even whisper. It wasn't that kind of flat.

Tiddles sauntered inside with her tail held high and her paws sinking into the thick cream carpet. Suddenly she jumped about a foot in the air and twisted her head from left to right before glancing over her shoulder at me.

'On my way,' I told her.

She sniffed, wandered off to her right and disappeared from view.

I took my time as I stepped carefully over the threshold. Carpets and cats weren't a particularly great combination, and *cream* carpets and cats were worse. Although this might only be a temporary address for Thane, I reckoned that carpet was there for a reason. Tiddles had avoided the area directly inside the front door so there was probably a concealed pressure pad that would be triggered if I stepped on it.

I hopped to the side and stayed well away from the danger area, then took a few steps forward until I reached the spot where Tiddles had leapt into the air. Interesting. I couldn't see any evidence of a tripwire. Perhaps Thane had decided to splash out and buy an expensive invisible version from one of the more well-appointed witchery stores.

I bunched my muscles and jumped, taking care to leave as much air between myself and the floor as possible. I landed a foot away and with a gallingly heavy thump.

There was a sudden loud purr from the far corner. Tiddles was beside a large leafy plant in the corner – and she looked as if she were laughing. Correction: she looked like she was *gloating*. 'There's nothing there, is there?' I demanded. 'You were gaslighting me.'

Her whiskers quivered in delight.

'The front door?' I asked. 'Is there a pressure pad there?'

Tiddles didn't answer but I knew Thane: there would be some sort of trap there even if there was no tripwire. 'You know it pays to be prudent when the situation calls for it, Tiddles,' I said. 'I'm not ashamed of being cautious.'

The ginger cat blinked and sauntered off once more. 'You could give me a modicum of respect!' I called after her.

She didn't react and I rolled my eyes. Cats. Honestly.

I half turned – and that was when my flash of humour dissipated. There were more spots of dried blood, a whole collection of them between the long black sofa and the glass-topped coffee table. Thane had always been careless with his own blood but this was ridiculous. And where the hell was he?

There was nothing interesting in the glossy, open-plan kitchen other than a very expensive brand of cat food that Thane had left on the counter. He was clearly spoiling Tiddles rotten. I swivelled away and followed her towards the bedroom.

From the moment I'd opened Thane's front door I'd been certain he wasn't home, but I was still disappointed when I confirmed that his bed was empty and he wasn't hiding in the bathroom or taking a shower. He'd made me give my word that I'd be here and I tried not to allow myself to feel hurt. There was bound to be a rational explanation.

Tiddles miaowed plaintively; she wasn't any happier about this situation than I was.

'He would have been hungry after last night,' I said. 'He might have gone out for food.' I marched to the kitchen and pulled open the fridge door. It was stocked full: steak, mushrooms, bacon, orange juice. Hell – there was enough food to feed an army.

'He's not gone out for food, then.' I pursed my lips. 'Maybe he went out to run an errand.'

Tiddles slunk out of the bedroom and miaowed again.

'Yes,' I said, 'I *did* promise that I'd come round this morning and he should have been here waiting for us. And, yes, I know that's his blood on the stairs and on the carpet, though there's not a lot of it. His wounds last night weren't life-threatening – a first-aid kit would have taken care of them.'

Tiddles' tail swished from side to side then she jumped onto the coffee table and started pawing through some papers. She raised her head and looked at me pointedly. When I didn't move, she pawed at the papers again and hissed.

I threw up my hands. 'Al*right*. Jeez. But when Thane is pissed off because I've been snooping through his private things, I'll blame you.' My threat didn't appear to faze her in the slightest.

I picked up the loose sheets and my breath caught when I realised what was on them,. There were several charcoal drawings and their quality was extraordinary. But it wasn't his skill that had given me pause, it was his subject matter.

Me.

There was one of me curled up in a chair with all five of my gorgeous cats around me, and one of me clutching a dagger and staring fiercely. There was one of me laughing, and one of me with my hand raised to a loose purple curl in a gesture I knew far too well. Each one was sketched not simply with exquisite realism but with a tenderness that made a lump rise in my throat. These pictures had been created with feeling, and that realisation played havoc with my normally tamped-down emotions.

'The different versions of Kit McCafferty,' I whispered. 'As seen through the eyes of Thane Barrow.'

Tiddles, still on the coffee table, huffed in impatience. 'What?' I asked. 'You wanted me to see these.' She huffed again.

I flicked through the last few drawings. Me. Me. Me. And... I stared at the last one. It was of a wolf, though it wasn't a self-portrait; this particular drawing was of a werewolf I'd seen only last night. Even rendered in charcoal, I recognised those narrowed eyes that reflected youthful malevolence. Thane had drawn a picture of Silver.

I noted the signature and the date in the lower corner: Thane had created this drawing two weeks ago. But why this wolf? I stared at it uncomprehendingly.

'What's going on, Tiddles?'

She only blinked at me in response – but I couldn't deny the uneasiness that was uncurling in my belly.

# SIXTEEN

I scribbled a note for Thane and left it on the coffee table beside the drawings. I reminded myself that I trusted him; there would be a good reason as to why he wasn't waiting here for me. That knowledge was far more worrying than reassuring, but I was limited as to what I could do. This was Coldstream. Because mobile phones rarely worked, I couldn't simply drop him a text message or call him.

Perhaps it would have been easier if I were a werewolf, but as a cat sith I didn't possess amazing tracking skills. I could buy a tracking potion, but I'd have to commission a witch to brew it for me and that could take hours, so that would be my last resort.

Thane was a big boy: he could look after himself and, until I heard otherwise, I'd have to assume he was alright. Keres, however, was definitely dying and her problems were my priority. Even so, I wiped away all Thane's damned blood from that staircase as I left. He could thank me later.

When we exited the swanky building I pretended not to see the concierge frown in my direction. Tiddles immediately turned left and pattered with feline determination along the narrow pavement. 'No,' I muttered as I caught up to her, scooped her up and returned her to my shoulder. 'We're going to Danksville.'

She hissed in my ear.

'If Thane wanted us to know where he was, he'd have left a note.' I ignored the flicker of anxiety in my stomach. 'We can search for him later if he doesn't show up. We need to focus on Keres.'

Tiddles nipped my earlobe hard enough to make me wince. 'I won't change my mind.' She dug her claws into my flesh but I remained resolute. 'I'm in charge here,' I said. 'Not you.'

This time she didn't respond but I knew she was still pouting. Tough. Searching for Thane right now would be a wild goose chase whereas I had a destination in mind when it came to Keres.

I was relieved that Tiddles settled down and allowed the journey to Danksville to proceed without incident. When I hopped off the tram at my usual spot, I didn't walk towards my own street: instead I turned right towards the fringes of the suburb.

According to her journal, Keres had been shrieking outside the door of a man called Colin Shellycoat. I vaguely recognised the name: as his surname suggested, he was descended from the shellycoats of times long gone. Hundreds of years ago they were infamous for being one of the many Scottish creatures who made a sport out of misdirecting travellers. Even now, it wasn't considered wise to ask a shellycoat for directions, although there were few of them left and they tended to be neighbourhood stalwarts who were active members of the community rather than outsiders with a penchant for mischief.

That was why Colin Shellycoat's name rang a bell with me.

After he'd died the previous month, vast numbers of people had attended his funeral to pay their respects. In fact, there were still several floral tributes outside the house. But I was certain that he'd been elderly and had died of natural causes.

His house was similar to mine with four floors, although none of them had been turned into flats. There was only one entrance and it looked as if he and his family had retained the building for their own use.

The scrap of garden at the front was the same size as mine and, by the looks of things, the remaining Shellycoats enjoyed spending time in it. It was well-kept, with butterflies, bees and small flies hovering around the multi-coloured flowers.

Tiddles was fascinated by a small water feature and jumped down from my shoulder to lift a paw and bat curiously at the gurgling bubbles. I left her to it; if a water fountain was what it took to distract her from Thane's vanishing act, so be it. I might consider getting one for my garden if it held her attention for more than a few minutes.

I went up the stone path. The front door was ajar, so rather than knock I called through. 'Hello? Is anyone there?'

Footsteps approached and a moment later an apple-cheeked woman wearing a flour-dusted apron appeared. She looked relatively young, probably only a few years older than me, which suggested that she was Shellycoat's daughter rather than his wife.

'Good morning.' I smiled at her. 'I'm Kit. I live a few streets away.'

She squinted at me then her expression cleared. 'You're the cat lady!'

I beamed. 'I see my reputation precedes me.' It was lovely to be reminded that people thought of me as the person with too many cats rather than the person who was too handy with a garrotte.

'I asked around a few months ago when I kept seeing a black cat wandering around,' she said. 'I wanted to be sure he had a proper home.'

'That would be He Who Roams Wide – he does his own thing. It wouldn't be the first time somebody thought he was a stray, and it probably won't be the last.'

'Cats are going to cat,' she said. On cue, Tiddles thrust her head into the gushing fountain then sprang back and glared at it for not letting her know beforehand that it was wet.

'You're a woman after my own heart,' I replied. I was pleased; this might prove to be an easy conversation.

She grinned. 'I'm Holly.'

'Nice to meet you. Do you mind if I ask you a few questions, Holly?' I took a gamble that she was indeed Colin Shellycoat's daughter. 'It's about your dad.'

Her expression dimmed. 'He's dead.'

'I know, and I'm sorry for your loss. I realise he passed away only recently so it must be very painful for you.'

Holly blinked rapidly. 'It's okay,' she said hesitantly. 'What would you like to know about him?'

'It's not him I'm interested in, it's the ban sith who was shrieking outside before he died.'

'Keres.' She whispered the name so quietly I had to strain to hear.

Uh-oh. I prepared myself for a bitter onslaught. 'Yes, that's her name.'

Holly wrapped her arms around herself. 'She was so wonderful.' She shook her head slowly. 'I don't think I can ever thank her enough.'

That certainly wasn't the reaction I'd been expecting. 'Please,' I said. 'Go on.'

Holly took a while before answering, not because she didn't want to talk about her father but because she wanted to choose the right words. 'My dad was ill for a long time and he was in a lot of pain. He had some good days but,' she sighed, 'most of the time it was a real struggle. He did his best not to let us see how much he was suffering – he came from that generation where you maintained a stiff upper lip and carried on rather than complaining.'

I nodded my understanding.

'But it was hard for him – months of sleepless nights when he was in agony.' She dropped her head. 'He'd tried every painkiller you can think of, magical and non-magical. They worked for a while but then his body got used to them and the pain crept in again. Sometimes, when he thought nobody was listening, I heard him cry out as if he couldn't keep it to himself any longer. It was brutal.' She looked up. 'And then Keres came along.'

I didn't say anything; this was one of those times when it was wiser to wait than to fill in any gaps with the sound of my own voice. Tiddles, however, sensed the shift in the atmosphere. She abandoned her attempts to kill the water fountain in favour of padding towards Holly's feet and sitting beside her. Sometimes she was smarter than she appeared. She didn't demand ask to be petted and she wasn't begging for food, she was simply reassuring Holly by her presence.

Tiddles was definitely a demon kitty but she possessed an angelic side, too.

Holly was silent for several moments as she reached down to tickle Tiddles under her chin. When she spoke again, her voice was calmer and her eyes were clear.

'Keres changed everything. The relief my dad felt at knowing the end was coming was extraordinary – it sounds contradictory but it gave him a new lease of life for his last few days. He stopped worrying about the pain and he got out of bed for the first time in weeks. At his insistence, we opened our doors and welcomed in his friends, distant relatives – everyone he wanted to see. It might sound macabre but we had a party to celebrate his approaching death.'

I didn't think it sounded macabre, I thought it sounded lovely. 'He got the chance to say goodbye properly. He didn't have to worry about what was coming because he already knew. He knew there would be an end to the pain and he could leave on his own terms.'

She nodded and gave me a meaningful look. 'He was so invigorated that we thought he would overcome his illness and he'd be alright. But he didn't think that because he believed in Keres and her powers. To my dad, her skirl made all the difference.'

That was the third time I'd heard someone describe the shriek of a ban sith as a skirl – Trilby, Martin and now Holly. 'You spoke to her at length?' It was the only thing that made any sense; Holly wouldn't use ban sith terminology unless she'd talked with a ban sith.

She nodded. 'My dad invited her into the house on the first night. At first I was horrified – I didn't want anything to do with her. But when I saw his reaction to her singing...' She shrugged. 'She was the best thing that could have happened to him. His final few days were spent in peace rather than fear. Keres gave him that.'

I felt an odd flicker of pride, which was ridiculous because I'd had nothing to do with Colin Shellycoat or Keres' actions in the days before his death. 'She sang for three nights? Did you see what happened on the final night?'

Holly looked puzzled. 'Her skirl was much shorter. I thought she would stay for the whole night but she stopped not long after she'd started singing and disappeared. Less than an hour after she'd gone, Dad passed away. I assumed she'd left us in peace for his final moments.' She twisted her fingers together. 'Was I wrong to think that?'

She didn't need to know what had happened to Keres because she'd only feel guilty about it and it obviously wasn't her fault. Better for her and the rest of her family to focus on the positives and the way that Keres had made Colin Shellycoat's final few days a little easier.

'No, no,' I said airily. 'I was only curious.' I paused. 'Did Keres have a particular spot where she, uh, performed?'

It was a question too many; Holly was suspicious now. 'What's going on?' she asked. 'What's this about?'

I offered a half-truth. 'I'm trying to understand as much as I can about ban siths. Lots of people are afraid of them and I'd like to change that.'

'I was one of those people,' Holly said quietly. 'But I was wrong to be scared of her. Come with me and I'll show you where Keres stood.' She smiled briefly. 'It's the least I can do.'

I STOOD in the patch of golden sunlight and frowned down at the ground. Keres had stood here for three nights, shrieking about Colin Shellycoat's upcoming death, and she'd lost her powers on this very spot, but there was nothing to see. There was no dark miasma or itchy sensation between my shoulder blades. I couldn't sense even a whisper of magic.

I glanced at Tiddles. She was totally uninterested, staring off into the distance as if she were occupied by more important matters. If there had been any flicker of the same darkness that was affecting Keres, she would have told me. There was nothing to learn here.

I scowled. Keres' powers had been ripped out of her; surely I could find *something*.

I turned around and allowed myself to think like an assassin rather than an investigator. If I had been contracted to kill Keres and I'd chosen to end her life here while she was singing to Colin Shellycoat, how would I have done it?

Like my home, the house was on a quiet street with little passing traffic so Keres would have noticed anyone approaching her, even after the sun had gone down. Given how people reacted to ban siths, she would definitely have been wary if someone had drawn near, so any attack would have had to be done from a distance. Sniper style would have been the easiest way, I decided.

I lifted my eyes to the row of houses opposite. They were of a similar height to the Shellycoats'; which one would have the best line of sight to this spot? Which one would allow me to hide effectively?

As my gaze travelled from house to house I spotted several possibilities, then I smiled grimly. There: a building with large chimneys that would provide plenty of cover and appeared to have a useful flat section of roof. That's where I would have lain in wait.

As I started to march towards it, Tiddles miaowed in protest. 'We're not done here yet,' I told her. She miaowed again and I glanced at her. She was certainly a stubborn moggy. She didn't want to follow me but she didn't want to wait around for me either.

I sighed. 'Alright,' I relented. 'Give me thirty minutes and then we'll go and look for Thane.'

She narrowed her eyes. For goodness' sake. 'Twenty minutes then.' She didn't move.

'Wherever he is,' I said, 'it must be to do with that young silver werewolf, right?'

She blinked once.

'In twenty minutes we'll visit Alexander MacTire. If anyone knows who that kid is, it will be him. It'll be faster than conjuring up an effective tracking spell.'

Her tail twitched but thankfully she acquiesced. Despite my earlier declaration, it was clear who was the boss here – and it certainly wasn't me.

# SEVENTEEN

I had thought it would be a simple matter to scramble up to the rooftop but it was far harder than I'd expected. Several times I wondered if I should ask Tiddles if I could use her fur to affect a feline transformation but I suspected that the answer would be no. She stayed where she was, enjoying the sunlight on the street, ignoring me. It was obvious that she felt this entire enterprise was beneath her.

I knew I didn't have much time so I ploughed on, shimmying awkwardly up an old drainpipe that was thankfully stronger than it looked, then clambering from one windowsill to another. Finally I stretched up and pulled myself onto the sloping tiles above me, arms straining with every inch of my progress. I'd been working out lately and I was much fitter than I'd been a year ago, but I still wasn't back to the level of my EEL assassin days. I suspected I'd never be that lithe or agile ever again and it was a galling thought.

Given the spate of local robberies, I didn't want any of the Shellycoats' neighbours to see me; I'd be hard pressed to prove my innocence if I were spotted on the rooftops. I crouched down and shuffled from one house to the next. There was only one large gap in the terrace where I was forced to jump, startling a resting seagull that squawked violently at my appearance. I muttered an apology but it only glared at me, flapped upwards then dropped a white splatter that narrowly missed my head. If Tiddles had witnessed the seagull's attempt at ruining both my hair and my outfit, she would have been highly amused.

I peered over the edge of the roof to look for her. She'd moved closer to the Shellycoats' garden gate and was pawing at something on the ground. Good.

It took another couple of minutes to reach the right spot. As soon as I landed on the flat-roofed section, I knew it was the perfect place for an attacker: the view to the Shellycoat house was unimpeded but the angle of the chimneys in front of me concealed me from the street. I might no longer be so adept at climbing up the side of buildings but I could still rely on my old instincts.

I searched the small area for signs of anything untoward. Some dried leaves had gathered in the far corner and there was a large puddle of dirty water that suggested the roof needed some minor repairs. I ignored them and moved to a dark patch next to one of the brick chimneys. It looked suspicious and when I was close enough to it to sniff the air, I was certain it was magical residue.

Not many spells left traces that the likes of me could notice, though there were plenty of witches and druids who would recognise the leftovers of magic spells. I couldn't – unless the magic was particularly powerful. The stronger the spell, the more obvious the residue – and this patch of black nastiness was very obvious indeed.

Although the more sensible part of my mind rebelled at the thought of getting too close, I hunkered down to examine it. Immediately my eyes started watering and I felt nauseous. I breathed in until I was absolutely sure, then retrieved a white linen handkerchief from my pocket. Taking care not to touch the stain with my bare fingers, I scooped up a small sample of the sticky substance and folded it into the fabric; there would be more than enough for testing. I didn't need the likes of Trilby to confirm that it was the same gunk I'd seen eating Keres from the inside out.

I straightened up, pleased to put some space between myself and the nastiness, and scuffed several other sections of the roof with the toe of my shoe. Whoever had been up here waiting to attack Keres hadn't left any other calling cards. I turned around and climbed back down the building to where Tiddles' tail was swishing angrily from side to side.

I checked my watch: I'd been gone for twenty-two minutes. 'I'm only two minutes late,' I told her.

She glared, suggesting I'd committed a heinous crime, then stood up and immediately headed towards the end of the street, determined to find Thane as quickly as possible. I turned to follow her but I stopped as I saw the white scrap that she'd been pawing at. I frowned and bent down. It was a shell.

I ran my finger over its smooth surface and glanced towards the Shellycoat house. From several metres away, Tiddles let out a wince-inducing wail. I ignored her and nipped into the small front garden.

'Holly?' I called through the open front door. 'Can I ask you another question?'

She appeared in the hallway carrying a cardboard box. 'I thought you'd gone already,' she said. 'What is it?'

I curled my fingers around the shell. 'There have been several home burglaries around Danksville recently,' I said. 'I don't suppose that you—'

I didn't get the chance to finish my sentence because she was already pulling a face. 'Yes, we were targeted. I suppose I should be thankful that we didn't notice the theft until after Dad had died.'

'What was taken?'

Her expression was a mixture of anger and sadness. 'His most treasured possession, his shellycoat. It had been passed down through generations.' She sighed. 'It wasn't worth anything but its sentimental value was incalculable.'

'You're talking about the traditional coat made out of shells that your ancestors wore when they were luring travellers astray?'

She nodded. 'Yeah. Dad hadn't ever worn it, but it was part of our history. He would have been devastated to know it had been stolen.'

I heard Tiddles wail again. 'I'm sorry,' I said.

Holly grimaced. 'Me too.'

My mind was still churning over the implications of what I'd learned from the Shellycoats when we arrived at the front gates to the MacTire mansion. I paused for a moment and looked over my shoulder at the buildings behind us. Thane owned the low-rise block of flats that was only barely visible from here and I knew he had hung around there watching the MacTires. I didn't think there was any chance he was there now, but I waited for a beat until I was sure there was no stirring in the air to suggest he was watching.

I sighed and faced the gate before thumping so hard on it that at least half the people inside would hear me. Tiddles added a miaow for good measure; it was unnecessary but I appreciated her support.

Within seconds the gate swung open and a pale face appeared. I recognised him immediately: Ribbit wasn't his real name, but he was one of the MacTire foot soldiers. He was less disciplined than the others and, not too long ago, I'd dislocated his knee when he'd attacked me without giving the matter proper thought first. From his pallor, he was suffering the after-effects of a particularly active full moon the previous night and his right ear was still pointed and furry, but his lingering wolf didn't prevent him from blanching when he saw me.

'What do you want?' he snapped in a voice that was as much of a whine as a snarl. I was on relatively good terms with Alexander MacTire these days and Ribbit knew it but he still didn't want to be my friend. He was scared of me. Smart guy.

'I need to speak to your boss.'

'He's unavailable.' Ribbit was already closing the gate. I thrust out my hand and stopped him. 'It's important.'

'It doesn't matter if the fate of the world rests on him,' he growled. 'He's not talking to anyone today.'

This was a familiar dance so I didn't lose my patience. 'He owes me. In case you've forgotten, I rescued his nephew from a horrible fate.'

'Nick isn't available either. It's the morning after the full moon, lady. Nobody is available.'

Tiddles had started to growl as I prepared to argue further but then a voice rang out from the courtyard. It was the crystal-clear feminine tone belonging to the one MacTire I would never, ever underestimate. 'I've got this, Mikey,' Samantha said. 'You can go inside.'

Ribbit didn't need telling twice and he vanished in a breath. A moment later, the familiar face of the MacTire beta wolf appeared.

'Hi Samantha,' I said cheerfully. 'How was your full moon?'

She didn't smile. 'Great.'

She appeared as poised as the last time I'd seen her, so it was hard to believe that only hours before she'd been padding the city streets with four paws and a tail. Samantha's inner wolf was very well contained.

'I assume that you're here for a reason, Ms McCafferty,' she said icily.

I beamed at her. 'Yep! I need to speak to Alexander as soon as possible.'

If Samantha was annoyed that I was on first-name terms with her alpha, she didn't show it. 'He's unavailable.'

'It's important.'

Her expression didn't change. 'He's still unavailable.'

When Tiddles arched her back and hissed, Samantha flicked her a narrow-eyed look. Shockingly, the cat backed down. Tiddles was more intelligent than she appeared and she'd recognised that Samantha MacTire was a true predator.

'Perhaps you can help me, then,' I said.

She folded her arms but at least she didn't slam the gate in my face. 'Go on.'

'I need to find a young werewolf as quickly as possible. I don't know his name and I've only seen him in wolf form, but I know he's not long out of adolescence. He's got silver fur and his tail is tipped with black. He's kind of bolshy, likes a fight, and,' I thought about Silver's trailing companions, 'despite his youth, he has alpha potential.'

Samantha stared at me without speaking.

'I don't expect you to know every werewolf in Coldstream,' I told her, 'but I have a feeling you might know this one. I have to find him. Do you have any idea who he is?'

She tossed her head and snorted. 'Of course I know who he is. The question is why don't *you* know who he is?'

I blinked. I didn't have the sense that she was being disingenuous. 'I don't know what you mean,' I said slowly.

'We all know who you spend your time with, Ms McCafferty. I thought that you and Thane Barrow were close – but perhaps you're not as close as you realise.'

'Go on.'

'The werewolf you're talking about is getting quite a reputation – he's been causing problems across the city, although that's not a surprise given his family connections.' She grinned. 'He's called Cayden. Cayden Barrow.'

I didn't move a muscle.

Samantha's eyes danced. 'He's Thane Barrow's half-brother.'

# EIGHTEEN

I didn't say a word to Tiddles until we were on the tram heading past Hirsel Street towards the outskirts of Migden where the old Barrow pack stronghold was located, then I asked her, 'Why didn't you tell me?'

Tiddles lifted a front paw and started to lick it before delicately washing her face. A leprechaun seated not too far from us turned and stared, apparently bemused that I was talking to a cat. I ignored her.

'Why didn't Thane mention it?' I demanded.

Tiddles changed position and raised a hind leg so she could groom her nether regions.

'This isn't a good time for family politics, not with everything that's going on with Keres,' I grumbled. The Barrow werewolves had stopped trying to kill Thane at every opportunity over the past few years and I'd thought they were softening their stance towards him. I'd obviously been wrong.

Tiddles paused in mid-lick with her shell-pink tongue sticking out, then continued her grooming. I rolled my eyes in exasperation. 'We're only doing this because I promised you we'd find him. After that, you and he will have to deal with

Cayden Barrow yourselves. Unless it's a matter of life and death, I don't want to get involved.'

The leprechaun raised an eyebrow before turning away. Thankfully she disembarked two stops before us.

With Tiddles on my shoulder, I stomped off the tram after muttering a quick thank you to the driver, then I stomped across the street, stomped past the crossroads and stomped down the road to the Barrow property. There was a great deal of stomping.

At least I was familiar with this area: I'd completed an EEL contract on a witch who had once lived near here, so I knew where the Barrows lived. I was aware that their pack didn't enjoy the same sort of wealth or privilege as the MacTires, but I was still shocked by their residence. It was only three years since I'd last passed this way and the deterioration was obvious. The Barrow werewolves were not prospering.

In terms of design it was similar to the MacTires' main house, albeit considerably smaller. There were gates in front that I knew led to a small courtyard and what looked to be three separate buildings inside. The gates, which had been stained and varnished once upon a time, were weather-beaten, the hinges were rusty and they looked as if a strong breeze might blow them down. The roofs of the inner buildings were visible from the street and they didn't appear to be in much better nick: there were slates missing, copious amounts of slick green moss and a crumbling chimney stack. Oh dear.

Before I could thump on the gates and alert the residents to my presence, there was a loud cough from behind me. My body suddenly relaxed. That was Thane; I was sure of it.

'See?' I muttered to Tiddles. 'I knew he'd be fine.'

She gave a warm purr, leapt off my shoulder and ran. I abandoned the Barrow gates in favour of following her as she disappeared down a narrow snicket. I arrived in time to see Thane shimmying down a drainpipe.

I crossed my arms and waited until his feet were planted safely on terra firma. Tiddles threw herself at him, leaping into his arms then rubbing her head across his chin in delight. Thane smiled and scratched her ears.

'She missed you,' I said pointedly. He didn't look up. 'We went to your silly bachelor pad this morning, as promised.'

Thane still wouldn't meet my eyes. 'It's not a bachelor pad.'

I snorted. 'If it looks like a duck and quacks like a duck…'

'It's a temporary place to crash, that's all.' There were two high points of colour on his cheeks. 'The mirrored ceiling in the bedroom isn't something I would have chosen.'

I raised an eyebrow; I hadn't noticed that particular bit of his décor. 'I broke in and looked around but I certainly didn't do any more than pop my head in your bedroom to confirm you weren't there. I'd been hoping,' I said with a melodramatic sniff, 'that we would go in there together. I was expecting hot sex, with or without a mirrored ceiling.'

'There still will be hot sex,' Thane said.

My tone was very, very dry. 'Oh, will there?'

He finally looked at me. When he saw my expression, he relaxed. 'I'll make it up to you. The sex won't just be hot, Kit – it will be sizzling.'

'That remains to be seen, Thane.'

His eyes glinted. 'You will scream.'

'That might not be the flex you think it is.'

He grinned cheekily. 'Trust me.' His expression softened. 'I'm sorry. I would have been there waiting for you but…'

'But you think something's wrong with your brother and you were worried enough to come here to check on him as soon as you woke up.'

Thane blinked. 'You know about Cayden?'

'I just found out.' I uncrossed my arms. 'How do you think I ended up here?'

'I was so pleased to see you that I didn't give it much thought.' He was trying to butter me up, but it was clear that lack of thought was the recurring theme of Thane's post-full-moon day.

I stayed focused on what was important and ignored my fleeting burst of warmth towards him. 'Is being here a good idea? He attacked you last night. He would have killed you if he could.'

'Normally I try to stay away. You know that. Nobody in the Barrow pack wants me sniffing around, least of all Cayden.'

'You were kicked out twenty-seven years ago, Thane. He must be ... what? Seventeen? Eighteen years old?'

'Eighteen.'

'Has he ever met you?'

Thane shook his head. 'We've come close a couple of times but no, we've never spoken to each other. Unless you count our meeting last night.'

'I think it's fair to say he doesn't want to be your friend.'

He sighed. 'I know. But something's wrong. He shouldn't have been out with so few other werewolves, not at his age and with his pack history. I've heard rumours that he's been causing trouble for a few months. Under normal circumstances my mother wouldn't ignore that. Not after what happened with me.'

'He's your maternal half-brother,' I said aloud. I should have realised; Thane's father had died too many years ago for him to have sired Cayden.

'A surprise late baby,' Thane told me. His mouth turned down. 'Or so I heard. Ashina, my mother, had me when she was very young and Cayden when she was forty-five.' He sighed. 'Cayden shouldn't have been allowed to take the lead with those other wolves last night. He was acting like an alpha, but he's little more than a kid. Something is up.'

I was inclined to agree. 'How are your wounds?'

He dismissed my concern. 'Fine. He didn't hurt me.'

'You left your blood all over the stairs at that swanky flat.'

Thane winced: he knew that was a stupid thing to have done. 'I was worried.' He waved a hand in the direction of the Barrow stronghold. 'I'm still worried. But I shouldn't have let that worry to distract me so much. Thank you for cleaning it up.'

'I never said I did that.'

He smiled slightly. 'I know you, Kit.' He paused. 'I really am sorry I wasn't there.'

I held up my hand. 'I figured there was a good reason for your absence. To be honest, I'd have left you alone to sort this out yourself if it weren't for Tiddles. She was genuinely concerned.'

The cat miaowed softly in agreement. Thane dipped his head and nuzzled her briefly while I tried not to drool. I licked my lips and composed myself. 'What's your plan?' I asked.

'I'm staking out the place to see if I can find out what's going on.'

'You could be here for days!'

'They kicked me out, Kit, but I still care. I wish it were otherwise but I can't change how I feel.'

I sighed. 'Has there been any sign of any movement today?' It was well past noon – someone should have been up and about even considering last night's shenanigans.

'Nothing,' he answered darkly. 'Not yet anyway.'

I sighed again. I'd meant it when I'd told Tiddles I wouldn't get involved, but Thane looked so lost. And if any of the Barrow werewolves realised he was watching them, there would likely be more blood spilt. 'Give me half an hour,' I said. Sometimes a cat lady's touch was required.

Thane's green eyes widened in alarm. 'What are you going to do?'

'Help you.' I wagged my finger at him. 'Not that you deserve my help. And I can't stick around for long because I've got other problems besides yours to solve.' Before he could argue, I turned on my heel and returned to the Barrow gates.

This time I didn't hesitate: I raised my fist and thumped on the wood loudly enough to wake the damned dead and I kept on thumping until somebody opened up and gazed blearily out at me.

It most definitely wasn't Cayden Barrow. The woman's skin was still patchy and she hadn't yet regained possession of her human teeth; she was thin, gaunt and about ten years older than Thane's half-brother.

'Who are you?' she growled. 'And what the fuck do you want?'

I wanted to get inside the Barrow enclave and there was only one surefire way I could achieve that without transforming into a cat, which would have been unwise. The Barrows would be wary of felines after last night.

I allowed myself to appear slightly intimidated by her attitude. 'I'm here because I've got some information about Thane Barrow that you will want to hear.'

She stared at me for a long moment. 'In that case,' she said eventually, 'you'd better come in.'

The unkempt, disorderly air was echoed in the courtyard. Perhaps it had once been pretty but the gravel was tinged green with moss and weeds were sprouting up everywhere. Rubbish lay haphazardly on the ground and there was a faint scent of rot, possibly from a dead animal of some kind. Given werewolves' strong sense of smell, it was a wonder that they'd not disposed of it before now.

The female wolf caught my glance. 'It was the full moon last night,' she muttered. 'We've not had a chance to clean up yet.'

This was far more than the detritus caused by a full moon, but I held my tongue. 'It's a lovely space,' I said. 'I wish I lived somewhere like this.'

The werewolf grunted at my obvious lie then directed me to a metal chair in the centre of the yard and told me to wait. I glanced at it, and the puddle of dirty water pooling in the centre of the seat, and decided to stand as she vanished indoors.

I was curious as to who would appear next. Thane's mother was still alpha of the Barrow pack; she'd been in charge since before Thane had killed his uncle and been booted out for his actions; in fact, I believed she was the longest-serving alpha in Coldstream.

I couldn't admire her, though; she'd allowed her only son to be thrown out of her pack when he was barely fifteen years old. Thane had never explained to me why he'd murdered his uncle, who had been the Barrow beta at the time, and I'd never questioned him about it. He'd tell me if he wanted me to know. I didn't judge him for past actions that I didn't understand, but I judged the hell out of his damned mother. Yes, it was possible Thane was the villain of the piece and his mother didn't deserve my censure but she had it nonetheless. Thane had been a *child*.

The figure that appeared in the doorway and paused to look me over before joining me was a grizzled older man. Something about his eyes and the way he held himself made me think that he was one of the older werewolves who'd been with Cayden last night; I reckoned this was the wolf who'd nudged Thane's brother away from the dryads. His bearing as a human looked similar.

I pasted on a tentative smile and offered him an awkward wave. 'Hi there. Thank you for coming out to talk to me.'

He drew close enough to invade my body space; he was at least a foot taller than me and he was using both his height and the lack of space between us to intimidate me. 'Who are you?' he asked. He didn't smile.

I played along; I was perfectly happy to act meek if it meant I got results. 'I'm Kit McCafferty.' I fiddled with my cuffs and looked at my feet.

'What do you want, Kit McCafferty?' He was overdoing the gruff antagonism. Sometimes less was definitely more; it wasn't the snarling, snapping monster that you had to be wary of but the smiling wolf in sheep's clothing.

I flinched, trying to give the impression that I was scared. Last night's full moon was working in my favour; even an older, more experienced werewolf such as this one would still be disorientated and off his game.

'As I said to the woman at the gate,' I told him, 'I have some information about Thane Barrow.'

The grizzly werewolf was unequivocal in his response. 'There is no Thane Barrow.'

I blinked rapidly. 'Oh,' I said. 'Oh. I thought...' My voice trailed away, then I sighed. 'I should go then.' I started to walk uncertainly towards the gates.

He shot his arm out to stop me. His hand was still a furry paw, complete with sharp-looking claws. 'Hold up.'

I was relieved that I'd read the situation accurately. 'What?'

'That man may no longer be worthy of the Barrow name but we are interested in him.' After twenty-seven years, that surely had to be the result of last night's brawl rather than concern about Thane himself.

I had to play my next move very carefully. 'I know where

he's staying. I heard something went down last night and I thought you might be interested in his whereabouts.'

Grizzly narrowed his eyes. 'What did you hear about last night?'

'There was an altercation between you and him. Plenty of people living nearby saw what happened – the stories are all over Coldstream.' I appealed to the man's pack vanity and exaggerated the numbers. 'Ten of you, one of him – and he still managed to beat you.'

'That's not what happened! It was one-on-one, and Thane attacked without provocation.' He bared his teeth. 'As is his wont.'

Yeah, yeah. We were both lying now. 'He's staying in my building at the moment. He's alone, vulnerable. You could take him unawares and beat him.'

Grizzly was watching me like a hawk. 'Why would you come to us with this information? What's in it for you?'

I tried to conjure up a blush and failed, so instead I looked away and shuffled my feet. 'I thought we could come to an arrangement,' I mumbled.

'Money?'

'Nothing comes for free.'

Unfortunately, Grizzly wasn't buying what I was selling. 'Not interested.' He pointed towards the gates. 'You can leave now. And don't come back.'

It looked like I'd screwed this up and I wouldn't get the chance to uncover the information I'd needed, but before I could attempt another ploy a door opened and a figure burst out.

In a blur of movement, a young man bounded towards me and wrapped his hands around my throat. He looked a bit like Thane and I was certain this was Cayden Barrow in human form. 'What's the address?' he spat, his body vibrating with rage.

It took everything I had not to react by grabbing him and body slamming him to the ground for putting his hands on me. Instead, I squeaked and looked scared.

'Enough, Cayden.' Grizzly was trying – and failing – to calm the young werewolf. The effects of the full moon were still running through their veins; Cayden was too focussed on his anger and Grizzly was too ineffectual in giving an order. Where the hell was Thane's mother? Any werewolf alpha worth their salt should have been out here dealing with the situation by now.

I widened my eyes and whimpered, 'Don't hurt me.'

Grizzly tried again. 'Cayden!' This time he spoke more forcefully.

The young wolf released me but he didn't back away. 'Where is Thane?' he demanded.

I swallowed. 'I'll tell your alpha. I'll talk to Ashina Barrow and nobody else.' It was quite a demand for someone in a supposedly powerless position but it worked.

The werewolves exchanged looks. 'She's not available,' Cayden said. 'So you'll have to tell us.'

I raised my hands to my throat and rubbed it pointedly. 'I'm not talking to you! You assaulted me! It's Ashina or nobody.'

Cayden snarled, 'I won't repeat myself. She's not available.'

I refrained from pointing out that he *had* just repeated himself. 'Is she dead? Are you alpha now?'

Something flared in his eyes and Grizzly stiffened, too. 'I think we're done here,' he said.

'No.' Cayden shook his head. 'She will tell us where the bastard lives.'

I knew I'd have to give them something. The swanky flat

didn't suit Thane anyway, and he had other places he could stay. I dropped my shoulders and whispered the address.

Cayden smiled coldly. And then he threw me out and shut the gates behind me.

CHAPTER

# NINETEEN

Thane and Tiddles weren't where I'd left them so I returned to the alleyway where Thane had used the drainpipe to clamber down from the rooftops opposite the Barrow household. I gazed upwards and sighed at the injustice of having to climb the side of a building twice in one day, then heaved myself up. At least there were no acrobatic jumps involved this time.

I found Thane flat on his belly next to a narrow chimney stack, watching the buildings across the street with steel-eyed focus. Tiddles was lying next to him; she appeared to be the only one out of the three of us who was enjoying herself. I joined them and lay down so that I wouldn't be spotted.

'Your brother is quite the antagonistic little bastard,' I said.

When he responded Thane's voice was level but I could sense anger vibrating from him. 'I saw what he did to you. Did he hurt you?'

'Not really.' That wasn't the point.

He sighed. 'I heard he used to be quite a sweet kid. I don't know what's happened to him or if what I heard was wrong.' He continued to peer at the Barrow stronghold opposite, even though we could only see half of the courtyard and it was now empty.

I licked my lips. 'I don't think your mother is dead but I suspect she's sick or seriously injured. She should have come out to speak to me, especially after Cayden kicked off. The fact she didn't – and no other senior Barrow werewolves appeared either – makes me think she might be ill.'

'I agree,' he said. 'Ashina wouldn't have allowed Cayden to act that way under normal circumstances, especially on Barrow property.' Thane clearly no longer wanted to call Ashina Mum and I didn't blame him.

'Cayden is fixated on you,' I went on. 'Whatever woes have befallen the Barrow werewolves, he seems to have decided they're all your fault.' I tried to soften the blow. 'You're an easy target – you're not there and you can't defend yourself.'

Thane only grunted. He shifted to the left and pressed against the chimney as he tried to see through the closed windows opposite. I frowned. One of the windows was boarded up and I wondered if it had only recently been broken. And if so, by whom.

'Perhaps,' I offered, 'you'll get a better view from the other side.' I pulled myself into a crouch. 'The angle will be clearer from the next roof.'

Thane didn't move. 'I tried that before,' he said. 'But there's some dark gunk on that side that I didn't like the look of.'

Tiddles raised her head and twitched her ears before giving me a long look.

I felt the blood drain from my face. With slow, deliberate movements, I crawled around the chimney to the other side of the roof. When I saw the dark 'gunk' that Thane had mentioned, my heart skipped a beat.

Shit. Oh, shit. No wonder Cayden and the other Barrow werewolves were dangling on a precipice of bloody violence.

Suddenly I had a very good idea as to what had happened to Ashina Barrow and quite possibly several others.

Steeling myself for the unpleasantness to come, I drew closer to the misshapen patch of black and crouched down. Even before I smelled it, I knew it was the same magical residue that I'd discovered opposite the Shellycoat house. It wasn't as strong but it was definitely the same stuff.

I rocked back on my heels, no longer worried that somebody from the Barrow household might see me. Suddenly, that was the least of my concerns.

I called out to Thane in a low voice, 'Did you get close to this … gunk?'

'Close enough to know that it's incredibly nasty. It reeks to high heaven of bad magic but, whatever it is, it's old. I figured something dark and magical died up here and rotted away leaving that crap behind. I wouldn't get too close if I were you.'

He didn't need to tell me twice. 'It's not death residue,' I told him. 'This is something else. I think I know what's happened to the Barrow pack.'

I glanced again at the boarded-up window as another thought occurred to me. Had the Barrows suffered a recent burglary as well as the Shellycoats? Uneasiness swirled around my belly: if Bin the trow had been involved, I'd had the chance to put a stop to him but instead I'd chosen to take a different path. If that were the case, I'd definitely chosen wrongly.

THANE and I sat together in the corner of a busy café. The noise of clinking crockery and the chatter around us was more than enough to mask the sound of our conversation; we were less likely to be overhead in a busy spot than somewhere with no customers.

It had taken some persuasion to get Thane to leave his stake-out, but for once Tiddles had been on my side and had nipped his fingers to encourage him to listen to me. Now she was curled up on his lap snoring.

'You're saying that you believe what happened to this ban sith has also happened to my mo—' he swallowed and corrected himself '—to Ashina Barrow?'

I didn't beat around the bush. 'The signs are there. If somebody could rip out a ban sith's voice, they could also rip out a werewolf's lupine soul. Ashina isn't dead, but if she can no longer transform during the full moon she'll be very sick, right? Sick enough for her pack to believe she's dying.'

Thane's skin was pale and his voice was distant. 'The pack had to work hard to prove themselves in the years after I left. They didn't want to appear weak, and that will still be a concern now.'

And that was the reason they'd not told anyone what had happened. I nodded.

'And last time I checked,' Thane continued, 'there were nineteen Barrow werewolves. Last night there were seven. What if it's not just Ashina who's been affected but others, too? What if it's not a coincidence that I only ran into seven of them last night?'

He met my eyes. 'That's why Cayden is so angry with me. All those years ago I weakened the Barrow pack and now he believes it's my fault this is happening to them.'

'It's only a theory,' I cautioned.

He sighed and rubbed a hand across his shorn, copper-coloured hair. 'But it fits.' Unfortunately it did.

'How long do you think a werewolf can go without transforming?' I asked.

'We don't have a choice, Kit. The full moon forces that transformation every month.'

I watched him. He knew what I was asking: if a werewolf was forced out of their wolf body and couldn't return despite the demands of the full moon, how long would they survive? Months at best because the shock to their system and the inability to accede to their natural cycle wouldn't be healthy. That could easily prove as lethal for a werewolf as Keres losing her ban sith wail. And it was obvious from the residue I'd found that the Barrow werewolves had been targeted long before the ban sith, so their time had to be running out.

'I'm not a Barrow wolf, Kit,' Thane whispered. 'They're not my family. Not any more. But I have to—' he choked.

I took his hands in mine. 'I get it, Thane. We'll help them.'

'How?'

'I'm already on Keres' case and I have a few ideas. You can't talk to the Barrows but you know other werewolves. Maybe ask around and see if anyone knows what has happened to them?' I gave him a warning look. 'Don't try and approach the Barrow pack yourself, will you? They want someone to blame and right now, for whatever stupid reason they've concocted amongst themselves, they're blaming you.'

'I'll stay away.' His voice was resigned.

'You have to promise, Thane.' I wanted my ginger werewolf to be safe; hell, I *needed* him to be safe.

He held my gaze. 'You have my word.' That was more than enough. 'There are a few people I can speak to who might know what's happening, and last night's full moon could work in my favour because I'll be more likely to catch them off-guard. They might be more willing to talk.' As long as Thane was in problem-solving mode, he wasn't focused on the trauma of what was happening.

I checked my watch. 'Let's reconvene this evening before the sun goes down.'

'Eight o'clock?' he asked. 'At your place?'

'I'll be there.' I drained my cup of coffee, which wasn't up to Black's standards but had been reasonably bitter and tasty nonetheless, and stood up. 'Take care of yourself,' I told him. I meant it wholeheartedly. 'Oh – and don't go back to your flat. It's not safe.' I pulled a face. 'Sorry.'

'A mirrored ceiling is a silly idea anyway,' he muttered.

I managed a small humourless smile then I left. I had business to attend to.

I FOUND it hard to believe that I'd accidentally come across the only people in Coldstream who'd had their powers ripped away from them. The idea that Keres and the Barrow werewolves were the only ones affected was nonsensical: there had to be others.

There were two people I could go to in order to confirm that dark theory.

The Magical Enforcement Team headquarters was smack bang in the centre of Coldstream. The last time I'd visited, the place had been in a considerable state of disarray having been attacked in the middle of the night. Now it sported a shiny new front door complete with an elaborate magical ward in place. In theory that was a good thing: the fast repairs meant that the MET appeared not only efficient but also prosperous. In reality, it was a pain in the arse because I could no longer stroll inside and demand to speak to Captain Wilberforce Montgomery. I had to wait on the step outside until I was deemed unthreatening enough to enter.

'Take a seat, Ms McCafferty,' stated the officious-looking druid who eventually allowed me into the building. 'Captain Montgomery will be here shortly.'

The MET were woefully under-staffed and the one contact I

could rely on was often out on the mean streets of Coldstream, dealing with the petty crimes that others hadn't mopped up. That Montgomery was already in the building looked promising but, alas, he didn't see it the same way.

His face dropped when he strode into the waiting room and saw me. 'Oh, it's you. I knew our paths would cross again at some point but I was hoping it would be later rather than sooner.' Clearly, the druidic staff sergeant had neglected to mention my name.

I smiled pleasantly; I still had my amiable cat-lady persona to maintain, although Montgomery's belief that I was nothing more than that was diminishing every time we met.

'Good afternoon, Captain.' My smile widened; I could be both deferential and polite when the situation called for it.

He gave me a long-suffering look that was filled with dread rather than pleasure. That was a shame. Maybe next time I'd drop by with some scones instead of problems – then again, given Dave's reaction to my baking attempts, perhaps that wasn't such a good idea.

'I suppose you'd better come this way,' he said. 'We can talk in the interview room and you can tell me how you're planning to ruin my day.'

'Ruining your day would never be my intention, Captain.'

He snorted. 'Yeah, yeah.'

I followed him into a small windowless space that appeared to have been renovated at the same time as the front door and the waiting area. Whoever had been in charge ought to have tried harder; even with a fresh coat of paint and newly plastered walls, it was depressing. I managed to stop myself from saying so and sat down.

Montgomery took the seat opposite. 'Alright then, Ms McCafferty. What's the problem today?'

'Call me Kit.'

His look suggested that he didn't ever want to be on first-name terms with me if he could possibly help it.

I got to the point. 'I'm here as a concerned citizen.'

Montgomery sighed. 'Go on.'

'I've heard reports that there are people in Coldstream who've had their powers stolen. Their magic has been ripped from their bodies with some force. Is this true?'

'You have nothing to worry about, Ms McCafferty. It's happened to very few people and there's probably a simple explanation. I expect they'll recover their magic soon enough.'

Shit. I'd expected there would be others but it was still awful to hear Captain Montgomery confirm it. 'How do you know that? Has anyone recovered their powers yet?'

'Well, I doubt the three affected would tell me if they had. The harpy has lost her ability to fly, though that makes Coldstream safer, and I suspect the leprechaun having a run of bad luck is simply feeling sorry for himself. The druid is a frequent complainant who is prone to exaggeration.'

I looked at Montgomery and he looked at me. 'Goddamnit,' he muttered. 'That's what you're here for, isn't it? You want information about who's been affected. Is there something else going on? Should I be concerned?'

I decided that it wouldn't hurt to have somebody else on the case. 'I think,' I said carefully, 'that you ought to investigate further. If the druids have been affected, maybe you ought to check with the witches' council to see if any of them have been having problems. The same goes for the vampires. It wouldn't hurt to tell the public to be on their guard.'

'Be on their guard for what exactly?' His eyes narrowed.

I grimaced but answered truthfully. 'I don't know. But I don't think any of them will suddenly recover their magic any time soon. And I recommend that they see a doctor, even if they're not feeling unwell.' I took out the handkerchief I'd used to collect the sample of nasty dark gunk from the rooftop over-looking the Shellycoat house. 'I'd also look for some of this residue. I suspect it might be connected.'

He gazed at the handkerchief. 'What is that?'

'I'm hoping you'll find out.'

Montgomery ran a hand through his hair. 'And what will you be doing while I'm running around the city asking questions?'

I blinked innocently. 'Me? I've raised my concerns with the appropriate authorities, Captain. Now I'm simply going home to Danksville.'

'Would you like any help with that?'

I'd started to suspect Wilberforce Montgomery was smarter than he let on. I hesitated then spoke aloud the thought that had been bothering me. 'A list of all the properties where residents have recently reported burglaries would be useful.'

'Why? Do you think there's a connection?'

It was tenuous: a nervy trow, a stolen shellycoat and a broken Barrow wolf window were all I had so far. 'Honestly? I'm not sure yet.' But I soon would be.

# TWENTY

Trilby was packing up their stall for the day by the time I arrived at the riverside market. They were placing several pretty coloured vials into a chest but the clinking of the glass wasn't enough to drown out Trilby's whistling. My eyes narrowed: that was the tune for 'The Lion Sleeps Tonight'. Hmm.

'Hello, Kit,' Trilby burbled without looking up. 'Having a stressful day?'

I crossed my arms and waited until they'd finished with the vials and raised their head to smile at me. 'That's quite the ear-worm tune you're whistling,' I commented.

Trilby grinned. 'It's been stuck in my head all day. I can't think why.'

Uh-huh.

'Is there something you want? I've sold out of silver-coated clover.'

That wasn't a surprise – and it certainly wasn't what I wanted. 'I need some information.'

'I'm afraid I don't know the way to a lone werewolf's heart. Perhaps try a candle-lit dinner and sexy underwear.'

Ha. Ha. I rolled my eyes and got to the point – even though I suspected Trilby already knew exactly why I was there. 'What do you know about people who've had their magical powers stolen from them?'

'Stolen magic? That must be a peculiarly nasty thing to happen to someone.'

That was something of an understatement. 'Potentially lethal in some cases,' I said.

Trilby abandoned their packing to give me a long look. Their expression was sombre and there was a dark ferocity in their eyes. 'Yes, that much is true.' They drew in a deep breath. 'I have heard of some cases.'

'You didn't think to mention them?'

'They only came to my attention in the last day or so. Unsurprisingly, those afflicted don't want to advertise what has happened to them. Nobody wants to appear weak, whether they are or not.'

That was as much true everywhere as it was in Coldstream. 'What exactly do you know?' I pressed.

Trilby's mouth thinned. 'It happened suddenly and there was no prior warning. The victims are from a range of different Preternatural groups and there's no apparent connection between them. In fact, I'd say they are notably disparate.'

'Is that important?'

'Perhaps.' They continued to eye me. 'Whatever has taken their magic has done it deliberately. I don't believe these events are the result of accident or illness.'

'Good to know.' I paused. 'I don't suppose you know if these people were also burgled recently?'

Trilby straightened slightly. 'You have a suspect in mind?'

Yet again, an image of Bin the trow flashed into my mind. 'I have a theory,' I agreed. 'That's all.'

'Interesting.'

I raised an eyebrow. 'That's all you have to say on the matter?'

'I'm sure you'll get to the bottom of it sooner or later, Kit. You are tenacious, if nothing else.' Trilby returned their attention to the vials. 'You know, if somebody were stealing magic, they would need receptacles to put it in otherwise it would dissipate into the atmosphere and be lost forever.'

I had the sense I was hearing something important – but there again everything Trilby said was important. 'What sort of receptacle?'

'I can't begin to imagine. This isn't the same as bespelling some herbs. This sort of magic is held within a person's body.' They touched the centre of their chest. 'It would take far more than glass to contain that power if it were ripped away from its natural home of blood and flesh and bone.'

Trilby made it sound even more gruesome than it was. 'Okay.' I waited another beat to see if any more information would be forthcoming, but they had moved their attention to another packing box. Our conversation was over. 'Thanks,' I muttered.

'No problem, Kit,' they said cheerfully, then glanced up and smiled. 'Don't forget what you are, will you?'

'Huh?'

Trilby waved a hand. 'And take care!'

My brow knitted in confusion but they had already lifted up the box and were walking away. They were done.

KERES WAS SITTING up in bed holding a bowl of chicken soup; although it was now lukewarm, with a congealed layer forming across its surface, according to Dave she'd consumed at least half of it. An appetite, even a small one, was a good sign but I knew I couldn't be too optimistic. If Fergus was right, this was only a temporary reprieve from her symptoms. Even so, I was extraordinarily pleased.

'I'm sorry to have caused so much bother,' she said in a strained voice. 'Regardless of your favour to Mallory, you didn't sign up for this.'

'Do not apologise for being sick,' I replied firmly. 'None of this is your fault.' I took the bowl from her and held her hands. 'And I'm working on the problem. I will find out who has taken your powers, Keres. I *will* get them back.'

Although I pushed as much heartfelt conviction into my words as I could, she didn't believe me. She was already resigned to her fate. I stared at her pale face, saw the bruised circles under her eyes and felt the shiver in her long fingers. Then I drew in a long breath. 'I give you my word, Keres. I will get your magic back.'

Her dark eyes widened and flew to mine. 'No! Don't do that. You can't make promises you can't keep. The consequences...'

I interrupted her. 'I'm well aware of the consequences.'

'But you're just a...' Keres stalled in mid-sentence.

I didn't mind. 'Just a cat lady.' I smiled at her. 'You don't know cats, do you? It takes a strong woman to be a cat lady, Keres, and I'm stronger than most.'

She clearly wasn't listening. 'Take it back,' she urged. 'I don't want your word.'

My smile grew wider. 'Tough. You already have it.' I leaned back in the chair. 'But I do need some help. I have some questions and this time I need you to answer them.'

Thankfully she didn't argue. I wasn't stupid: I knew that Keres still didn't trust me completely and she certainly didn't trust that I could find the bastard who'd done this to her. But she was beginning to accept that I was on her side and for now that would do.

Keres was weak and needed to rest so I focused on what was most important – and what would help me most. 'Tell me exactly what happened on the night your powers were stolen.'

Her eyes took on a distant sheen. She swallowed, composed herself and began to speak. 'I was at a house not far from here. There was a man inside dying – I'd felt the pull of his approaching passing from across the city and I knew that his end was near. On the third night, I took up position outside. I wasn't expecting to be there for a fourth night – I wasn't expecting to be there for more than a few hours.'

She met my eyes. 'Death enveloped him and his home,' she whispered. 'It pulsated through the ground and it was impossible to ignore. I think he was glad.'

From what Holly Shellycoat had told me, he definitely was. I didn't say anything. I didn't want to distract Keres from her story.

She shook her head slightly. 'There was no warning. The death skirl was building in me but I'd not yet reached the crescendo. I changed key, sang louder and then,' her eyes filled with tears, 'and then I felt the pain.' Her hands were trembling more violently. 'It was like nothing I've ever experienced.'

Recounting the moment was clearly not cathartic for Keres and I certainly didn't need her to describe how awful it had been when her magic had been ripped from her body. She didn't need to re-live the moment for me.

'Did you see anyone or sense anyone nearby? On the rooftops behind you, perhaps?'

She didn't hesitate. 'No, not before. And if there was anyone there afterwards, I was in no state to see them.'

That was disappointing but not surprising. I wetted my lips. 'Why did you agree to come and stay so close to where it happened?' I asked softly.

Keres flicked her eyes up to me and away. 'It sounds silly but

I thought that maybe I'd find myself again if I was close.' She gave a short, humourless laugh that wrenched at me. 'As if I'd lost my house keys and not my damned soul.'

I waited for a moment or two so she could compose herself. 'Speaking of losing things,' I said quietly, 'can I ask about your wedding ring?'

Alarm flashed across her face. 'How do you know about that?'

'When you were unconscious I went to Barton Road and spoke to your husband. He doesn't know where you are,' I added quickly. 'And I won't tell him unless you want me to.'

Keres exhaled. 'Thank you. It's not that Harvey is a bad man. He's not, he's really not. But he doesn't understand what this is like for me. If he knew I was here, he'd want me to go home and I don't want to be there. I don't want other ban siths coming to visit. If I stay there, I'm a burden on the community. A cautionary tale.'

She assumed a soft, self-mocking tone. 'Look at Nessie Johnson's great-granddaughter. That's what happens when you get your powers too young. That's what happens when you get too big for your boots. That's what happens when...' She choked, unable to finish her sentence.

'You don't have to explain, Keres,' I told her. 'Staying away is your prerogative. I'm not judging your decisions.'

'It's not just the other ban siths. I love Harvey and I still want to be married to him but I can't be near him when I'm like this. I can't explain it. He's so anxious, so worried all the time, and he hovers around me until it's suffocating. He makes me feel worse. And in the long run, he'll be better off without me,' she added sadly. She looked up at me. 'But for the record, I didn't leave my wedding ring behind. It was stolen.'

Suddenly I stopped breathing. 'Stolen?'

She nodded. 'It must have been. I took it off to wash the

dishes and then the doorbell rang. I went to answer it and when I returned to the kitchen it had gone. The window was wide open – somebody must have sneaked in and taken it.'

'When was this?'

She pursed her lips. 'Almost two months ago. I should have bought a replacement but my life was overtaken with far bigger concerns than jewellery.'

'Your ring was taken not long before your magic was stolen?' I pressed.

'Yes.'

'Can you remember what time it was?' I demanded. Her brow creased. 'Was it day time?'

'Oh.' Her expression cleared. 'No, it was still dark. I'd not long got home from skirling outside a block of flats for a woman who lived there. It was around four in the morning.'

Trows were nocturnal; perhaps Bin hadn't limited himself to thefts in Danksville . My suspicions about his involvement rose another notch. 'Thank you,' I said. 'That's helpful.'

From the doorway, Dave coughed pointedly. 'I think it's time Keres got some sleep.'

He was right. I smoothed down my top and stood up. 'Who was at the door?' I asked Keres as I left. 'Who comes calling at four in the morning?'

She smiled. 'Another ban sith, my friend across the road. She wanted to complain about silvered clover. She doesn't always have much success when she skirls and she thinks it's because of charms like that. Sometimes it is, sometimes it's not.'

She shrugged. 'She doesn't feel death as strongly as I do – as I *did*,' she amended. 'I don't feel anything now, and I miss that as much as I miss the magic. There's something beautiful about death that few people except ban siths understand. It's like when you come to the end of a great book, it's sad and it's certainly not pleasurable but somehow it's...' Her voice trailed off.

'Satisfying?' I offered. That was how I used to feel about death. Mostly when I'd caused it.

'Yeah,' Keres said. 'Satisfying.' Her smile returned for a moment but it was tinged with melancholy. Then her eyes closed and I left her in peace.

# TWENTY-ONE

'What the fuck, Kit?'

My response was mild, even though Thane looked incandescent with rage. I stroked She Who Loves Sunbeams, cooed at She Without An Ear, and grinned at He Who Crunches Bird Bones as he batted a determined paw at Tiddles. 'I gave Keres my word that I would find her magic and return it to her,' I repeated,

'And if you can't?' he demanded. 'When you're writhing on the floor and screaming in agony because you gave your word to a dead woman?'

'Keres isn't dead.'

'*Yet.*'

'She needed to hear me say it, Thane. She'll cling on to life for longer if she believes there's a chance that she'll get her powers back. All it means is that I have to succeed.'

'*All,*' he scoffed.

I gazed at him. With his hands on his hips and his face in a scowl, he looked remarkably cute. 'It'll be fine. Stop fretting.'

He threw me an irritated look. 'I've spoken to several people and I think you're right that the Barrows are also victims.

Nobody has seen Ashina for weeks. Other Barrow pack elders have also been absent, and they've been buying up all sorts of random medical supplies from witchery stores. I'm certain they've been attacked in a similar way to Keres.'

His voice darkened. 'What would you have said to me if I hadn't vowed to keep my distance and stormed up to Cayden to give him my word that I'd save the entire Barrow pack from extinction?'

'I wouldn't be happy,' I conceded. That was an understatement. Another confrontation with any of the Barrow were-wolves, let alone with Cayden, would result in more bloodshed. A lot more.

Thane raised his eyebrows to emphasise his point. I waved a hand at him, indicating that I understood his feelings but it was too late. I couldn't unsay what I'd already said: the vow had been made.

'You're not normally this rash, Kit.'

He was right. 'I guess I feel a sort of kinship with her. We both have an odd relationship with death that's unlike other people's experience.' Thane continued to look unimpressed. 'Besides,' I continued, 'I think I might know who's behind all this.'

'Who?'

I told him about my encounter with Bin. 'Since then I've learned that the Shellycoats were burgled not long before Keres lost her powers.'

'Okay.'

'Keres was burgled not long before she lost her powers, too.'

This time his answer was more drawn out. 'Okaay.'

'And one of the windows at the Barrow stronghold had been broken and boarded up,' I finished, 'I think they might have also been burgled.'

His green eyes narrowed. 'By this same trow?'

'I don't have any proof of that, and I'm not saying he's definitely involved – at this point it's little more than a punt. But it does seem strange, doesn't it?'

'It's worth investigating,' he agreed reluctantly. 'Although it might be an unlucky coincidence.'

'Captain Montgomery is coming up with a list of recent home burglaries. If it matches more of the magic-loss victims, we'll have Bin the trow bang to rights.'

'How long will that take?'

I shrugged. To be fair to Montgomery, he was a busy man. 'A few days, I guess. Maybe longer.'

Thane's frown deepened. 'Does Keres have that much time?'

I certainly hoped so. 'We don't have to wait for the list.'

'Why not?'

'Because Bin told me where he lives.' I checked my watch. 'And if we go now, we can catch him before he heads out for the night. The sun won't set for another two hours.'

Thane was already moving towards the door. 'Then what are we waiting for?'

WE TRAVELLED *SANS* CATS. I checked over my shoulder several times to make sure that Tiddles wasn't following us but it appeared that while she was unwilling to accept *my* orders to stay at home, she was prepared to do what Thane told her.

'Cat caviar,' he informed me, after I glanced behind me for what was probably the twentieth time.

I blinked. 'Huh?'

'I import it from Edinburgh specially. It costs a fortune but when I give it to Tiddles, she does exactly what I tell her. It's worth its weight in gold.' I stared at him. 'Don't worry,' Thane continued. 'I left some for your furry family, too. It's special –

it's not like normal caviar because that's not safe for cats. This stuff is good for their health as well as their behaviour.'

I wondered which came first, the cheeky behaviour or the expensive caviar? I sneaked a look at Thane's expression; it might be wise not to suggest that Tiddles was actually training him to give it to her. Besides, I didn't disapprove, far from it. 'Okay.'

'Have I gone overboard?'

'That's not for me to say.' I paused. 'Just don't try to tame me into submission with expensive treats.'

Thane grinned. 'I wouldn't dare.'

'I saw your stocked fridge when I broke into your flat.'

'You mean the flat I can no longer go back to?'

I pulled a face.

'It's okay, Kit. There are other places where I can stay.' The purple sparks of the approaching tram appeared. It slowed to a stop in front of us and the doors slid open. 'But I did buy that food for you. I wanted to cook for you, and I will. After we've enjoyed some sizzling sex, I will make you dinner. Or breakfast. Or,' he smiled slowly, 'whatever you want.'

The tram driver looked impressed. Thane winked at her, dropped two tokens into her outstretched hand and walked towards the nearest empty seats.

'Cat caviar,' I whispered to myself, then I smiled at the driver and joined Thane.

The journey to the stop nearest to Green Humbleton, where Bin the trow had told me he lived, was pleasantly long.

To begin with there was a reasonable gap of about three inches between Thane and me but it didn't take long for it to close. Thane initiated the move and shifted closer to me. When his thigh was pressed against mine and we were shoulder to shoulder, I realised how comforting his body heat was. He possessed a warm, reassuring solidity.

I dropped my head onto his shoulder. 'I'm glad you're here,' I mumbled. 'I missed you during the full moon.'

Thane took hold of my fingers and squeezed them. 'Is that some genuine emotional honesty from the cat lady?'

'Yeah,' I said. 'It is.'

I heard the answering smile in his voice. 'I missed you, too. I'm still sorry I wasn't there when you came around with Tiddles.'

'You should have left a note,' I agreed. 'But it's okay. You don't need to apologise twice.' I paused. 'I'm not sorry I gave my word to Keres, though I should have told you what I was doing first.'

'I don't want anything bad to happen to you, Kit, but your decisions are your own. I only want to know you're doing everything you can to stay safe.'

Feeling a wash of relief, I snuggled closer. 'Ditto.'

We lapsed into silence for the remainder of the tram ride, enjoying the peace we brought each other. There were different ways to compromise within relationships and I decided I liked this way very much; in fact, I was almost disappointed when the tram pulled into its final stop – but then I thought about Keres, pale-faced and shaking.

I jumped up, straightened my shoulders and strode off the tram. I could be a snuggly kitty and a ferocious tiger. Both were good.

'I know this area,' Thane said as he alighted behind me. 'The fastest way to Green Humbleton is through those trees. I come here sometimes during the full moon, though it's been a while. The last time I was here, I ran into a clump of concealed wolfsbane.'

I glanced at him. 'Just lying around?'

'Yeah.' He pursed his lips. 'I wasn't sure if someone had left it deliberately or it had been dropped by accident.'

Given the price of wolfsbane recently, I doubted it was the latter. 'And yet you've not been back to this area since,' I pointed out.

Thane scratched his chin and we exchanged looks. A beat later, we both picked up the pace.

Green Humbleton couldn't be described as a large settlement. It was too far from the city limits to count as part of Coldstream and too small to be considered a village in its own right, not to mention that there were no visible buildings. But there was still magic bound into the land.

Usually you had to be close to the border between Scotland and England to feel the natural ground enchantments and Green Humbleton was several miles away, yet the thrum of magic was tangible.

This was protected land. As far as I was aware, annals that went back five centuries had decreed this land should be maintained as a green space as much as possible. Those laws certainly suited the trows, who lived in holes in the ground. Tourists visiting the area would probably have likened them to fictional hobbit holes, but tourists weren't allowed here. This was a place for a peaceful rural life, not social media, and it helped that it looked like an uninspiring field rather than a magical fairy landscape.

Thane frowned as he surveyed the area. 'It's one thing finding Green Humbleton, it's another locating a trow in Green Humbleton.' He waved an arm. 'All I can see is grass. I can't scent much, even though my senses are still heightened from the full moon.'

I smiled serenely. 'Don't worry. We'll find Bin.'

'You have a contact here? Somebody you know from your EEL days who can pinpoint his home?'

'Nope.'

'He told you his address?' He cast a dubious glance around the empty green space.

'Nope.'

'You've formulated a tracking spell?'

'Nope.' Maybe I could have used the shell that Tiddles had unearthed outside the Shellycoat home to come up with something like that, but I'd not kept it. And anyway, there hadn't been time to make spells.

Thane's frown deepened. 'What then?'

'Patience.'

He squinted. 'Patience? That's your big plan?'

'It's the assassin's greatest weapon – well, that and a lovely sharp dagger.' I glanced up at the sky, which was darkening to a deep magenta. 'Although given the way dusk is settling in, we won't have to be patient for long.'

There was a muffled rumbling noise and Thane raised an eyebrow. 'Not long at all. I've never been here at the right time to see any trows wandering around.'

'Well, now's your chance.'

The first trow to appear was a female who emerged from the ground about a hundred metres away. Given the growing darkness, the only way I could tell she was female was by the shape of her bonnet, which was typical of those worn by all trow women. She was followed immediately by another trow-shaped figure, probably a male.

Over to the left, three more appeared. In front of us eight more emerged in a line from the ground as if Mother Earth had given birth to them. Thane whistled.

'It's quite a sight, isn't it?' I whispered.

'I can't make out any of their faces, Kit. How will you tell which trow is ours?'

I grinned. 'That part's easy. Bin will be the trow who's running.' I delved into my pocket and withdrew a slender torch.

I wouldn't use it to light any faces; there was a far faster way to locate the trow I wanted from this crowd which, now that the sun had disappeared, numbered around three dozen.

I flicked on the torch and angled it up to illuminate my features.

'He's met you,' Thane breathed as several of the trows turned in our direction. 'And he's scared of you.'

'Got it in one. I give it five seconds.'

Thane scanned the area. 'Five,' he said, counting down. 'Four, three, two...'

A single figure broke away from the others and sprinted in the opposite direction away from us. 'One.' I smiled coldly.

Then, for the second time that week, I ran Bin the thieving trow down.

# TWENTY-TWO

Last time I'd grabbed Bin within seconds of his attempt to flee but that had been on my home turf in Danksville. This time, the trow possessed the advantage because he knew the area. Short legs or not, his sprint was impressive.

He was heading for the same trees through which Thane and I had marched on our way here. I knew that if Bin reached them, there was every chance I'd never find him because he'd hunker down away from the main paths and wait for the danger to pass. I was determined not to let that happen.

I gritted my teeth and pumped my legs faster. Just as I thought I was gaining on him, my toe caught the edge of a hole in the ground and I stumbled. I managed to stay upright but I lost all my momentum, and now my damned ankle – and my pride – hurt.

I gave myself a fleeting second to acknowledge the pain then worked on quashing it so I could focus on the hunt. Before I could pick up speed again, Thane passed me sprinting far faster than I was capable of. Bin the trow might be able to beat a cat lady in a race on home soil, but he couldn't outrun a determined werewolf a day after the full moon.

By the time I'd recovered enough to return to full speed, Thane had grabbed Bin's cloak and hauled him backwards until he was gripping the trow by his upper arm.

Panting slightly, I caught up to them. Thane glanced at me. 'Thought you'd been training lately?'

I rolled my eyes in mock irritation; I was fit and I could run fast, but I wasn't super human. My throbbing ankle proved it.

Bin was already screeching, 'Lemme go!' He twisted against Thane's hold but couldn't break free, so he switched tactics and started kicking repeatedly at Thane's shins.

'Hey! Stop that!' Thane tried to angle his body away but Bin was determined. Some of those sharp kicks must have hurt.

I moved until I was facing the trow. 'Enough,' I growled. The menace in my tone made him falter. 'You're outnumbered here, buster, and we've got some questions that you will answer before we consider releasing you.'

There was a polite cough behind me. 'Actually,' said a clipped female voice. 'I think you'll find that you two are the ones who are outnumbered and that *you* will answer some questions before *we* let you go.'

I turned around slowly and gazed at the miniature army of trows. Several were holding weapons and all of them looked cross. 'This doesn't concern you,' I told them snippily.

One of the trows stepped forward, probably the one who'd already spoken. She was wearing a bonnet like the other women but she had a heavy gold chain around her neck. Nobody else was displaying such visible jewellery.

I made an educated guess. 'You're the mayor of Green Humbleton?'

Her eyes glittered in the darkness. 'I am, therefore this matter concerns me. Binhamatin is one of ours. You have no right to assault him in this manner.'

Bin emphasised the trow mayor's words by launching

another series of kicks at Thane. 'Exactly!' he said shrilly. 'Let me go!'

'I think that he's the one who's guilty of assault,' Thane grunted. 'All I've done is stop him from running away before we can speak to him.'

I nodded. 'He's not the upstanding citizen you think he is. He's guilty of a series of thefts across Coldstream. Binhamatim here is a criminal.'

The mayor's expression was placid. 'I know,' she replied. 'Who do you think put him up to it?'

I blinked at her. 'You?' I asked stupidly.

'Desperate times call for desperate measures.'

I stared at the assembled trows. None of them were backing down. I turned to Thane and met his gaze. He acknowledged my glance and cleared his throat. 'All of us need to sit down,' he said, 'and have a serious conversation.'

Perceived wisdom suggests that embattled parties joining together for talks should meet on neutral ground because to do otherwise gives one side an unfair advantage. In theory, that was true for Thane and me. Entering the underground network of concealed trow living spaces could have been a very bad idea indeed; we didn't know the layout and it would be easy for them to gain the upper hand and attack us both. And given that Thane's height meant he would have to stoop, he was already at a disadvantage.

On the other hand, there were reasons why walking into a trow space wasn't such a terrible idea. For one thing, I used to be an assassin and my job had centred around entering enemy territory to complete my missions. For another, offering the small concession of literally yielding ground to the trows would relax them, and if they felt less threatened they'd be less unpredictable. And, of course, we didn't have much choice in the matter. We could have walked away, but given Keres' condition that wasn't really an option. Although it was possible that Bin and the other trows had nothing to do with the stolen magic, this was the only real lead we had.

The mayor, who formally introduced herself as Tanavantia, took us to an unmarked spot in the centre of the empty Green Humbleton field and waved her hand. There was a brief rumbling sound and a moment later a narrow gap opened up leading downwards. We squeezed in after her and found ourselves in a wide space lined with wooden benches. Doubtless this was the trow version of a town hall.

Tanavantia offered us space on a bench near the front and I eyed it dubiously. Trows were relatively small creatures and I wasn't convinced it would hold my weight, let alone Thane's, so I elected to sit cross-legged on the floor in front of it. After a moment's pause, he joined me.

As soon as we were seated, six trows flanked us to the left and the right, their expressions grim. Although I wasn't daft enough to underestimate their abilities, I wasn't worried. Not yet, anyway.

Tanavantia gestured at Bin and he shuffled forward, a bag in his hands. I recognised it immediately as the same drawstring bag he'd been carrying when I'd confronted him in Danksville. He moved to the centre of the room and emptied its contents.

'There you go,' Tanavantia said. 'Take what is yours.'

I gave her a steady look. 'None of it is mine.'

She sighed and jerked her head at Thane. 'You, then. Take what belongs to you.'

He didn't hesitate. 'None of it is mine, either.'

Her gaze switched between us. 'You are not members of the

Magical Enforcement Team, and you are not stalwarts from the druids, the witches or the vampires,' she said, naming the three largest and most cohesive Preternatural groups. 'You,' she said to Thane, 'are a lone werewolf. And you,' she addressed me, 'are a cat sith.'

I didn't bother looking at Bin; I already knew he was the one who had informed the mayor as to what I was. 'We might be independent beings who are not aligned with any other groups but that doesn't mean we are not community minded,' I pointed out.

'So you are here on another's behalf?' she enquired.

'You could say that,' Thane replied.

Tanavantia shrugged. 'You have come all this way. You may take what you wish from what is here. Then,' she added with a harder edge, 'you will leave and never return.'

Thane kept his voice deliberately soft. 'Why steal in the first place if you're only going to hand back the property?'

She hissed, 'Our motives are not for you to question. Binhamatim's actions have been well thought out. We only take that which is no longer required or that which we do not believe possesses sentimental value. Mistakes are inevitable, but our intentions are profit, not pain.'

I felt a ripple of anger. 'A shellycoat?' I asked. 'A one-of-a-kind family heirloom? Its loss has caused undue pain.'

Tanavantia looked at Bin. He sniffed. 'The owner of that item hadn't worn it in decades. He was dying. Nobody needed it, nobody wanted it. I doubt its absence was noticed.'

It might have taken a few days but Holly Shellycoat had noticed. It had meant a lot to her. I folded my arms and glared at him.

'Is that why you're here? To take back the shellycoat?' Tanavantia asked. 'It has been some weeks. We have already sold it.'

I wasn't surprised but I was still pissed off. 'What about the ban sith's wedding ring? You can't tell me that you believe a fucking wedding ring doesn't have sentimental value.'

Again Tanavantia looked at Bin. This time he only frowned. 'We have stolen no such item,' she said. 'And we have not targeted any ban siths.'

Thane growled. 'What about werewolves?'

She looked at him cooly. 'What about them?'

His growl increased in volume and I placed a hand on his arm.

'What is it that you really want?' Tanavantia asked.

'We want the magic,' I bit out.

'What magic?'

I made a decision. The fastest way to confirm or deny the trows' involvement was to accuse them directly and gauge their reaction. I hardened my gaze. 'The magic that you ripped out of Keres Johnson, the ban sith. The magic that you stole from the Barrow werewolves. The magic that you yanked out of the bodies of a druid, a harpy and a leprechaun. They are all in danger of losing their lives as a result of your actions.'

Tanavantia didn't blink. She didn't turn pale or blush or twitch or shuffle – but somehow I knew exactly what she would say next. 'I have no idea what you're talking about.'

Damn it. I stared at her. I knew deep in my bones that she was telling the truth. The trows were guilty of a great deal but they were not responsible for what was happening to Keres. My heart sank to the soles of my feet. The trows were a dead end.

'What is this?' Tanavantia asked. 'What is this terrible thing that you're talking about?'

I had no reason not to tell her. 'Somebody has been pulling the power from different Preternaturals, extracting their magic through foul means and leaving them with nothing. The shock to their bodies is overwhelming.'

For the first time, the trow mayor looked genuinely disturbed. 'I can believe that.'

Thane leaned forward. 'There was reason to believe that the victims were also victims of your burglaries.'

Her expression darkened and she turned her head to Bin. 'What do you know of this?'

'Nothing,' he said, his eyes wide.

'Has anyone else approached you about your thefts?' I asked with a flicker of lingering hope that this wouldn't be a wasted visit.

His answer was unequivocal. 'No.'

'Have you seen anyone following you during your nightly activities?'

Bin's lip curled. 'Only you.'

'What about your fence? Who do you sell your stolen goods to?' Thane asked.

Tanavantia answered. 'We have different contacts in Coldstream. I will not give you their names without good reason. We need to maintain their goodwill.'

'Why?' I met her eyes. 'Why are you thieving at all?'

For a moment I thought she would refuse to answer, but my revelations about the stolen magic had unsettled all the trows. Something had shifted in our favour.

Bin sucked in a breath as Tanavantia gave him a long look. She nodded reluctantly and this time he answered. 'We are trying to save our home,' he said simply. 'We are trying to save Green Humbleton.'

'I don't understand.' I frowned. 'This is protected land.'

Thane agreed. 'Ancient law decrees that Green Humbleton must remain green.'

Tanavantia's voice was resigned. 'Who is to say what is green? The dryad's groves are green, the witches' gardens are green. The land here is powerful and there are plenty of groups in Coldstream who would seek to take control of it. We don't own the land, we only pay rent.' Her expression soured. 'Generation upon generation of trows don't count for very much when there is the possibility of making a profit.'

The wolfsbane that Thane had remarked on was starting to make sense. The owner of this space would want to keep it werewolf free if he or she were planning to sell it. Such assurances would doubtless increase the selling price.

Thane shook his head. 'There are still laws to protect you. As long as you pay your rent, you have every right to remain.'

'What if the rent is increased beyond our means?' Tanavantia said quietly. 'We're trows. We don't waste our time worrying about money. We make do with what we have – but what we have only goes so far.'

My sympathy only went so far, too. 'You're stealing to pay your rent.'

She inclined her head. 'We are. We take from those who seek to take from us.'

That wasn't strictly true, although part of me understood her reasoning how ever twisted it was.

'But I can assure you that we would not steal anyone's magic,' she continued 'We don't wish to harm anyone physically – and we certainly would not kill. We are not monsters.'

I didn't say anything.

Thane was already getting to his feet. 'I apologise,' he said stiffly. 'We thought you were involved. It is clear you are not.'

I wondered how much money the trows owed. The collection of items from Bin's drawstring bag wouldn't sell for much: most of it was junk. Despite his many nights of burglary, he'd snagged very little – a battered brass cup, a small wooden witchery chest, a little white box, an ugly china ornament.

I stood up and winced slightly. Sitting cross-legged for long periods of time wasn't a good idea. I stretched my joints but I didn't make any move to join Thane; instead I walked over to the small pile of items, crouched down and picked up the white box. It was surprisingly heavy and had an elaborate seal.

'Bone,' I whispered. 'This is made of bone.' I looked at Bin. 'Why did you take this?'

He glanced at Tanavantia and she nodded at him to answer. 'The man had lots of those boxes,' he said. He shuffled his feet. 'I didn't think he'd miss one.'

'Lots?' I asked sharply.

He dropped his gaze. 'Hundreds.'

I thought of Louise's collection of thimbles as I turned over the box. Trilby's words were echoing in my head; they had pointed out that whoever ripped away magic would need a receptacle to hold it in, something that could contain extraordinary powers that were usually encased within flesh and *bone*.

I sniffed the box but there was no trace of magic on the outside of it. I twisted the elaborate catch and opened it. It appeared to be unused. What purpose could it have? Nothing sprang to my mind.

I returned it to the pile of pilfered objects. As I straightened up, my head scuffed the ceiling of the trow hole. 'I'll make you a deal.' I pointed at the box. 'I will solve your landlord problem and in return you tell me who you stole that box from.'

Then I smiled. This hadn't been a wasted visit after all; in fact, it might provide the solution to all our concerns – trow, werewolf and ban sith alike.

CHAPTER

# TWENTY-THREE

'It sounds like we're replacing one wild goose chase with another,' Thane muttered as we walked away from Green Humbleton.

'What other reason can you think of why someone would possess a hundred bone boxes?'

'We're talking about Coldstream, Kit. People do weird things, have weird hobbies – though I'll agree it's worth investigating further. But the trows' attitude towards us had already relaxed. They'd probably have told us where they got the box without you making a deal with them.'

I stopped walking, put my hands in my pockets and gave him a long look.

'Oh,' he said.

I nodded. Now he understood.

'You want the trows to accept your help without it appearing to be charity.'

'Stealing is out of character for their kind, regardless of how they justify it to themselves. They're desperate but they're also proud. It's the same reason the Barrow werewolves haven't asked anyone for help or advertised their problems.'

'We live in a fucked-up world,' Thane muttered.

I didn't disagree. 'It's why I prefer spending my time with cats.'

'Cats?' he asked archly. 'And perhaps the occasional lone werewolf?'

I half smiled. 'Perhaps.'

We jumped onto the next tram heading into the city. Unfortunately it was busy with all manner of nocturnal-living Preternaturals, so Thane and I had to stand for the whole journey wedged between a huffing basilisk, who took up far more space than should have been allowed, and a trio of chattering vampires. But even though we couldn't maintain the same physical contact we'd had on the outward journey, the tension between us continued to grow.

Thane's gaze brushed against mine repeatedly. When the basilisk stretched, towering over me so that only the top of Thane's head was visible, I ran my eyes over his copper-coloured hair, which was longer than usual because of yesterday's full moon. I imagined running my fingers across it and wondered if he'd purr like Tiddles did when I stroked her ginger fur.

The tram lurched as it curved around a particularly sharp corner, which made the basilisk shift position. Thane's eyes were on me once again as he tilted his head and wet his lips. I inhaled deeply, scenting past the basilisk's earthy smell and the iron-rich tang of the vampires until vetiver tickled my nostrils.

Thane had dropped his right arm to his side and placed his left foot in front of his right one; he was mirroring my stance, unconsciously or not. I shifted my weight and altered my posture and he followed suit a moment later. My heart rate picked up a notch.

His eyes lingered on my mouth then he raised one hand to his lips and scraped them gently with his thumb. I reached up to my neck and slowly traced a path downwards with my fingertips until I reached my chest. Two high points of colour appeared on Thane's cheeks. A moment later, he upped the stakes and raised his T-shirt several inches from his waist as if to absently scratch his skin. My breath caught sharply.

That was when two of the vampires nudged each other and smirked at me. Suddenly I felt my own cheeks warming and I dropped my gaze. It was a relief when the tram reached the Danksville stop at the top of my street and I could step out into the cool night air with Thane by my side.

'I don't have anywhere to stay tonight,' he said, breaking the silence. 'I can't go to the flat and I've not had time to arrange an alternative.'

I pretended to consider the matter. 'Tiddles is already at my house waiting for your return. It's late and it's been a long day for both of us.'

'It has.'

'It will be another long day tomorrow.'

'Mmm.'

'I suppose one more stray won't make a difference to the McCafferty household.'

Thane's eyes gleamed.

'For one night,' I added, in case it needed to be said aloud.

'One night,' he agreed. 'We both want to maintain our independence.'

I was glad we were on the same page. I started to smile – but a beat later my smile turned into a scowl and I stopped dead in the middle of the cobbled street.

'Kit?' Thane asked, immediately aware of the abrupt shift in my mood.

I bared my teeth and marched over to the Dinsbury house. For fuck's sake.

The Dinsburys had erected a sign in their small front

garden. I strongly suspected that Arthur had watched me leave earlier with Thane and decided it was the perfect opportunity to put it up. He probably thought I'd notice it on my way home and immediately cave to public pressure. Well, he thought wrongly – very wrongly.

*Keep Our Neighbourhood Safe! Keep Ban Siths Out!*

I glared at it. The ornery bastard.

Thane gave a low whistle. 'Jeez. Your neighbours are kinda crazy.'

'They're afraid,' I muttered. 'But fear doesn't give them the right to act like this.' It was incendiary, nasty and uncalled for. I hissed, giving my best impression of She Without An Ear when she was forced to endure some petting, then I clambered over the Dinsburys' garden wall and yanked the sign out of the ground.

I returned to the street with it clamped under my arm. As Thane raised an eyebrow, I proceeded to smash it against the ground until I'd turned it into kindling. A light went on in the Dinsburys' house and the curtains twitched. I didn't turn my head: let them stand behind their window and watch the show if they wanted to. They should have expected this sort of reaction.

'Feel better now?' Thane enquired.

'Not really.'

'I'll get the next one for you,' he promised.

I frowned, then realised that there was a similar sign on display in Slasher's garden further down the street. Maybe I should have been pleased that there were only two signs to deal with, but I knew it was unlikely to stay that way. This was pack mentality. Even though Keres hadn't emerged from her bed since she'd arrived, more of my neighbours would follow suit with anti-ban sith rhetoric. Under other circumstances, I'd have dealt with the situation more diplomatically but I had bigger problems eating into my time.

Thane was true to his word. He pulled up Slasher's sign and destroyed it easily, then hand in hand we walked to my house. There would be considerable fall out from our actions – but I wasn't sure I cared.

As soon as we reached home, I let Thane in before heading upstairs to check on Keres in her flat. Dave was asleep on the sofa, his chest rising and falling with wheezing regularity. I reckoned I could have bashed a pair of cymbals next to his ear and he wouldn't have woken up. Keres, however, was a different matter. Whether it was because of her illness or because she was unused to sleeping during the night, her eyes opened the moment I poked my head into her room.

'Hey,' I said quietly.

Keres blinked in return. Instinctively, I realised she wasn't feeling chatty. 'Do you need anything?' I asked.

She swallowed. 'No,' she whispered. She continued to watch me, a question in her eyes.

'Nothing concrete yet,' I told her. 'But I'm chasing something that might prove useful.'

Her body sagged and I registered the worry in her eyes. She wasn't concerned for herself, she was worried for me because I'd given her my word I'd find a way to help her. It was possible that rather than boosting her confidence and well-being I'd only made things worse.

'I've got this, Keres,' I told her, trying my best to sound confident.

She nodded but I sensed that she didn't believe me. She had a point: my assassin skills were superlative but my investigative skills could do with some improvement. I might do well to sign up for some sort of private eye training programme.

I filed the thought away for the future. As useful as training might be, right now there wasn't any time. Keres' life was on a clock.

I refreshed the jug of water by her bedside and went back downstairs. When I walked into the kitchen, Thane was leaning against the counter saying, ' ...and please, Tiddles, behave yourself. We're guests here.'

The ginger cat sniffed balefully.

'Have you run out of cat caviar?' I asked.

'I'm saving the rest for tomorrow,' Thane said. Tiddles offered me a narrow-eyed look. 'I can only find four of your five, but I've said hello to them all in turn.'

'He Who Roams Wide will be out and about.'

Thane nodded then looked at me more closely. 'How's Keres?'

'Much the same.' I met his eyes. 'Not good.'

He stepped forward and drew me into a tight hug. 'We'll sort out the trows' landlord tomorrow,' he murmured. 'And then we'll know more. We'll find whoever is behind this.'

'Yes.'

'You're Kit fucking McCafferty,' he declared.

'I am. And you're Thane fucking Barrow.'

'I am. Keres is lucky to have us on her team.'

I wasn't so sure about that but I didn't disagree.

The corners of his mouth quirked up. '*I'm* lucky to be on your team.'

That part was definitely true. I grinned, then I hooked my arms around his neck and kissed him.

Tiddles growled from her place on the table, though it was a half-hearted effort for her. This was a fait accompli and we all knew it. She huffed faintly, jumped onto the floor and padded away.

Thane deepened the kiss, his hands reaching for my waist so he could pull me in closer. I allowed it for a moment then I stepped back, pulled my T-shirt over my head and dropped it to the floor. It was followed immediately by my sports bra.

'Bathed in moonlight,' Thane whispered, watching me. He gave me a questioning look and I nodded. He moved closer, dipped his head and trailed hot kisses from my neck to one breast then the other. His tongue lapped gently at my nipples, circling each one with agonising slowness, while the base of his thumb caressed the long silvered scar along the edge of my ribcage.

'Knife?' he asked.

'You'd think so, but actually it was a parasol.'

'With a concealed blade?'

'No.' I grimaced. 'It was a bog-standard parasol, inasmuch as any parasol can be considered standard.' They were hardly everyday objects, especially in this chilly part of the world. 'I'd been contracted to take out a druid. He had several bodyguards, each of whom I'd clocked beforehand and managed to finagle my way around – but I didn't pay any attention to the woman by his side. She was far more lethal than her manner and bearing suggested.'

Thane raised an eyebrow.

'Yeah, I fucked up,' I admitted. 'I was still pretty new to the whole assassin thing. Let me tell you, though, that after being stabbed with the blunt end of a damned sunshine umbrella I never made that mistake again. I also never again made the error of thinking I was invincible.'

'She must have put incredible force behind the blow to pierce your skin.'

'I felt every ounce of that energy.'

Thane crouched down until his mouth was level with the scar and kissed it gently, making me shiver, then he stood up and pulled off his own T-shirt. He didn't make any move to pull me to him; instead he gestured towards a scar located perilously close to his heart.

'Bullet wound,' he whispered. 'It was supposed to be silver and if it had been, I'd be dead. But my aunt who pulled the trigger had been scammed and it was a dud.'

My eyes widened. 'Your aunt?'

'To be fair,' he said, 'she found me standing over the bloodied corpse of her husband, my uncle.'

'Thane...'

He turned around so I could see his back. I'd caught glimpses of those scars before but I'd never really examined them. Although they were clearly old, they still told a brutal tale.

Thane pointed to a long thin mark that wrapped around his back and reached under his armpit. 'This was the first one – I lost track of the others. But you always remember the first time you've been whipped to within an inch of your life.'

A sound escaped my mouth. It wasn't a whine or a squeak, it was a growl because it wasn't pity for Thane that I was feeling but rage. 'How old were you when that happened?' I bit out.

'It was the day after my tenth birthday.'

Every single one of my words vibrated with fury. 'Your uncle did that to you?'

He nodded.

'Why? For God's sake, why would he do that? And *keep* doing it?'

Thane ran a hand over his head. 'I've asked myself the same question many times. He was the Barrow beta and my mother was alpha. Perhaps he wanted to make sure I stayed in my lane and wouldn't ever think I could make a bid for her spot.'

'He wanted to succeed her as alpha,' I spat.

Thane shrugged. 'It's a theory. But they were a similar age and he wouldn't automatically have taken her place if something had happened to her. He might have been beta, but he wasn't popular with the rest of the pack – not all of them, anyway.' He paused. 'So sometimes I've wondered if it was my fault.'

'You were a fucking child!'

'Maybe I provoked him. Maybe I should have been better behaved. Maybe he was trying to teach me to be strong.'

'Thane—'

He held up a hand and I quietened. 'I think the truth is that he did it for no other reason than because he could. My mother was busy with pack business, my dad was already gone, the Barrow wolves were in real trouble. There was every chance that one of the larger packs would try to gain control. As a pack, we'd have ceased to exist.'

I snorted. 'That's no excuse.' I held his gaze. 'I'm glad you killed him.' I meant it.

An odd light was reflected in Thane's green eyes. 'That's the thing, Kit,' he said starkly. 'I don't remember killing him. It must have been me – I hated him enough to do it, and I was strong enough. But I don't know if I stabbed him because my memory of that whole day is a blank.'

'You're saying that it might *not* have been you?' I said slowly. 'Someone else might be responsible?' It was a given across Coldstream that Thane Barrow had killed his uncle twenty-seven years ago when he was only fifteen years old. Nobody had ever questioned it – hell, *I*'d never questioned it and I was well aware of the link between trauma and amnesia.

'It must have been me. I had motive, opportunity and ability.' He hesitated. 'But sometimes I wonder.'

I bet he bloody did.

'I've never told anyone else outside my own family that I don't remember what happened. My own pack believed I'd killed him so why would anyone else listen to me?'

'I'm listening,' I whispered.

'I know. I trust you. More than anything.'

We stood there looking at each other, half naked. It wasn't the lack of clothes that made us vulnerable, it was us. I allowed the moment to draw out then I straightened my shoulders and moved towards him.

I dipped my head towards the bullet-wound scar and kissed it gently, then moved to his back and did the same with cross-hatched shadows of old pain, trailing my fingers and my lips across every raised line. I felt Thane's body tremble but I didn't stop. Eventually my mouth reached the first one, the long thin scar that was seared into Thane's memory. It was more than a foot long and I kissed every inch of it.

I would give him something new to remember.

'Kit.' His voice was hoarse.

'Is it too much?'

He answered immediately. 'No.'

I smiled and moved so I was facing him again. 'Good,' I said. I started to unzip my jeans. 'Because I'm just getting started.'

# TWENTY-FOUR

It would have been lovely to luxuriate for several lazy hours against Thane's warmth. We could have gone for another round of mind-blowing sex and, with growing confidence in each other's bodies and reactions, it would have been even more pleasurable. It would have been equally wonderful to make a delicious breakfast together. I could have popped plump sweet strawberries into his mouth while he flipped pancakes on the stove. We could have gazed into each other's eyes over steaming cups of delightfully bitter coffee.

Naturally, none of those things happened because there wasn't time. We only dozed through the first few golden fingers of dawn before both of us got up with impressive alacrity.

The only cat pleased by the early rising was Tiddles; there were distinct rumbles of disquiet from all five of my moggies – even from He Who Roams Wide, who had been taking advantage of having two warm bodies to snuggle beside. My furry bunch were older cats who appreciated a lie-in, but not Tiddles. She began miaowing for her breakfast in earnest before I'd even stood up.

Thane groaned and rubbed his head. 'Ten minutes,' he

promised her. 'Breakfast in ten minutes. Let me sort myself out first.'

Tiddles swiped a paw at my foot as if the delay was all my fault. I didn't take offence; she was a one-man cat and I respected her for that. But I did dart for the shower before she decided to swipe at me again.

Although I didn't want to waste any time, I took longer getting ready than usual. Today I wasn't a cat lady, today I was a dark assassin and I had to prepare accordingly. Unfortunately I hadn't counted on Dave dropping by for coffee and to give us an update on Keres' condition.

He was already in the kitchen with Thane when I strolled in. The look in Dave's eyes when he saw me wasn't one I'd seen before. His gaze travelled from my tightly bound hair, with the lethally sharp clips holding each purple curl in place, to my skin-tight, flame-retardant, moisture-wicking, black T-shirt and trousers.

Then he noticed the leather straps encircling my biceps that held the smaller pieces of equipment I might need. There was a bulge where my favourite curved dagger snuggled against my spine and another where a small handgun nestled against my left calf. Jet-black trainers with tiny, concealed compartments in their rubber soles encased my feet.

Dave was used to seeing me dressed in colourful loose-fitting clothing covered in cat hair. This was definitely a departure as far as he was concerned.

'Kinky sex games,' I told him, gesturing to Thane who responded with a saucily raised eyebrow.

Dave grunted and tried to dissemble, though he couldn't quite manage to disguise the shocked awe in his eyes. 'Always knew you were weird.'

I took the cup of coffee that Thane was holding out to me. 'How's Keres?'

'Better than she was – she's sitting up and talking. That medicine is working. You were right about your doctor friend. He knew what he was doing.' Unfortunately we all knew that if Fergus was right, Keres' days were numbered but nobody wanted to say that aloud.

'Good.' I nodded briskly and gulped down several burning hot mouthfuls of caffeine. I reached for a banana, unpeeled it and started to munch while I measured out kibble for the cats with my other hand. Within seconds, it wasn't just Tiddles who was miaowing; all five of my own kitties were suddenly milling around my feet.

Dave winced at the cacophony and pulled himself into the corner out of their way.

'You can stay for breakfast,' I offered. I finished the last mouthful of banana and dropped a piece of kibble into my mouth.

Even Thane looked disgusted. 'I kissed that mouth,' he said.

'Salmon flavour. It's tastier than you think.' I held some out. 'Try it. You too, Dave.'

My druid neighbour was already shaking his head. 'You are a vile lady.' He opened the door. 'I'll head home for a few hours where I will eat some real food, but I'll be back to check on Keres again soon.' He glanced over his shoulder and his expression altered. 'These kinky sex games,' he said quietly. 'Will they help find the bastard who's done this to Keres?'

'That's the plan,' I said quietly.

'Good.' He paused. 'If you need any handcuffs, rope or whips, let me know and I'll sort you out.'

I had no idea whether he was still talking metaphorically. 'I will.'

As soon as Dave had gone, Thane glanced at me. 'You eat cat food?'

I grinned. 'Not as a rule but I needed to get rid of Dave and it was a surefire way of doing it.' I crouched down to give each cat their bowl. 'I love him to bits but we can't hang around here talking. I don't want him to know what we're up to and I don't want to delay any longer than is necessary. We need to deal with that damned landlord before nightfall so we can return to the trows.'

Tiddles miaowed sharply and I glanced down. She didn't appear to be passing comment on my plans for the day: her problem was her food. Apparently my kibble wasn't good enough for her, even though I'd watched her chow down a bowl of it the previous day.

'Don't you worry, sweetie.' Thane bent down, picked up the bowl and covered the kibble with a layer of his expensive cat caviar. When he returned it to Tiddles she quivered with happiness and – finally – began to eat. 'Stop judging,' he murmured to me. 'You know you want a man who's well-trained.'

I pursed my lips but it was hard to argue with that statement. 'Come on,' I said. 'We have to get going if we're to reach Broughton and get into that building to deal with the trows' landlord before they open for business for the day.'

Thane uttered the magic words before he bowed in my direction 'You're right. Let's go.'

I HAD HEARD of Tobias Hollow long before Tanavantia had whispered his name to us last night while the rest of the trows were busy crossing themselves. He wasn't the devil incarnate; as far as I was aware, he wasn't particularly evil, not in the Coldstream sense. No, Tobias Hollow was simply another rich schmuck who spent his days trying to get richer as if all that mattered in the world were money.

He lived in the well-heeled suburb of Migden in a penthouse flat that would have made the architects of Thane's last place blush with shame. It was a million miles away from the likes of Green Humbleton, and I doubted that Hollow had given the trows and the other rural residents on his land a single thought. His concerns were purely financial; it wouldn't have occurred to him to consider the consequences his actions would have on an entire community.

He was a selfish dick and he would have been a contract I'd have enjoyed fulfilling when I'd worked for EEL – but I no longer worked for EEL. I didn't have easy access to the resources that would have helped me scope out the Migden apartment and its security. I also had limited time, which was why Thane and I avoided Migden altogether and headed for Broughton instead. It would be far easier to get into his office there than his home, and far quicker.

Even if I hadn't already heard of Tobias Hollow, I'd have recognised that he was wealth obsessed as soon as I saw the building where he worked. It was a large sandstone affair. There were pretty magicked window boxes outside with perfectly manicured flowers, and the sign for Hollow Estate Management was small and discreet. The size of one's exterior company lettering was a good indicator of the size of one's company bank account: typically the smaller the former, the larger the latter.

As far as I could tell, Hollow shared the building with two other companies with similar aspirations, although his office had its own private entrance. I was pleased by that: it would make it easier to gain access – and to leave quickly, if necessary. There would be no need to bother anyone else. In my experience, other people were rarely anything but a hindrance.

Thane was examining the building's posh façade. 'There's unlikely to be a rear entrance – it's not that sort of place.' He brushed his fingertips lightly across the front door. 'And there's a ward. It's not a strong one, but it will slow down our progress.'

I nodded thoughtfully. 'The ideal scenario is that we get inside before Hollow arrives. If we're waiting for him when he gets here, we can surprise him. This will be an easier conversation if he's off-balance.'

Thane agreed. 'Because we can't kill him.'

'Indeed.' Tempting as it might be, ending Hollow's life might only amplify the trows' problems in the long run.

We didn't have the time to investigate what contingencies were already in place in the event of Hollow's death or who would inherit his interests, or if any Hollow heir would end up being even greedier than he was. Sometimes it was definitely a case of better the devil you knew.

Thane tapped his chin thoughtfully. 'If unnerving him from the start is our first goal, why be coy about it? We shouldn't worry about flashing our bare ankles or giving him a glimpse of tantalising decolletage.'

I eyed him; I didn't know where he was going with this, but it was certainly an interesting analogy.

He smiled slowly. 'We don't bother with a striptease, Kit. We offer him full-frontal from the beginning.'

'Uh...' I scratched my head.

'We break in,' he suggested. 'We trip the ward, make a noise and a mess. Do you think Tobias Hollow's first instinct will be to call the authorities?'

Suddenly my expression mirrored his. 'No. He has an image to present to the world and he doesn't want to appear weak. He won't want the likes of the MET officers rummaging through his private papers. Hollow is supposed to be a man who can defend his own interests – that's why he scatters wolfsbane around his property. It's why his office is in this building with that tiny sign. He likes to take care of matters himself and he doesn't want to attract attention.'

Thane nodded at the door. 'Shall I?'

I stepped back. 'Be my guest.'

And with that, Thane used brute force to smash his way in. He was right: sometimes it was prudent to use tweezers and sometimes a sledgehammer was more appropriate.

With the full moon only just over and strong echoes of Thane's werewolf still lingering beneath the surface of his skin, it only took three shoulder shoves and two well-placed kicks to warp the door enough to force it open.

Panting slightly, he moved to the side as it swung open. I gazed at the gap. The shiver of magic from the barrier ward in place was raising goosebumps on my arms. This was going to hurt.

When I stretched forward and passed the tip of my index finger across the threshold, pain flashed through me and there was a faint smell of burning. I considered the situation for a moment or two. The ward wasn't that strong; plus Tanavantia had told me that Tobias Hollow wasn't a witch or a druid so there wouldn't be any lasting injury. I didn't want to over-think the problem.

I drew in a breath then leapt through the doorway and inside the building.

As soon I was in, I stumbled and fell forward onto the marble flooring. Bloody hell. That had hurt.

'You alright, Kit?' Thane called, not sounding overly concerned since I was clearly still conscious and breathing.

I raised my hand to indicate that I was okay, then scrambled to my feet, turned around and examined the damage. Despite the swanky building, Tobias Hollow was something of a cheap-skate. Breaking the ward had hurt but only fleetingly because it had been designed for show rather than keeping out undesirables. As soon as I'd crossed it, the ward had snapped. Thane could pass through the door without any ill effects.

When I beckoned him forward, he sauntered through the doorway and kicked the bottom of the door to make it obvious to anyone with eyes that it had been broken into. 'Thanks for taking care of the ward,' he said.

'Thanks for taking care of the door,' I returned. We grinned at each other like we were Bonnie and Clyde; much more of this behaviour and I'd start to embarrass myself.

'What do you think?' Thane asked. 'This way?' He pointed towards a set of double doors.

I shrugged. 'Let's find out.'

Thane opened the doors to reveal a fairly large office. There was a welcoming feel to the space and I noted a small vase of fresh flowers; this was probably where Tobias Hollow's PA worked. It wasn't impersonal enough for a man whose bottom line was pure profit without any regard for his fellows.

Thane apparently agreed. He looked around the room then immediately strode towards the next set of doors.

The second room met my expectations. The air contained the lingering scent of strong, expensive aftershave – the sort that the wearer wanted you to recognise as a named brand. There was a bank of leather-bound books on the shelves at the far side of the room, none of which appeared to have been opened much less read from cover to cover. In the centre of the room was a large oak desk that wouldn't have looked out of place in the Oval Office. This had to be the right place.

Thane sat down in the leather chair behind the desk and started opening drawers, although from the expression on his face there was nothing useful in any of them. I circled the room several times to establish that there were no more magical wards or booby traps, then I took up position by the side of the door.

We didn't have to wait long. Less than ten minutes after Thane and I had entered Tobias Hollow's inner sanctum, a sharp, feminine cry sounded from outside followed swiftly by footsteps. *Two* sets of footsteps. I crossed my fingers that one set belonged to Hollow.

A young woman with delicate elfin features and a tight skirt that restricted her movements came in and stared in horror at Thane, who was still seated in Tobias Hollow's chair. His feet were propped up on the desk and there was a lazy grin on his handsome face.

'Who are you?' she burst out, her voice trembling.

Thane didn't speak or get up; he waited until a well-dressed man in a sharp suit barrelled in past her and yelled. 'I've called the MET!'

Thane continued to smile. 'Tobias Hollow, I presume?'

Although Hollow exuded magical power, it wasn't immediately apparent what sort it was – and I didn't like that. With his broad shoulders and large frame, he could have been mistaken for troll but he didn't have their facial bone structure. Without knowing what he was capable of, I would struggle to predict his actions but I realised that I was looking forward to this confrontation.

Intimidation, brow-beating victims and leaving my targets alive were not what I was used to; when I'd worked for EEL, I'd rarely even spoken to them. It would be interesting to see if I could find it in myself to bring this affair to a satisfactory conclusion without killing Tobias Hollow.

'Get out!' Hollow screeched. 'Get out of my office!'

Thane stretched out his arms languidly and linked his fingers behind his head. 'Why don't we wait for the MET?'

Hollow spluttered in response, confirming that he'd not contacted them. I pushed myself away from the wall. The young woman started when she saw me but her boss only gave me a cursory glance before he turned his attention back to Thane. 'Who are you?' he snarled. 'What do you want?'

'My name is Thane Barrow and this is my friend, Kit. We're here to represent the interests of the Green Humbleton trows.'

Hollow's face screwed up. 'Who?'

This time I answered. 'The community who live on your land, Mr Hollow,' I said softly. 'The people who've been there for generations and who you are trying to kick out by raising their rent to unaffordable levels.'

There was a moment's silence while Hollow absorbed this information, then he visibly relaxed. 'Oh,' he said. '*Them.*' He affected a nasty smirk. 'Ground-dwelling neanderthals.'

I glared with enough force to make the woman flinch, but Hollow paid me no attention. 'It's my land,' he said. 'I can charge them whatever I like.'

'You know you're being unreasonable,' Thane said. 'Your goal is to force them out so you can sell their land at inflated prices.'

'It's not *their* land.' Hollow paused for dramatic effect. 'It's *my* land. My family has been too good to those creatures for too long. It's about time they realised what it means to live in the real world.' He bared his teeth. 'I have nothing against the trows per se. It's only business.'

Thane didn't miss a beat. 'That's exactly why we're here.' He waved a hand between the two of us. 'This is only business.'

Tobias Hollow's smile was broader now; Thane was talking a language he thought he understood. 'You're interested in purchasing Green Humbleton? I already have several interested parties so your offer will have to be a good one.'

My eyes narrowed. 'The trows are still living there. How can you already have potential buyers?'

'Because the trows will leave. They're already several months behind their rent and I know they can't afford what I'm demanding. They'll be under orders to vacate by the end of the month.'

'So you admit you're deliberately trying to force them out?'

Annoyance flickered across his face. 'As I said,' he bit out, 'it's only business.' He glanced at his assistant. 'Why don't you take this lady outside and fetch her a cup of tea or something?' He looked at Thane. 'Then the two of us can talk properly without interruption. *Mano a mano.*'

'Oh,' Thane murmured. 'This is simply *too* delicious.'

I sent him a small smile and slid out my dagger, then I leapt forward in a blur of movement and pressed it to Hollow's throat. 'Perhaps we've not made ourselves clear. This isn't a negotiation. We're the ones in charge.'

Hollow's eyes widened and he squeaked.

'*You're* in charge, Kit,' Thane drawled.

I grinned and pressed the blade a fraction deeper until a bead of blood appeared. 'If you insist, Thane,' I said. 'Now, Mr Hollow, I'm sure we can come to an agreement that suits all parties.'

# TWENTY-FIVE

I f I'd been under any illusion as to how seriously the trows took their problem with Tobias Hollow and how much trouble and angst that shit had caused, I wasn't now. A mass of trows of all ages, sizes, genders and creeds were standing in front of Thane and me, every face anxious and expectant.

Even Tanavantia looked nervous; she was twisting her fingers together and occasionally reaching up to touch the heavy gold chain of office around her neck. The burden of responsibility lay heavily on her and I was genuinely pleased that I could ease it. The satisfaction I gained from helping people was even greater than that from stroking a sleek cat or executing a perfect kill. Of course, I mused, being able to kill effectively was a large part of what enabled me to help.

'Nobody is perfect,' I whispered under my breath.

Thane glanced at me. 'Tiddles isn't far off.'

'I wasn't referring to cats.'

The corners of his mouth tugged upwards.

Tanavantia cleared her throat. She was keen to get down to business. 'You have news?' she asked.

'Yes. Very good news.'

Thane held up the parchment. 'The next two hundred years at Green Humbleton are guaranteed as long as you maintain rental payments, which will return to their previous rates. Your rent can only be increased every five years and only in line with inflation. And it is clearly stated in magically binding ink that rent negotiations with future generations beyond the two hundred year mark are to be favourable and fair.'

Several of the younger trows couldn't contain themselves and gasped aloud, clutching at each other. One of them shouted, 'How? How did you get that wanker to agree to that?'

Tanavantia gazed at me then nodded slowly. 'It is better to avoid questions to which one does not wish to hear the answer.'

A dozen cheering trows crowded around Thane and I stepped backwards, out of their way.

'I never thought a wolf would be our saviour!'

'Thank you, sir! Thank you so much!'

'I didn't do anything,' Thane protested. 'It was all...' I glared at him and his shoulders dropped. 'It was all in a day's work,' he finished lamely. I smiled and the trows' rousing cheers grew louder.

'Thank you,' Tanavantia murmured. She'd sidled up and was now standing beside me, watching the celebrations.

There was no point in pretending Thane had done all the heavy lifting so I accepted her words. 'You're welcome.'

'We owe you far more than information.' She drew in a deep breath and I had the appalling notion that she was about to present me with her first-born. There was only one thing I wanted and I was determined to walk away with nothing else.

'It's only information that I need,' I said before she could speak again. 'We had a bargain and I expect you to stick to it.'

Something flitted across her eyes but she nodded and gestured to Bin, who was ignoring the ongoing celebrations around Thane and standing close by. 'Binhamatin,' she intoned. 'You must speak freely now.'

The trow shuffled forward. If anything, he was more scared of me now than he had been the first time we met and I felt a flicker of irritation. I wasn't trying to be scary, not here; I was trying to be their friend. But maybe you could take the cat lady out of the assassin but you could never completely take the assassin out of the cat lady. Perhaps Bin was right to be afraid; perhaps I had to learn that I would never be viewed as harmless even by those to whom I meant no harm.

'I took the bone box from a house in Danksville,' he mumbled. 'I don't know the address – I don't understand your system of numbering.' He sniffed. 'City folk do things in a daft fashion. All those buildings, all tightly packed together. It makes no fucking sense and...'

'Binhamatin,' Tanavantia cautioned him, gently.

He stopped his complaint in mid-sentence and wiped his nose with the back of his hand, then lifted his head and met my eyes. 'I'll have to show you where it is.'

That worked for me. 'Great,' I said, smiling at him. Unfortunately he only flinched. 'There's no time like the present.'

IT TOOK FAR LONGER than I liked to extract Thane from his adoring fans, and it also took far longer than I'd anticipated to travel back to the heart of Danksville. Bin was more terrified of the tram than he was of me, and after nearly ten minutes of trying to persuade him that it was the fastest and safest way into the city, I gave up. Sometimes you had to know when you were beaten.

'Fine, we'll do things your way,' I said. If we walked it would be dawn before we got close. There was no chance that Bin had walked into Danksville on his previous visits; he had to have another mode of transport.

He grunted and scurried off, leaving Thane and me to follow.

'Is this a good idea?' Thane asked in a low voice. 'Maybe we should meet him there. We can take the tram and he can travel in a way that suits him.'

'We don't know where we're going,' I pointed out. 'And Bin doesn't understand our system of addresses. Sticking close to him will be easiest.'

Thane nodded. 'Uh-huh. Especially now that he's just disappeared.'

I blinked and looked around. Shit: a moment ago Bin had been in front of us and now there was no sign of him.

Thane frowned. 'He wouldn't run off. This is part of our agreement.'

'He's scared of me,' I muttered. 'Maybe...'

There was a shrill voice to our left. 'I have not run off! I am right here!'

Thane and I exchanged looks and turned. Neither of us had spotted the concealed trow hole only a few metres away from which Bin's head was poking out. And he was furious. 'Of course I'm scared!' His high-pitched voice bounced around in the darkness. 'I know what you are! I know what you're capable of! If I wasn't scared, I'd be fucking stupid!'

'He has a point,' Thane murmured.

It was my turn to flinch.

Bin wasn't finished. 'Scared or not, I'm still here. I won't run away from you. I know what I did was wrong and I know I scared people by breaking into their homes, but I had my reasons. I'm not a monster and I don't wear a mask – I am what you see. But you are not what you appear to be, and that makes you more terrifying than me. We're grateful to you for what you achieved with Mr Hollow, but Mr Hollow told us who he was from the start and we always knew what he wanted. Who are *you*? What do *you* want?'

Thane's eyes glittered. 'You need to take this down a notch.'

'Or what?' Bin demanded.

I put a hand on Thane's arm and thought of Keres. This was only a flavour of what she experienced on a daily basis and she managed it with considerable grace. 'It's fine.' I met Bin's angry gaze. 'I'm Kit. I'm many things to many people, but all I want as far as you're concerned is help. I wanted to help you, and now I want your help for someone else. Nothing more, nothing less.'

Bin bared his teeth in a semi-snarl. He didn't trust anyone from the city, but he had specific reasons for not trusting me in particular. 'I don't like cats.'

'Okay.' He was lying; he'd been friendly enough when he'd first met me and I'd been in a cat's body.

'And I don't like you.'

'That's okay, too.' This time he was telling the truth. That was alright; I didn't need him to like me.

He huffed loudly then his head dropped back into the hole in the earth. When he reappeared, he was carrying something. 'This is better than any scummy tram,' he declared.

I gazed at the rickety bicycle that appeared to be made out of wood. I dreaded to think what its suspension was like. 'Fabulous,' I said.

'Take it, then.'

I did as I was told.

'Wolf!'

Thane started. 'Yes?'

'This one is for you.' Bin produced another bike, slightly bigger than the one I was holding though it didn't appear to be any sturdier.

'Wonderful.'

Bin managed a smile. He pulled out a third bicycle, heaved himself out of the hole and smacked his lips in satisfaction. 'Now we can go.'

I gazed at him. 'What?' he asked. 'I thought you were in a hurry. The faster this is over and done with, the better.'

True. I sighed and clambered onto the bike. It was designed for trows and I was far too large for its wooden frame. Thane didn't look any more comfortable. 'The Three Damned Stooges,' he muttered.

I stifled a laugh. 'It could be worse.'

'Could it?'

Bin was already cycling, pulling away from us and gaining speed with each turn of the heavy wooden wheels.

'It's all for a good cause, Thane.'

'Tell that to my arse when we finally get to Danksville.'

I started to pedal. There was no doubt in my mind that we would both be rubbed raw in that tender area before we got close to my home suburb. 'Play your cards right,' I told him, 'and I'll kiss it better.'

NINETY OR SO MINUTES LATER, when we finally trundled into the dark and empty riverside market, I felt even worse than I'd expected. It was bad enough when we were cycling along paths and grassy walkways, but when we reached the city streets and the uneven cobbles it became a genuine nightmare. I was no stranger to pain but my bottom felt as if it were on fire and I wasn't sure there was any skin left on it. When I climbed off every muscle screeched and even walking was painful.

'This way!' Bin chirped, pirouetting off his bike and dancing up the slope that led away from the market.

'Torture,' Thane whispered, his horrified expression a mirror of my own. 'We should have taken the tram.'

'Indeed.' I certainly had a newfound respect for the hardiness of your average trow.

I stretched my legs as best I could and set off after Bin, though it took several shuffling steps before I managed anything that approximated a normal stride. It would have been galling if Thane hadn't also been struggling.

We heaved ourselves up the narrow hill and away from the market. Once we reached the summit and the network of dark cobbled streets, I realised that there was no sign of Bin. Goddamnit. I kept my voice low and called his name. There was no answer.

Thane tried, his baritone penetrating further through the darkness than my voice. 'Binhamatin! Where are you?'

Given the way he'd spoken to us at Green Humbleton, I didn't think Bin had run away. It probably hadn't occurred to him that our longer legs would require recovery time after so much painful cycling. I swivelled on the spot, trying to peer into the darkness and identify which direction he'd taken.

'I think...' I began, then froze.

Thane glanced at me. 'What is it?'

'Something's wrong.'

'What do you mean?'

I swung my head from left to right. It wasn't anything specific but there was a definite sense of wrongness. The air was shifting in a way that suggested encroaching evil and I knew that if I'd been in cat form, every single hackle along my spine would have been raised. 'You can't feel anything?'

'No, Kit.' Thane frowned. 'There's...'

I didn't find out what he was planning to say because that was the moment my whole body was wracked by searing pain. The bone-crunching agony was like nothing I'd ever felt before.

My knees gave way and I fell forward. Thane was by my side in an instant, trying to help me up and calling my name but I was only dimly aware of his presence. The trauma of what I was experiencing was too great for me to focus on anything but myself.

Violent shivers shook my limbs and I gasped for air. I choked and spluttered and writhed. There was a growing pressure in the centre of my chest, as if a hand had reached into my heart and was squeezing it, but this was far more than a heart attack.

A scream clawed its way out of my throat. Dark magic – the darkest magic. Suddenly I knew exactly what was happening to me: it was what had happened to Keres, a harpy, a leprechaun, a druid and quite likely several Barrow werewolves. Something – some*one* – was ripping the magical essence out of my body and it hurt like fuck.

I rolled to my side. With the market to our left, there were few places this magical killer could be hiding so they had to be on the rooftops. I was in no state to go hunting – I could barely do anything beyond twist in pain – but Thane would understand if I could just communicate with him.

I gritted my teeth and forced my eyes open. His face swam in front of mine. His lips were moving and he was saying something, but I couldn't hear him through the roaring in my ears. I raised a hand to the roofs opposite and tried to point, then touched my chest to indicate through the blasting pain that my cat sith soul was being ripped from my body.

Another jolt surged through me and I was unable to continue.

I would rather have been stabbed by any number of parasol tips than experience this. I'd rather have had any number of witches perform rigor spells upon me. I'd rather have been shot, stabbed, drowned, strangled and burned than go through this. I was powerless. I couldn't fight this enemy, couldn't defend myself, couldn't do a damned thing. The magic inside me was being ripped away and I couldn't stop it.

*Don't forget what you are.*

Trilby's last words to me echoed around my head.

*Don't forget what you are.*

Cat sith. I was nothing without that part of myself. It was me: I was it.

*Don't forget what you are.*

Cat sith. My heart burned. Cat sith. Cat… I drew in a shuddering breath. Cats weren't just cats and I wasn't just a cat lady. Cats were from the netherworld; they were demons – and that made me a demon lady. A demon wouldn't allow its essence to be stolen and neither would I.

I bared my teeth. I was stubborn and hardy and strong – and my roots were in at least some people's version of hell.

A strangled whisper escaped my lips. 'I am a demon lady,' I gasped. 'You … cannot … take … this … from … me.' And with that, I curled my hands into fists and clung onto every shred of what was myself with claws and teeth and fur.

# TWENTY-SIX

I had no idea how long my internal fight lasted but I knew the exact moment when the onslaught ended. And I also knew I had won this round. I was still me. My cat – my *demon* – remained within me. Thank you, Trilby.

A quavery voice broke through the air above me. 'Are you alright?'

I blinked, opened my eyes and gazed up at Bin, whose face was white with fear. I licked my lips; my mouth was as dry as sandpaper. 'Yes,' I croaked. 'Yes, I'm okay.' I flicked my eyes to the side then sat bolt upright as terror shot through me yet again. 'Where's Thane?'

Bin lifted a shaky hand and pointed to the row of terraced houses behind us. 'He went that way. He climbed up to the roof of one of those houses and disappeared.'

'When?' I demanded. 'How long ago?'

'Ten minutes, maybe? He told me to stay here with you. He told me not to leave you.'

I was already pulling myself to my feet. There was a dull ache in my chest but other than that I felt surprisingly alright. Thane had clearly understood my desperate mute flailing and gone in search of the bastard attacker. But ten minutes was a long time: he should have been back by now.

'Don't go anywhere,' I ordered Bin. 'Stay right here.'

The trow was disturbed enough by what had happened to hold up his hands in submission. He was still terrified. I couldn't blame him.

I softened my voice. 'Please,' I said. 'I need to find Thane and make sure he's alright. I won't be long.'

He nodded. 'I won't go anywhere.'

I touched his shoulder and this time he didn't flinch. Perhaps watching me writhe around in agony had diminished some of my commanding stature. I didn't pause to dwell on it but spun around and sped towards the houses. I'd sent Thane in this direction: this was on me.

Although the terraced houses looked higgledy-piggledy, they were all relatively low-lying; even the tallest was only three-storeys high. It made sense to aim for that one to get the best vantage point. It was also the likeliest place for the magic thief to conceal themselves.

I grabbed hold of the sturdy, cast-iron drainpipe, checked its strength and shimmied up it. I'd climbed up the side of enough buildings in the last few days to become more confident of my abilities. It was just like old times.

*Don't forget what you are, Kit,* I whispered to myself. And then I climbed even faster.

I expected to see Thane as soon as I reached the rooftop but there was no sign of him. There was no sign of anyone.

I resisted the urge to call his name; revealing my presence to whoever was behind this devastating attack could do more harm than good to my copper-haired wolf. Instead I examined the rooftop. It looked empty and nothing seemed out of place – except a strange dark lump that was mostly obscured by a squat chimney stack. I drew in a sharp breath and darted over.

As I'd feared, it was Thane and he was out cold, lying face down on a section of flat roof. My instinct was to focus all my energy and worry on him but I quashed it down in favour of checking the area again. This could be another trap, a quickly planned but cleverly created ambush.

Nobody was lurking behind the chimney stack or hanging off the edge of the roof waiting for the right moment to reappear. There was nothing in the air above me. Whoever had attacked Thane – and me – was no longer here, but there was a patch of dark, miasmic gloop. I glared at it briefly, as if a monster made out of black gunk were about to appear from its centre. Then I crouched down and carefully turned Thane onto his back.

He was still breathing; his eyes were closed and his skin was pale, but his chest was rising and falling with reassuring regularity. I ran my fingers around his head, his neck, his arms, his torso, and up and down his legs to check for wounds but there was no blood. This hadn't been a physical attack.

The ice running through my veins wrapped its way around my heart. I had little doubt that whoever had tried to rip my cat sith soul from my body had taken the wolf from Thane. I leaned closer. 'Thane?' There was no answer. I tried again. 'Thane?'

His fingers twitched and I was rewarded with a very brief, very soft groan. I swallowed hard, aware of the tears pricking at the back of my eyes. I knew what had happened to him, which meant I knew what I could do for him next. Unfortunately, there wasn't much.

UNDER NORMAL CIRCUMSTANCES, it took me twelve and a half minutes to walk from the riverside market to my house. On this particular occasion, it took more than two hours.

The hardest part was dragging Thane's unconscious form down from the rooftop onto solid ground. I was concerned that the soul stealer would return and, as a result, I was painstakingly vigilant. Shimmying down a drainpipe was a no-go, so I was forced to rummage through several dark garden sheds until I located a ladder tall enough to suit my purposes.

I pressganged Bin into holding the base of the ladder steady while I manoeuvred Thane's dead weight down it. It wasn't easy; in the end, I placed Thane's body at an angle and sandwiched him between myself and the ladder with one arm between his legs and one awkwardly positioned at his shoulder so that he didn't fall. It made for slow progress – and it didn't help when the homeowner, a grizzled witch, woke up and came out to see what all the commotion was about.

'You ain't that dirty thief that's been stealing from the good folks here, are you?'

I didn't look at Bin. 'No.'

'Then what were you doing up my roof?'

I wasn't in the mood for lengthy explanations. 'Looking for my friend.'

'And what was your friend doing up my roof?'

I gritted my teeth. 'Looking for that dirty thief.' In a manner of speaking.

The witch narrowed his eyes, clearly disinclined to believe me, then a flash of recognition crossed his face. 'Wait,' he said. 'I know you.'

Bin squeaked, 'My name is Bin. I live in Green Humbleton. I...'

'Not you.' He pointed at me. 'You. You're that crazy cat lady.'

I exhaled. 'Yeah.'

'You've got like, what – twenty cats?'

'Five.'

'Nah, it's more than that.'

I didn't want to get into a spitting contest about my own damned life. 'If you say so.' I eyed him. 'If you won't help me get my friend home then can you get out of my way?' If he didn't move soon, it was likely that I'd actually kill him.

'What's wrong with him? Drugs?'

I didn't answer.

'Betcha it's drugs.' He paused. 'Do you know the going rate for weed these days? Even normal weed, not magicked weed?'

He needed to get out of my fucking way. I hissed loudly and glared. 'This man requires urgent medical attention.'

'I can call a doctor for you,' he offered.

'All I need is for you to get out of my way.' I injected every word with the menacing venom that I wanted to direct at whoever was responsible for this.

The witch frowned and looked for a moment as if he would continue jabbering. He glanced at my face and thought better of it. 'Can I have my ladder back?'

'It's all yours.' I hefted Thane into a fireman's lift, pushed past the witch and walked away without a backward glance.

'You look angry,' Bin muttered once we were out of earshot. I was incandescent with rage but I merely grunted in response. 'What's wrong with the wolf? And what happened to you back there?'

I only had one answer for him. 'Evil,' I said. Pure fucking evil.

# TWENTY-SEVEN

It was three hours before Thane opened his eyes. I had laid his inert form on my bed, given him several drops of the same alder-stirred mixture that Keres had swallowed, and waited by his side. Tiddles waited with me, her ginger-furred body quivering with anxiety. She refused to take her eyes off Thane and every time he stirred or his breathing changed, she lifted her head and tensed.

As soon as his eyelids fluttered open and he could focus his gaze, she'd moved onto his chest. I wasn't sure if it was because she needed to be close to him or she wanted to make sure he stayed where he was and didn't try to get up. Either way I was glad she was there; her presence would calm Thane and another pair of eyes was always welcome.

'Hey,' I said softly.

He exhaled loudly. 'You're alright. Thank God, Kit. Thank God you're alright.'

I wasn't the one in serious trouble. 'Shh,' I said. 'Don't try and talk too much. You need to rest.'

Thane clearly wasn't listening. 'When I saw you on the ground, I panicked. Are you hurt?'

'I'm fine.'

'It was the same bastard who stole Keres' ban sith voice, wasn't it?' His tired green eyes roved across my face. 'Did they ... did they ... did they...'

I didn't look away; Thane deserved my direct gaze. 'Not from me.'

The faintest shadow crossed his face then his nostrils flared. 'Oh,' he whispered.

I leaned forward. I had to be sure. 'Thane? Your wolf. Is it...?'

'Gone.' He looked more stunned than appalled. 'There's a hole in my heart. An emptiness.' He gave a strangled noise and I squeezed his hand tightly. Tiddles was already licking his chin, her small pink tongue rasping across his stubble.

I was still holding his eyes with mine. 'I'll get it back, Thane. I'll get your wolf back.' I drew in a breath and met his eyes.

Thane was already shaking his head in alarm. 'No. Don't do it. Kit, don't you fucking dare do it.'

Of course I'd do it. 'I give you my word I will bring your werewolf back.'

'Goddamnit, Kit!'

I picked up the cup holding Fergus's brew. 'Here. Drink as much of this as you can, it'll help with the aftermath.' From what we'd gleaned about the Barrow pack, Thane would be able to hold out for far longer than Keres but he would still suffer. My heart wrenched. 'Drink it all,' I told him.

He was a better patient than I expected and he drained the cup dry before leaning back against the pillows. 'So empty,' he murmured. 'So tired.'

'Get some rest. Sleep is the best thing for you.'

'You're an idiot, Kit.'

'I know.'

'You shouldn't have given me your word.'

I shrugged. 'It's too late now.'

'Don't leave me.'

This time I didn't reply.

'I need you, Kit.' His eyelids were already closing again.

'I need you too, Thane.' Which was exactly why I *had* to go. I turned to Tiddles. 'Don't let him leave this room.'

Her ears twitched. I nodded grimly, then pulled back my shoulders and strode into the kitchen. Bin was seated on one of the chairs with He Who Crunches Bird Bones curled up on his lap. 'We've got about forty minutes before dawn,' I said briskly. 'It's already too late for you to return to Green Humbleton. You'll have to stay here.'

He nodded. I knew he wasn't pleased by this outcome but he wasn't surprised by it. As soon as I'd found Thane's unconscious body, Bin must have expected something like this.

'Before that happens,' I continued, 'you will show me where this house is.'

He Who Crunches Bird Bones flicked his tail, opened his eyes, stretched out his front paws and jumped onto the floor.

'Now?' Bin asked.

I nodded. 'Right now.'

'What if you're attacked again?'

'Then I'll resist again.'

'What if I'm attacked?'

'I'll help you.' I waited. I knew Bin would make the right decision; I didn't need to force him into it.

'Okay.' He stood up, his face a dark, unyielding mask. 'Let's go.'

We slipped out of the front door. When I reached the garden gate and unlatched it, Bin murmured, 'We're being watched.'

Dave was on his porch. His face was shrouded in darkness but I didn't need to see his features to know his eyes were on us. I raised a hand, he raised one back. 'How's Keres?' I called softly.

'Really good. She's feeling better and she's been moving

around. I checked on her just now. I'm heading to bed for a kip.' He paused. 'What's going on with that wolf of yours?' He must have seen me hauling Thane home.

If I told him what had happened it would make it true, so I said nothing and simply waved. Dave, who was far smarter than he usually let on, didn't say anything more. Instead he pointed into my garden: all five of my cats, even She Who Loves Sunbeams, had come outside. Oh.

'No,' I said firmly. 'Go inside.'

None of them moved.

I folded my arms and glared. There wasn't so much as a flick of a tail in return. Bloody hell. 'Nothing will happen right now. This is about locating an address. Nothing more, nothing less.'

Five unblinking pairs of eyes gazed at me.

I huffed. 'Fine.' As I stepped out of the gate alongside Bin, all the cats followed.

We walked ten metres. Bin glanced over his shoulder. We walked another ten metres and he glanced over his shoulder again. 'Are they coming with us?'

'It appears that way.'

The trow was clearly baffled. 'Why?'

I considered my response. 'Why did you spend so many nights breaking into houses and stealing?'

He pursed his lips. 'To save my community.'

I smiled slightly. 'There's your answer.'

'But they're cats.'

'Exactly.'

Bin frowned. 'Don't worry,' I told him. 'They can look after themselves.' I did, however, glance over my shoulder and check on She Who Loves Sunbeams. Her whiskers twitched when she noticed my gaze. Somewhat mollified, I faced the front again. She wouldn't do anything stupid – not unless I did.

Bin led me to the bottom of my street where the road forked

towards the riverside market. We both stiffened. I wouldn't have been surprised if we were attacked again but this time nothing happened. Bin pointed right. 'This way,' he said. He cast a nervous glance up at the sky, worried about the impending sunrise. Trows weren't vampires and he wouldn't spontaneously self-combust, but he would find the effects of the early sun painful.

'Is it far?' I asked.

'No.'

Good. Then I began to worry. What if this really was a wild good chase, as Thane had suggested? What if the bone box Bin had stolen from this place was simply an icky trinket? I drew in a shaky breath. I wasn't sure what I'd do if this lead turned out to be a waste of time.

'You *did* find hundreds of these bone boxes in this house, right?' I asked.

'Right.'

'And they were all the same as the one you took?'

'Mostly.'

I paused. 'Mostly?'

'Some had labels on them.'

'Written labels? You didn't mention that before.'

'I didn't think it was important,' Bin said. 'There were hundreds of boxes. Only a few had labels.'

Getting irritated with the trow wouldn't help anyone. 'What was written on them?'

'Different things. House mouse. Field mouse. Dormouse.'

My heart dropped to the soles of my feet. Oh no.

'Tea Rose. Garden Rose. Damask Rose.'

I stopped breathing.

'I figured the guy was some kind of naturalist. A collector.'

Blood was roaring in my ears. This wasn't right. The bone boxes were a dead end. I'd jumped to conclusions and...

'Then I saw some of the other labels,' Bin continued. 'Wolf. Beta wolf. Alpha wolf. Leprechaun. Harpy.' As I gasped and gulped in air, Bin shot me a curious look. 'Are you alright?'

'Yes.'

'Because if you collapse in the middle of the street again, I'm out of here.'

'I'm fine. Just peachy, in fact.' I gave him a wide-mouthed, brilliant grin and he immediately recoiled. Ah. Too many teeth. 'Just show me the house,' I said. 'Then your side of the bargain is over.'

He started to move faster. We passed the first and second streets on our left, but when we reached the third one Bin turned down it. I looked behind. Yep: all five cats were following us in single file. I inclined my head towards them to acknowledge their efforts, then plunged after Bin.

There were quite a few people around. In any other city in the country, that would have been unusual because it was just after five in the morning, too early for most joggers to get in their day's exercise before work and too late for any but the most determined partygoers to be heading home on a week night. But this wasn't a typical city and the hour preceding dawn was rush hour. In a way that was good because it meant that neither Bin nor I looked out of place.

Two hurrying vampires, one of them in bat form, passed us at high speed. A heavy-set troll clomped towards us from the other end of the street and swung into a pretty cottage just before we reached him. I caught a glimpse of a yawning dryad performing a sun salutation in her front garden alongside a smirking druid who was trying to mimic her movements and failing miserably.

'There,' Bin said. I jerked to a halt. 'That's the house.'

He pointed to number nineteen. There were at least three hundred houses along this street and for some reason I'd expected it would be further down. Number nineteen made perfect sense, however, because I knew exactly who lived here.

'Jimmy Leighton,' I whispered. I'd known all along that he was one of Bin's burglary victims; all this time the bastard who'd destroyed Keres' life – and quite possibly Thane's, too – had been right here. I should have realised.

As I stared at the front door, my cats gathered at my feet and did the same. 'Gotcha,' I whispered. 'How did you get inside?'

'Back door,' Bin said. 'I picked the lock.'

I chewed on my bottom lip.

'Can I go now?' he demanded.

I didn't glance at him. 'Yes. Thank you. Let yourself into my house and help yourself to whatever you like. The fridge is stocked up and there's a bed made up for you in the back room. You can rest there without being disturbed until sunset tonight.'

The trow scurried away but I didn't watch him go; my focus was entirely on Jimmy Leighton's property.

There was no point trying to get in through the same back door as Bin. Having already been burgled, Leighton would have ensured it was properly sealed against further intrusions. With luck the other entrance points wouldn't be heavily warded.

There was one easy way to find out.

I glanced down at the cats. 'Ready for some criminal activity, kitties?'

# TWENTY-EIGHT

I hung back with She Who Loves Sunbeams. I was concerned about her; her joints were old and she was far more used to long naps than illegal incursions. Besides, I needed an excuse for loitering for the passersby who were on their way to and from their homes.

It helped that I recognised most of the people because, like the annoying witch whose ladder I'd borrowed, they would recognise me as the cat lady from around the corner. It wouldn't appear out of the ordinary to see me lingering on this street and chatting to a furry beast.

The other four cats didn't waste any time. Usually they were contrary moggies who didn't take kindly to instruction, but now they understood what was at stake. Although they wouldn't enter Jimmy Leighton's house, they would find the best way for me to go in.

As I'd expected, it didn't take them long to scamper into Jimmy Leighton's front garden and start investigating the property perimeter.

'Morning, Kit.' It was Natasha, the troll who ran the butcher's stall at the market and who was doubtless on her way to set up for the day.

'Morning!' I smiled and tried to negate the tension that was inveigling its way into every bone, sinew and muscle of my body.

'I don't normally see you out at this time.'

I gestured to She Who Loves Sunbeams; hopefully that would be enough of an answer for her. Out of the corner of my eye, I spotted the other four cats assembling by a front window on the ground floor of Leighton's property. Excellent.

'Ah.' Natasha smiled and bent down to scratch a delighted She Who Loves Sunbeams beneath her chin. 'Herding cats. That sounds like you.'

'It's a dirty job but someone's gotta do it,' I murmured.

'Ain't that the truth.' She straightened up. 'Drop by my stall later if you get the chance. I've got some tasty titbits that might help you corral your kitties in future.'

'You're fabulous.'

She grinned, waved and went on her way. As soon as her back was turned, I gestured to the cats. They'd done their job; now it was down to me.

'Go home,' I told them once they'd clustered around my feet. I doubted they'd listen to me any more than they'd done fifteen minutes earlier, but I had to try. 'You can't come inside with me. I need to do this alone – I can't be worrying about you guys while I'm in there.'

I received five identical baleful stares. Even She Who Loves Sunbeams bristled.

'You're a bunch of stubborn, idiotic, contrary cats.'

She Without An Ear headbutted my shin. He Who Roams Wide licked a paw and looked pleased with himself. The others purred briefly.

I sighed. 'Fine. But stay here and stay out of the way.' I gave all five of them a hard glare. 'No matter what happens or who shows up.'

I glanced up and down the street. It was empty but it wouldn't remain that way for long. I darted across until I was standing in front of Leighton's ground-floor window.

There was an argument to be made for swallowing a clump of fur so I could sneak into the property in cat form but I'd be vulnerable during the moments of transformation, and I needed to be on two legs with opposable thumbs if I wanted to confront Leighton in person. Sometimes a human body could be more effective.

I smashed the window pane, reached inside to unfasten the latch and climbed in.

There was a strong probability that Leighton had heard the glass break so he'd be on high alert, not just because of what he'd been up to lately but also because of the recent break-in.

I waited for several beats, hoping he'd burst through the door to his front room and confront me because that would be the fastest and easiest way to bring all this shite to an end. Unfortunately, there were no sounds from the rest of the house and there was definitely no sign of the man himself.

I clenched and unclenched my fists. Fair enough. I started to look around.

The front room was unremarkable: a living room, with a nondescript sofa and chairs, a few plump cushions, a coffee table and a grey rug. The mantelpiece held a vase filled with dried flowers and a framed photo of Jimmy Leighton with an older couple, probably his parents. I picked it up.

Leighton's mum and dad looked as ordinary as his living room. His mum had the bearing of a witch and his dad displayed the tattoos of a druid, although the blue marks were simple in design and likely hinted a lack of extensive magical ability. Jimmy Leighton, who appeared to be around forty years old in the photograph, was bearded with brown hair and sallow skin, though his pallor might have been little more than the effect of his clothes. He appeared to have a penchant for stark monochrome: black cap, white T-shirt, black scarf, black trousers, white trainers.

I squinted. His style reminded of me something. I pursed my lips – then I realised what it was.

'Magpie,' I whispered. He was dressed in a way that put me in mind of the black bird with an alleged penchant for stealing shiny things. It figured.

I returned the photo to its original place and moved to the door that led to the rest of the house. I paused for a moment, my hand on the doorknob. I still couldn't sense anything or anyone, and there was every chance that Jimmy Leighton was still out searching for more victims.

Even so, I took my time; I wasn't daft enough to be lulled into a false sense of security. I slowly twisted the knob and opened the door a fraction. The air beyond was still and stale. I opened the door an inch further and prepared to step into the hallway. That was when I heard the whisper of a footstep behind me.

I didn't hesitate: within a single beat I'd drawn my curved titanium dagger, spun around and raised it to swipe with lethal force at whoever was there. Muscle memory is an extraordinary thing; Keres was lucky that she didn't bleed out in front of my eyes.

I hissed, yanked back my hand and glared at her. 'What the fuck? You should be in bed resting!'

The ban sith blinked at me. 'I'm feeling much better.'

'I don't care! Get out of here!'

I caught a glimpse of the same steel-willed woman who'd shown herself to me when we'd walked home from Mallory's place. 'You're here because of me,' she stated. 'Is the person who lives here responsible for what happened to me?'

I prevaricated. 'Nothing has been confirmed…'

'I knew it! So I have more right to be here than you do.' She looked around the uninspiring room. 'And that's saying something, given we've both broken in. This guy took *my* voice. He stole *my* magic soul.'

'It's dangerous, Keres.'

She shrugged. 'I've got nothing else to do with my time apart from wait to die.'

I cursed to myself. Keres wasn't trained, and there was every likelihood that she would get in my way and compromise my actions. Nothing about this was a good idea.

'How did you know I was here?' I would have noticed her following me – I hoped.

'I saw you leave with the trow. By the time I'd grabbed my stuff and managed to sneak past Dave, there was no sign of you but I figured you hadn't gone far. I saw the trow turn out of this street then I saw all the cats.' She managed a tight smile. 'Ta-da!'

For goodness' sake. 'Clever,' I acknowledged. 'But still not sensible.'

'I'm not leaving.'

I exhaled loudly. 'This could get very nasty.'

'I hope it does,' she said calmly.

I pinched off a headache. Nothing I said would change her mind; I could try knocking her out, but she was already halfway to death's door. 'Fine,' I muttered. 'But stay behind me and don't get in my way.'

She bowed and I rolled my eyes. If this all went tits up, I'd only have myself to blame and Keres' blood to mop up. But this wasn't just about Keres, it was about Thane, too. I shook my head, then returned to the door.

I was almost certain that Jimmy Leighton wasn't home; if he hadn't noticed intruders in his house by now, he had cotton-wool for brains and sludge in his ears. Even so I took my time, stepping carefully and keeping a close eye for any magic wards or booby traps.

The small bathroom opposite was clean, tidy and smelling faintly of bleach. Next to it was a cupboard containing neatly folded towels and sheets. Jimmy Leighton certainly wasn't a slob.

I padded down the hallway with Keres on my heels. Although the kitchen was old-fashioned, with wooden cupboards stained an unnatural shade of brown that had gone out of fashion decades ago, it was also very clean. And empty. Next to it a set of stairs led both upwards and downwards. Given the choice of peeking into some neat bedrooms or venturing down to a creepy basement, there was no decision to make.

Keres found a light switch and flicked it on. 'Behind me,' I growled. 'At all times.'

'Yes, ma'am.'

We descended. The stairs were carpeted, muffling the sound of our footsteps. I wondered if Jimmy Leighton's house included a basement door that led to the underground vampire city – at that point it wouldn't have surprised me – but the stairway took us into a large room lined with lots of shelves. There were no more doorways.

'There are so many boxes,' Keres breathed. 'They look as if they're made out of…'

'Bone,' I finished. Bin hadn't been exaggerating: there were hundreds of them and many of them were labelled. I saw labels for numerous plants and animals but there were others, just as Bin had described. Oh God.

According to these labels, Jimmy Leighton had stolen the

magic souls from about fifty people. With a sinking feeling, I realised that Thane's box wouldn't be here yet. If Leighton hadn't been home all night, he would still be carrying it. We were too damned early.

Keres gave a strangled gasp. 'Kit.'

I turned to see her reaching for one of the boxes. 'Don't touch anything until we've established there are no traps,' I began but I was too late: she was already holding a box with *Ban sith* printed in neat cursive script on the side.

She turned it over and held it up, her eyes wide. 'Is this it?' she asked. 'Is this me?'

'I don't know – but don't open it,' I warned her. 'We don't know what's in there or how it is contained – and we certainly don't know what will happen if we open it. I think we need to...' I halted mid-sentence.

Keres opened her mouth to speak but I darted towards her and pressed a hand over her mouth. A moment later, we heard a creak from the staircase. I slowly withdrew my hand and Keres stepped back while I slid my dagger out for a second time.

The stairs creaked again. I cocked my head and listened hard: there was more than one person coming towards us. If Jimmy Leighton wasn't working alone, this would be far, far harder. I stiffened.

Then an oddly familiar female voice called out. 'Aha! I knew it!'

# TWENTY-NINE

When Slasher walked into the room, her eyes glittering and triumphant, I was genuinely astonished. She'd been in on this damned business from the beginning? Unbelievable.

Then I saw who had followed her down the stairs. That wasn't Jimmy Leighton, it was Arthur bloody Dinsbury. Suddenly I knew exactly why they were there. Those absolute idiots would ruin everything.

'So you're in this together,' Slasher crowed. 'I suspected as much. I knew there was more to you than meets the eye.'

Uh-huh. I studied her as I wondered how to play this situation. Bizarrely, although Slasher was dressed in black from head to toe, she was wearing the same scarlet lipstick; it wasn't yet six o'clock in the morning, she was on a complicated spying mission – and she had perfectly applied lippy. That showed true dedication to the cause of make-up.

I found my voice. 'Let me guess,' I said. 'You decided to gang up and stake out Keres. You followed her here.'

'It's as well that we did!' Dinsbury nodded at the dagger in my hand. 'You're going to kill that poor bugger Jimmy Leighton, aren't you? You're in this murder business. You're planning to be a killer, not a cat lady!'

*Oh, if only he knew.* 'You've misunderstood this situation,' I began calmly.

'I don't think we have!' Slasher yelled. 'And don't try anything. My husband knows exactly where we are. If anything happens to us, you'll be hunted down in an instant!'

I winced. 'Keep your voice down!'

'I will not! I don't care what sort of weapon you're wielding, I will not stay quiet. You've been caught bang to rights!'

Nothing about this was good. Leighton could return at any moment. I returned the dagger to its sheath. 'The weapon has gone. Now please, indoor voices – in fact, indoor whispers.'

'She's holding something,' Dinsbury said. 'That *thing* behind you has a weapon too.'

'It's not a weapon.' I gritted my teeth. 'And she's not a thing.'

'Do it, Arthur,' Slasher hissed. 'Use it!'

He reached into his pocket and withdrew a black-linen bag about two inches wide. My heart sank; I already had a bad feeling about what was inside it.

Dinsbury cleared his throat and held it up. 'This,' he declared, 'is death powder.'

*Thank goodness.* I relaxed slightly. 'Really.' My voice was flat.

He smacked his lips together. 'Really.'

'It's fresh,' Slasher said. 'I got it from the witchery store where I work yesterday.'

I held my patience. 'If you work there you should know that death powder almost never works.'

'Of course it works!'

I raised an eyebrow. 'Really? One pinch of powder applied to someone's skin and they suddenly die? Don't you think that if it had any effect then lots of people would use it? You must know that nobody buys that stuff.'

'Because it's dangerous!' she spat.

'No, because it's next to useless,' I said patiently. 'The worst you'll get is a mild rash.'

'So why is it called death powder if it doesn't cause death?'

'Because it kills common sense,' I muttered under my breath. 'Look, let's all take a beat and...'

'Drop that damned box!' Dinsbury shouted at Keres.

Slasher immediately matched his energy. 'Drop it!' she shrieked. She ran forward, pushing past me to get to her. I lunged for Slasher as she lunged for the bone box and tried to wrestle it from Keres' hands.

'Stop it!' Keres screamed. 'It's mine! It's *me*!'

I grabbed Slasher's arm and hauled her back just as she gained a decent grip on the box, then for one strange moment everything seemed to stand still. Keres' face was a rictus mask of fear and Slasher's wasn't much different. Arthur Dinsbury was holding aloft his bag of silly powder.

Slasher tried to grasp the box as I wrenched at her arm, and in the confusion it slipped from Keres' fingers and fell to the floor, breaking into shards and releasing what was inside it.

The ban sith cried out sharply and fell to her knees, but it was already too late. A strange mixture, not quite a liquid and not quite a gas, was leaking from the broken box. It was sliding across the floor and rising up at the same time, as if it couldn't make up its mind what it was.

It certainly didn't look like the black miasmic goop that had been left behind after Leighton had performed his magic thefts. It glittered and sparkled and contained threads of black, royal purple, iridescent yellow and glowing green.

This was magic; this was the ban sith power that had been ripped from Keres' body – and it was leaking everywhere.

Keres threw herself towards the substance and tried to gather it up. One tendril had already snaked towards Arthur Dinsbury's foot and was coiling around his ankle and his shin; another had reached Slasher and, horrifyingly, was entering her body via her open, lipsticked mouth.

I looked down as a thin ribbon attached itself to my arm. My skin tingled and I realised my skin was absorbing the power. Bloody hell.

Slasher was choking, while Arthur Dinsbury was slapping violently at his leg as he tried to beat the substance away. I scratched vigorously at my arm, but I knew that some of Keres' magic was already seeping into me. It was only a fraction of her power because most of it was being reabsorbed into her body, but it was still magic that didn't belong to me and that I didn't want.

'Get off!' Dinsbury roared. 'Get off me!'

Slasher wheezed. 'I can't breathe! Help me. *Help* me!'

Keres was smiling beatifically, her expression one of pure ecstasy. 'Mine,' she whispered to herself. 'Me.'

And suddenly a fourth voice entered the mix. 'Who the fuck are you lot and what are you doing in my house?'

I looked up. Oh. Jimmy Leighton was home.

I stopped caring about the unfamiliar magic soaking into my skin and sprang to the far corner where hopefully I'd be behind him when he came into the room. With three mostly innocent people here, the game had changed and I had to react appropriately.

If Leighton had any nous he'd lock us in until he found a magical grenade to toss in and end us all, but I doubted he was used to confronting his victims. Hopefully the shock of finding four people inside his home would be enough to encourage him to come into the basement to see who we were. He would also want to protect his bone boxes – and their gruesome contents.

When he clumped down the last few stairs and barrelled towards Keres, I knew my guess had been right. 'What are you doing?' he demanded. 'That's my box! That's my magic!'

Keres was still smiling broadly – and that was chilling, considering the circumstances. 'No,' she murmured. 'It's mine. It's all mine.' She touched her chest and gazed at Leighton as he clenched his fists and prepared to swing at her. 'I am whole once again.'

'Fuck you!' he shrieked. 'Fuck you!' He punched her on the side of the head and she went reeling.

My dagger was already back in my hand but I hadn't yet moved in Leighton's direction. I had to get this right; an ill-thought-out move might ruin everything. Unfortunately getting my moves right was easier said than done given the presence of both Arthur Dinsbury and Slasher.

Slasher, whose choking fit appeared to have been more psychological than physical, was staring open-mouthed at Leighton. 'Beautiful,' she said. 'So beautiful.'

Then Dinsbury got in on the act. The tendrils of magic around his leg had almost disappeared and he was gazing at the bearded, thieving bastard with genuine awe. 'I've never seen anything like it in my life.' He reached forward as if to stroke Leighton.

*What the hell...?* Then I saw what they were seeing.

Jimmy Leighton, resident of Danksville, son of witch and minor druid, stealer of souls, destroyer of lives, was glowing. I couldn't think of any other way to describe it. A silvery light that resembled nothing I'd seen before in my life was emanating from his pores.

Something deep inside tugged at me; a deep desire was forming in my gut and I wasn't sure I could quash it.

'You broke into my house!' Leighton howled. 'You destroyed my box!' He raised his leg and kicked Keres then rounded on

Dinsbury and smacked him in the face before taking a flick knife from his pocket and releasing the blade to wave it in Slasher's face. 'You bastards! You've tainted my collection!'

Slasher didn't look at the knife, she just smiled tenderly and opened her mouth. It wasn't a scream that escaped her lips or a cry for help but a song. I winced: she was mostly tone deaf.

Her lack of singing ability didn't affect Arthur Dinsbury. Within a few seconds, he'd added his baritone voice to hers. Then, despite the attack she'd received, Keres joined in from the floor. A similar sound involuntarily left my own lips.

All four of us raised our voices, gaining in pitch and tenor with every beat. The sound was discordant but that didn't matter; I could no more have stopped singing than I could have stopped my heart from beating. It was extraordinary.

Suddenly I realised what was happening: we were singing the skirl of Jimmy Leighton's impending death. We could all see it coming and we couldn't stop it from happening.

Leighton snarled, 'Shut up! Shut the fuck up!'

We sang louder.

The silly man didn't understand what the rest of us had already recognised. He thrust his pocket knife towards Slasher's throat but it was too short and blunt to cause any real damage. The woman put up no defence but even so Leighton only scratched her skin; obviously close combat wasn't his forte. It was one thing to attack someone from a distance, it was another to try and take their life when you could feel the warmth of their breath.

He tried throwing all his hatred and rage into his voice instead of his blade. 'I'll rip your magic from you. I'll leave you as husks of people. Once I'm done, there'll be nothing left of you. You'll be useless hunks of flesh!'

I smiled, changed key and sang more loudly, as did the others. Leighton reached into his pockets again and this time produced a small grey sphere that throbbed with dark magic. There were sticky patches on its surface, traces of the same nasty gloop that had been left on the rooftops of Coldstream.

He held the sphere in both his hands and started to murmur an incantation.

Something sharp twisted in the centre of my chest as if a thin corkscrew had been thrust through my ribcage. I knew the others felt the same because the skirl of our voices faltered.

Panic lit Keres' eyes for the first time since the bone box had smashed at her feet.

'What?' Slasher stepped backwards. 'What are you doing?'

Arthur Dinsbury's hands clutched his chest and he gave a strange noise that was half song, half croak. As I watched, he scrabbled at his shirt in growing panic. The drawstring linen bag was still looped around his thumb.

I pushed away the pain in my chest, and the urge to shriek and sing, and smiled. 'He wants to try and kill us all,' I said. 'He'll reach inside and yank out our magic. He'll take what makes us what we are and leave us with nothing.'

'You bet your fucking arse I will,' Leighton snarled, breaking his incantation. 'My collection is just about to grow even larger. I have plenty of boxes waiting for you.'

I tightened my grip on my knife hilt. There was a sudden loud thump as Slasher slid to the floor. Keres' eyes were rolling back in her head. 'The powder, Arthur,' I whispered. 'Use the death powder.'

At first I wasn't sure he'd heard me but then, with an effort, he removed his hands from his chest. He managed to open the little black bag and throw it in Leighton's direction. It smacked the bastard in the chest then fell to the floor.

Tears of pain streaming down her cheeks, Slasher reached for it. She hauled herself up to her feet and tossed the powdery contents into Leighton's face. A moment later, she collapsed again.

I was already moving to the centre of the room. Leighton saw me coming. He turned to me, rage and desperation glittering in his eyes. 'You,' he spat. 'You resisted me before. What are you?'

I opened my mouth and answered him with a high-pitched shriek that should have impressed even Keres.

Then I stabbed him in the chest.

'Where's the wolf?' I asked. 'Where did you put the wolf soul you stole a few hours ago?'

He didn't answer, though his eyes flicked in the direction of the staircase. That was enough for me. I twisted my curved blade hard enough to be absolutely sure.

In the very moment that Jimmy Leighton's heart stopped beating, the overwhelming urge inside me to sing and shriek at the top of my lungs vanished. He was dead. My skirl was no longer required.

# THIRTY

Keres was moaning faintly from the corner of the room. I glanced at Slasher and Dinsbury; their eyes were closed but they wouldn't stay that way.

I turned to Leighton's body. The grey sphere had dropped to the floor by his side. I left it where it was then raised his arm and draped it across his chest to conceal the stab wound. I wiped the blade of my curved dagger and returned it to its sheath.

Keres was the first to recover fully. There was a large bruise on the side of her cheek and she was moving stiffly, but the return of her ban sith voice was more than enough to spur her into speedy consciousness.

I helped her to her feet and looked into her eyes. 'Follow my finger,' I ordered, moving it from left to right. 'You might be concussed.' She did as I asked. 'What's your name?' I demanded.

'Keres Johnson.'

'What are you?'

She smiled. 'A ban sith. And I'm fucking proud of it.'

She would be alright, but I was still squinting at her. 'I don't think that all your magic has returned to you.'

'It's enough – more than enough. I'm fine now. I'm myself again.'

'You're sure?'

Keres nodded. 'Oh yes.' She gave me a long, very direct look. 'I can see what you've done, Kit McCafferty,' she said. 'I can see what you are.'

I took a wary step backwards. She placed her finger to her lips and smiled again, although this time it was tinged with sadness.

Slasher groaned and sat up. Despite all she'd been through, her scarlet lipstick hadn't smudged or smeared. Magical setting spray, I guessed; whatever it was, it was extraordinary.

She rubbed the back of her neck, looked around and turned pale when she saw Jimmy Leighton's body. She glanced at her hands and the empty black-linen bag she was holding, then she swallowed.

'It's okay,' I said quickly, in an attempt to keep her calm. 'The threat has gone.'

Arthur Dinsbury stirred and immediately touched his chest. He gulped in air and passed a hand in front of his eyes. 'What was that?' he whispered. 'What the hell happened?'

I gave them a quick precis; it was the least they deserved. 'Jimmy Leighton has been attacking people and ripping the magic out of their bodies. Keres was one of his victims.'

Dinsbury looked blank. 'Who's Keres?'

I just managed to avoid rolling my eyes.

'I am,' Keres said.

He looked down at his shoes. 'Oh.'

'We came here to confront Leighton,' I continued, 'then you showed up. He came home and tried to take our magic souls. Fortunately he didn't succeed.'

'I threw that powder in his face,' Slasher whispered.

Arthur Dinsbury turned to her. 'I helped.'

I watched them both but was careful to say nothing.

'We did what we had to do,' he added more firmly.

Slasher nodded. 'I already knew he would die. That's why...' she flicked a glance towards Keres '...that's why I was singing.'

'We were all singing,' I said, trying to be supportive.

Slasher didn't notice. 'That stuff that came from the box,' she said to Keres. 'That was your magic, wasn't it?'

'I think so,' Keres replied in a small voice.

'It's in us now? Forever? Will we be like you?'

'I don't know.' She shrugged helplessly. 'I have no idea.'

Slasher looked at Dinsbury. 'I think I wouldn't mind so much if we are. When I knew what was happening to that man ... when I saw what was inside him, I knew it would be...' Her voice trailed off.

'Beautiful,' Arthur Dinsbury said. 'Cold and terrifying but beautiful, too.' Death wasn't always beautiful, of course, but nobody needed to hear me say that aloud.

Slasher walked unsteadily towards Keres and held out her hand 'My name is Suzanne.' I supposed that counted as an apology in her world.

Keres was a better person than I was. She shook Suzanne's hand warmly. 'Hi,' she said. 'It's nice to meet you.'

Arthur Dinsbury did the same. 'We should get out of here,' he said, when the awkwardness between the three of them became too much. 'Call the MET or something.'

'Good idea,' I said briskly. I pointed to the staircase. 'Lead the way.'

As soon as Dinsbury and Suzanne had left, Keres grabbed my elbow. 'You let them think that powder killed him, but it was you. You ended that man's life.'

'I'm not sorry he's dead.'

'Neither am I.'

I nodded. 'The truth about how Jimmy Leighton died will soon be revealed, but it won't do those two any harm to believe that they killed a man for a few hours. Absorbing some of your magic has altered their perspective, and believing they're responsible for the end of someone's life will solidify their new outlook.' Or so I hoped.

'I don't suppose your neighbours will think of you as capable of killing,' Keres added. 'He was a fucking bastard,' she whispered.

I looked at the white bone boxes that surrounded us, the boxes of death. 'That will be even more true when the full extent of his actions come to light.'

Keres glanced at his corpse. 'Why did he do this?'

'We'll probably never know, except that he was a nasty wanker who enjoyed other people's suffering and liked collecting weird shit.'

Keres pursed her lips then she shrugged. From the top of the stairs, there was a very loud miaow followed by another and another and another and another. 'I told you lot to stay outside!' I called.

Keres smiled. 'Maybe it's time you introduced me properly to your furry family.' Maybe it was.

Back on the ground floor, I glared at the five cats, scolded them all in turn – and then fussed over each one in the manner of their choosing. Keres held back nervously, but when She Who Loves Sunbeams padded up and nudged her shoe with her pink nose, she crouched down and offered her a pat. Soon He Who Crunches Bird Bones, He Who Must Sleep and He Who Roams Wide had joined her.

She Without An Ear stayed where she was. Frankly I'd have been concerned if she hadn't.

I picked up the backpack in Jimmy Leighton's hallway and

found three bone boxes inside. Only one had a label: *Lone wolf.* I clasped it tightly. I was holding Thane's wolf in my hands.

He would be alright. *We* would all be alright.

'We need to get out of here,' I said. 'I have to get this to Thane as soon as possible.' I took a couple of steps towards the front door then stopped. Hmm.

Keres looked at me curiously. 'Is everything okay, Kit?'

'Yep. Just … give a minute. I need to fetch something else from the basement.'

He Who Crunches Bird Bones miaowed. 'It's okay,' I told him. 'I won't be long.' I knew what I was doing.

I DIDN'T WAIT outside Leighton's house with Keres, Suzanne and Arthur Dinsbury. The news of a dead body in circumstances such as these would bring Captain Montgomery and other members of MET running. Montgomery knew where I lived and he'd find me when he needed me. My immediate priority was my werewolf.

The moment I stepped across the threshold of my home, I knew that Thane was alert and conscious – mostly because I could hear him yelling at Tiddles through the bedroom door. 'I'm fine! Get out of the way and let me leave!' Several seconds passed. 'Goddamnit, Tiddles!'

I smiled. That ginger cat was very impressive. It was tempting to linger in the hallway and continue to listen but it wouldn't be fair. I knocked on the door and called, 'It's Kit. Can I come in?'

I heard a shuffling sound. 'Yes! Come and rescue me from this damned ginger monster!'

I opened the door and stepped inside. Tiddles was on all

fours, her tail whipping from side to side, her ears flat against her head and her claws at the ready.

'I am *not* in denial about what's happened to me, Kit,' Thane said as soon as I walked in.

I gazed at his face. He looked better than when I'd left now that the initial shock had worn off and he'd had some sleep, but without the return of his wolf soul that recovery could only be temporary.

His tone softened. 'I'm not pretending that everything is hunky dory but I feel alright. Neither you nor Tiddles can make me stay in this room like some sort of invalid.'

'You should give your cat more credit,' I said. 'She couldn't stand to be in the same room as Keres because of the magical residue left inside her after her ban sith voice was stolen, yet your wolf has been taken and Tiddles has been alone with you with the door closed for a couple of hours. Whoever thinks that feline loyalty doesn't exist ought to get themselves a Tiddles of their own.'

She purred briefly.

Thane glared. 'I cannot believe you're on her side.'

'Her side is your side.' I looked down at the cat. 'You may stand down now.'

Tiddles twitched her nose then she blinked at me and sat down.

'Unbelievable,' Thane huffed. 'You know that trow is here? He's asleep in the spare room. I can hear him snoring.'

'You should be sleeping, too.'

'It's daylight.' He squared his shoulders. 'I don't need to sleep. Let's wake Bin up and find out where this magic-stealing bastard lives.'

'Let him sleep. Bin has already done what we asked of him.'

Thane's green eyes widened. 'Great. What are we waiting for? We can go now. I'm ready – I feel good. We can take care of this bastard and retrieve my wolf magic, Keres' voice and every other poor bugger's powers.'

I tilted my head. 'Uh...'

'We shouldn't delay, Kit.'

I removed the backpack I'd taken from Jimmy Leighton's house from my shoulders, opened it and took out the bone box labelled *Lone Wolf*. I held it out to him.

Thane stared at me. 'You've already done it.'

'Yep.'

'You've saved the day, retrieved the magic and...'

'Killed the bad guy.' I nodded. 'Yep.'

His shoulders dropped. 'Oh.'

I understood his disappointment because I'd have felt the same if I were him. He ran a hand across his head and managed a wry smile. 'I never thought I'd be the one in distress who needed rescuing by a fair maiden.'

'Stick around,' I said cheerfully. 'I'm sure you'll get to return the favour one of these days.'

A low growl rumbled in his chest. 'You can bet every curl of your purple hair that I'm sticking around.'

'Good.' I raised my eyebrows. 'You're not moving in, though.'

'I wouldn't dream of it.'

'There won't be marriage. Or a ring.'

Thane held up his hands. 'Kit, I get it. I'm the same as you. Independence is to be cherished – but I'll still be close by for as long as you want me.'

I was beginning to suspect that would be for a long time.

He looked at the box in my hands. 'Can I have my wolf back?'

I handed it over. 'Wait until I'm out of the room – Tiddles too – then open it. That's all you need to do. Your wolf magic will find its way into your body. It knows where it belongs.'

The relief in his expression was stark but there was still a question in his eyes.

I was fully aware of what he needed to know. 'There were many more boxes. Several were labelled as belonging to were-wolves. It didn't say which pack they were from but…' I took a second box out of my backpack and held it up. 'I left most of them where they were for the MET to deal with, but I took this one.'

Thane gazed at the neatly printed label. 'Alpha wolf,' he said. He swallowed. 'You think that box contains the wolf magic belonging to Ashina Barrow? To my mother?'

'It seems likely.' Suddenly I felt as if I were on shaky ground and my voice dropped even lower. 'You know I'm very capable of being a hard-arsed bitch when the situation calls for it.'

Thane looked at me and I looked at him. Several seconds passed before he responded. 'Yes,' he said eventually. 'I know.'

# THIRTY-ONE

I suspected Captain Montgomery was standing stiffly to one side because he was worried about getting cat hair on his smart clothes. I didn't take offence; I simply signed my statement and handed it to him.

'The sphere,' I said. 'The … thing that Leighton used to extract magic. Where is it?'

'It's been destroyed,' Montgomery said. 'It's too dangerous to keep around even as evidence. We're looking into how he created it in the first place. We can find nothing to suggest there are any other such spheres in existence and we don't expect any further occurrences of magic soul theft now he's gone.'

'I certainly hope not,' I murmured. 'I suppose it helps that Jimmy Leighton has taken the secret of the sphere with him to his grave.'

Montgomery eyed me. 'Indeed. Although it's interesting that dead bodies seem to accrue when you are around, Ms McCafferty.'

I tried – and probably failed – to look innocent. 'If you want to arrest me for my actions, Captain, I understand.' I held out my hands to indicate I was ready for his handcuffs. Both Thane and Keres stared at me. Fortunately they were too sensible to say anything, although their expressions spoke volumes.

'That will not be necessary, Ms McCafferty.' He paused. 'This time.'

I blinked in mock disbelief at the implication that there would be another time when our paths would cross. Then I thought of something else. 'Captain,' I said, 'if someone were to seriously consider becoming an adjunct to the MET, would any training programmes be available?'

Thane's eyebrows shot upwards though Montgomery only looked mildly amused. 'An adjunct? One is either in the MET or is not. There is no such thing as an *adjunct*.' He folded his arms. 'Certainly not an *official* adjunct. The Magical Enforcement Team must abide by very strict rules, you know that. There are limits to what we are allowed to do and many areas where we cannot tread.'

I held up my hands in mock surrender. 'I was only curious.'

His eyes gleamed. 'Of course, there are many reasons as to why an *unofficial* adjunct might be useful. I'll look into training programmes. It might not be a bad idea.' He produced a sheet of paper. 'To illustrate my point, this is a list of recent burglaries and home invasions in Coldstream. I've cross-checked it against those who have also reported the violent sundering of their magic souls.'

'Let me guess,' Thane said. 'No matches, no connections, No links.'

I grimaced. In my previous career mistakes were never an option, but as far as Bin was concerned I'd made several, and I'd probably done the same with Tobias Hollow. Only time would tell with that ornery bastard.

'Nary a one.' Montgomery pursed his lips then his eyes crinkled kindly. 'In my experience, investigative failures and mistakes narrow down possibilities and help lead to eventual success.' He waved the list of names. 'You have a way of looking at situations that can shed new light on old problems, Ms McCafferty.'

I tilted my head. 'Was that a compliment, Captain?' From the kitchen table, He Who Crunches Bird Bones purred loudly.

Montgomery sniffed. 'Don't let it go to your head.' He nodded. 'I'll take my leave. For now.'

I walked him to the door and smiled as he veered around She Who Loves Sunbeams, who had elected to take advantage of the morning sunshine and plonk herself in the middle of the garden path. Then I turned to Keres. 'Are you ready to go?'

She shouldered her bulging bag. Thane gave her a tight hug. 'Stay safe,' he murmured. 'And stay in touch.'

'You're not coming?' she asked.

He sent me a brief sideways glance and shook his head. 'No. I've got to find a new place to stay. My old flat is … unavailable. I need to find somewhere new that will suit Tiddles and me.'

I frowned. I hadn't seen Tiddles for a couple of hours and I suspected that meant trouble, though Thane's ginger cat had proved she could take care of herself. Most of the time.

'Come on,' I said to Keres. 'Let's make a move. Would you like me to help you with your bag?'

Her expression softened. 'No, I can manage it, Kit. Thank you.'

Fair enough. Not every facet of our character was open to change and it appeared that Keres was still struggling to accept help, but we were all works in progress in our own way. I stepped back and allowed her to take the lead.

Dave was waiting by the gate with a scowl on his face. 'You're leaving, then?' he asked gruffly, even though he knew the answer.

'It's time,' Keres said. 'Thank you so much for all you've done for me, Dave.'

His scowl turned ferocious but, unable to stop himself, he reached forward and pulled her into a bear hug. 'You look after yourself, you hear? I'll come over to Barton Street next weekend for a visit but if you need anything in the meantime, you get in touch.'

Keres sniffed into his chest. 'I will.'

Eventually, they parted. Dave's bottom lip jutted out and the creases in his forehead were deeper than ever when we turned away and walked down my narrow street. I suspected he would stay by the gate until long after she had disappeared.

As soon as we reached Slasher's – or rather Suzanne's – house, there was a cry of delight. Kate, her daughter, flew over the fence in a move that I heartily approved of then zipped towards Keres, pigtails bouncing behind her. 'I made you a goodbye card!'

She thrust a folded sheet of paper into Keres' hands. There was a scribbled drawing of a skull and crossbones on the front. Okay, then. 'Are you going to sing now? Are we going to die?'

'Not today.' Keres smiled as she held up the card. 'Thank you for this. It's beautiful.'

'My mum says she hopes you'll come and visit some time,' Kate burbled.

My eyes met Suzanne's as she hovered by her front door.

'And I hope you will, too,' Kate said. 'Mum says that next time you can come and have some cake with us.'

Suzanne smiled.

A few doors down, Arthur Dinsbury gazed at us for a long moment before lifting a hand towards Keres, either in greeting or farewell. Probably both. Not for the first time, I wondered if the three of us still possessed vestiges of Keres' magic. I guessed we'd find out soon enough.

'I'd like that a lot,' Keres told her.

Harvey Johnson was waiting at the end of the road. He was pale faced and sweating but he broke into a beaming grin when he caught sight of Keres. She rolled her eyes but she was smiling. 'I thought we agreed to meet at Crackendon Square,' she said to her husband, sounding faintly exasperated.

'That was the plan. But this is Danksville.' He glanced around nervously. 'I thought I should meet you here instead. There are all sorts of strange people in this neighbourhood – sorry, I don't mean you, Ms McCafferty. I don't mean any offence.'

'None taken,' I replied while Keres' right eye twitched.

Harvey took her hand and squeezed it. 'I'm so happy you're coming home. I planned to get you flowers,' he said, 'but I can actually go one better.' He reached into his pocket. 'I found it wedged down the side of the kitchen cabinets. It must have fallen down there by accident.' He unfurled his fingers and revealed a glinting gold ring. 'It wasn't stolen at all.'

Keres allowed Harvey to slide it onto her ring finger. 'It still fits,' she said and leaned forward to kiss him on the cheek. He crowed with delight and pulled her into his arms.

I left them to it: the last thing either of them needed was the likes of me hovering around them. Nipping across the road, I jumped on the first tram that appeared.

I didn't know whether Keres and Harvey would last the distance, given that her instinct when the shit had hit the fan had been to run away from him, but the couple deserved the space and the freedom to find out without interruptions from a nosy cat lady. My work as far as Keres was concerned was finished.

Besides, I mused, as the tram trundled away, I had a far more serious errand to run before all this business could be wrapped up.

Unlike last time, I didn't have to beg for admittance into the Barrow werewolf stronghold. I had an appointment and they were expecting me. Hell, they *wanted* to see me. Desperately.

Two smiling werewolves wearing full kilted regalia were at the front gate as I approached. Clearly the clan was making a point: *We're all fine here and we're open for business.* I enjoyed the sight of a man in a kilt as much as the next woman so I didn't complain, and I had to admit that it was pleasing to have the red carpet rolled out for me; it was a rare occurrence.

Both werewolves bowed and greeted me. 'Welcome, Ms McCafferty,' intoned the one on the left. 'We are pleased to have you here.'

Uh-huh.

The wolf on the right smoothly picked up the thread. 'Alpha Ashina Barrow is waiting for you inside. I will show you the way.'

I inclined my head as if I hadn't been unceremoniously thrown out of these very same doors only a few days earlier. 'Thank you,' I murmured. 'That would be wonderful.'

'May I offer you some iced water?'

'No, thank you.'

'Room-temperature water?'

'No, thank you.'

'English breakfast tea?'

This could go on for some while. 'I don't want anything to eat or drink,' I said. 'Just take me to your leader.'

If the wolf was amused by my clichéd words, he didn't show it. 'Of course. Right this way.'

We stepped through the gates and into the small courtyard. It already looked like a different place. The rubbish had been cleared away and the weeds had been uprooted. I nodded approvingly as someone called out from the rooftop to my left. I glanced up and spotted two workmen carefully replacing the broken window.

The wolf beside me followed my gaze. 'A game of football that went wrong,' he said wryly.

I smiled faintly, then he led me inside.

There were very few circumstances under which I would have openly entered the Barrow wolf stronghold on my own. For that matter, there were very few circumstances when I'd have openly entered *any* werewolf stronghold without extensive back-up. Right here, right now, however, I definitely had the upper hand. No wolf, not even Thane's hot-headed half-brother would lift a finger against me.

Captain Montgomery had returned the bone boxes and their painfully extracted magic to their original owners – apart from the box belonging to Ashina Barrow. I still had that one. The Barrow alpha wouldn't receive her wolf until she'd satisfied my conditions. It wasn't fair, but I didn't care. Thane was on board with my actions and that was all that mattered.

I was taken through a long hallway with wooden floors and dust-free corners to reach a large anteroom with closed double doors at the far end. The wolf gestured to a chair set against a wall. 'I will inform Alpha Ashina that you are here,' he said. 'Please wait one moment.'

I didn't bother sitting down; instead I walked over to the wall opposite. Doubtless the real reason for the delay was to give me time to peruse the large display of photographs of important Barrow werewolves from the past eight decades. Naturally there was no picture of Thane, though young Cayden was deemed important enough for a spot.

I glanced at the picture of Ashina Barrow then flicked my narrowed gaze towards Mark Barrow, Thane's dead uncle. There were laughter lines around his eyes and mischievous amusement in his face. He looked friendly, approachable and kind. I snorted derisively and turned my back on him. It was a tiny rebellion but I felt better for it.

The double doors swung open and a loud male voice invited me to enter. As I walked into the room, I absently plucked at some strands of cat hair that had seemingly glued themselves to my sleeve and allowed my peripheral vision to do my work for me. The room was large, well-appointed and dominated by a large chair in the centre. There were antique cabinets and unremarkable paintings on the walls. There was also a window ajar on the right-hand side.

Five werewolves, including Cayden Barrow, were present. Ashina Barrow was in the centre, seated in the chair with a blanket draped over her. She was very pale, sunken-eyed and almost skeletal. Clearly she'd been struggling with the loss of her wolf for some time.

'You will understand, Ms McCafferty,' she said in a papery whisper, 'why I do not get up to greet you.'

I met her eyes; they were the same vivid green as Thane's although her hair colour was brown rather than coppery red. 'Sure,' I said with a dismissive wave of my hand. 'Stay where you are.'

The man to Ashina Barrow's left, whom I immediately recognised as my old pal Grizzly, straightened his shoulders and spoke up. 'I cannot help noticing that you are empty-handed,' he said.

I deliberately played dumb. 'I was told that weapons wouldn't be allowed. I gave my word that I wouldn't bring any.' He glared. 'Oh,' I said. 'Are you saying that I should have brought a gift? Some flowers perhaps?'

Grizzly wasn't the only member of the Barrow household who looked pissed off.

'He's saying,' snapped Cayden, 'that you should have brought the box containing my mother's wolf.'

I smiled. 'So you could wrap your hands around my throat and wrest it from me?' I clicked my tongue. 'That wouldn't be a very clever move on my part, would it?'

'I apologise for my son's actions,' Ashina Barrow interjected. 'That should not have happened.' For someone knocking on death's door, she was managing remarkably well.

'Although you are not blameless yourself, Ms McCafferty,' she said, eyeing me with a sharp coldness that continued to belie her immediate health problems. 'We have investigated you and we know that you are friendly with my other son, regardless of what you may have suggested during your last visit here.'

I tilted my head. 'Oh, I'm not just *friendly* with Thane.' I allowed my smile to extend until I was grinning ear to ear. 'He's been in my house. He's slept in my bed. I've kissed him.' I paused. 'Not just on his mouth. I've seen every inch of him naked.' I didn't look away from Ashina Barrow. 'Including the deep scars on his back.'

She stiffened. Doubtless she was little more than a shadow of the woman she usually was, but she wasn't without strength. Her green eyes glittered coldly and I felt the temperature in the room drop by several degrees. I looked away, glanced at the open window then returned my gaze to her.

'So it's true then,' she whispered. 'You are here on his behalf. What does he want? Money? Blood? Does he want to see me suffer?'

I was surprised that she didn't click her fingers for mournful violins to accompany her words. Was I supposed to feel sorry for her? 'Thane has no need of your money. He's far richer than the entire Barrow pack.'

'Yeah, right,' Cayden spat sarcastically.

Ashina reached across and placed a trembling hand on his arm. He continued to huff and bristle but he shut up. Small mercies.

'Nor does Thane want blood,' I continued as if Cayden hadn't spoken. 'He has no great desire for vengeance, no matter how much is owed.'

Cayden snarled again; so did Grizzly and the other werewolves, for that matter.

Ashina Barrow flinched. Her reaction was barely perceptible but I noticed it. I licked my lips and lifted my chin. 'In return for the bone box containing your wolf, all I ask is for some information. If you tell me what...'

She interrupted before I could finish my sentence. 'Leave us.' She wasn't talking to me.

Grizzly stiffened but he didn't need to be told twice. He threw a quick glance at Ashina's face then marched out of the room with the other three werewolves beside him.

'You too, Cayden,' Ashina whispered.

'But...'

She didn't raise her voice because she couldn't but her tone was unmistakable. 'Leave. And close the door behind you on your way out.'

Hurt flashed across his face before he nodded and did as he was told. Finally.

As soon as we were alone, I spoke again. 'You were hoping I'd ask for money, weren't you? The right information is far, far more dangerous to you than losing the meagre contents of your bank account.'

Ashina Barrow bared her teeth. 'Name your terms, cat lady.'

It was nice to be properly acknowledged so I curtsied. 'In return for the bone box containing your wolf, you will tell me what happened when Mark Barrow died.' I smiled coldly. 'You will tell me who really killed him.'

Her expression betrayed little. 'Thane was there. He knows better than anyone what happened to Mark.'

'He has no memory of it. Either he has blanked out the trauma of what occurred or,' I paused, 'a memory spell was used on him.'

Ashina Barrow's responding glare was icy. 'I do not appreciate your insinuation.'

I didn't move a muscle except to say, 'I don't care.'

'If my son blanked out what happened it's because he cannot deal with the guilt about what he did.'

I noted that she wasn't saying that Thane *had* killed Mark Barrow. I eyed her dispassionately. 'You are alpha of this pack. You know exactly what happened that night. Give me your word that you will speak the full truth of those events as you understand them and I will return your wolf to you. This offer is non-negotiable. I will make no further compromise.'

Ashina opened her mouth, but before she could form any sort of answer she started to cough and wheeze. There was a rattling in her throat, her skin flushed red and she was forced to clutch her chest and gasp for air.

It wouldn't have been a good outcome for anyone if she'd died at that precise moment but I stayed exactly where I was. Let the cards fall where they may.

A thick vein throbbed in her forehead as she managed to croak out a response. 'No... ...deal. You ... will ... leave ... now.'

I tilted my head and examined her curiously. Huh. Even though it had always been a possibility that she would take this route, it still surprised me. I glanced again at the window; I could feel a faint breeze drifting in from outside, rippling my hair.

'You will die without your wolf,' I said, matter-of-factly.

Ashina didn't flinch. 'So be it.'

I looked at her pallor then into her unwavering green eyes. That was when I knew exactly what had happened. 'It was you,' I said softly. 'You killed Mark Barrow. You murdered your own brother and blamed it on your son.'

'I told you to go.'

'I've met some cold-hearted wankers in my time,' I murmured, 'but you rank at the very top.' I shook my head. Then I turned on my heel and headed for the double doors.

The moment my fingers brushed against the cold metal of the handle, there was a loud feline yowl. It was about time.

I turned around to see a ginger blur as Tiddles vaulted from the window and landed on all fours in front of Ashina's chair. Her fur was on end and her sharp teeth were bared. She meant business.

Thane's mother half-choked, half-laughed. 'A cat?'

'I wouldn't be quite so dismissive if I were you.'

Tiddles extended her claws and growled, more than prepared to go paw to paw with an alpha werewolf. Given Ashina Barrow's condition, Thane's kitten might do her some serious damage.

I waited, prepared to see how this would play out without interference from me. Several seconds passed until Ashina opened her mouth again. This time I had to strain to hear her words. 'She smells of him,' she whispered. 'Almost as much as you do.'

I gazed at her, unsure if she would speak again, but then she said, 'It wasn't my fault. I had to make a choice.'

I froze.

'I had to choose between Thane and the rest of the pack.'

Both Tiddles and I stared at her. Neither of us moved.

'I knew about the beatings – of course I did. I told Mark to stop but he was a law unto himself. I couldn't kick him out of the pack because we needed him. We were weak.'

She drew in a shaky breath. 'We needed someone with his strength in order to survive and not be subsumed by another wolf pack. In a few years, Thane might have been able to take his place but he certainly wasn't ready at fifteen. And my son never had the same sort of steel as Mark.'

'Because Thane is a good guy,' I said.

Her response was cool. 'Sometimes you need a bad guy on your side to succeed.'

I rolled my eyes but Ashina didn't react. 'I could control my brother up to a point but it was getting harder. The night he died we had an argument. He told me he had endured enough.' She laughed harshly. 'He was planning to make a play for alpha. I knew that he would win if he did. What happened after that would be a disaster for everyone, especially Thane. So we argued. We fought.' She sniffed. 'And I won.'

'So why not tell everyone that? You were alpha – you are still alpha. Dealing with someone like Mark was your responsibility. You would have been forgiven.'

'I doubt that. Mark had as many supporters as detractors. If they had learned what I'd done to my own beta – to my own brother – they'd have demanded that I step down.'

I swallowed hard. It was an incredible effort to keep my voice even. 'So this was about maintaining your own position?'

'Don't be naïve! It was about the future of the Barrow pack. The vultures were already circling. I knew we'd barely survive losing Mark. Dissension in the ranks would have finished us off.'

I curled my hands into fists, my fingernails digging painfully into the flesh of my palms. 'Unless you could offer up a sacrificial lamb. Your own son.'

'His exile satisfied the more aggressive and vocal Barrow

wolves. In time I was able to increase my authority over them and matters settled down. I'm not proud of what I did but the Barrows needed to survive. This was about more than Thane, it was about the survival of my pack for the generations to come. As alpha, I didn't have the luxury of caring only about *my* son, I had to care about *everyone*'s sons.'

For fuck's sake. 'Did you use a memory spell on him?'

For a moment she didn't answer then her whisper drifted across the room. 'Yes. I called him to me. I placed the knife in his hands and I cast the spell so he wouldn't remember.'

I half-closed my eyes.

'It was the right thing to do,' she said. 'Thane survived. In the long run, he thrived and so did the Barrow pack. We grew stronger. We were able to put off our enemies and increase our numbers. In the end everyone won.'

'If you believe that,' I said, 'then you're more of a fool than I realised. Memory spells are very dangerous and incredibly expensive – they always have been. You wouldn't have simply had one lying around the place in case you needed it, you'd have had to go out and buy it in advance. You planned Mark Barrow's death and you planned that Thane would be blamed.'

There was a defiant tilt to Ashina's chin. 'I won't deny it – and if I went back to that time, I would make exactly the same decision. I did what was necessary, no matter how much it hurt.' She hesitated. 'How is Thane? Is he happy? Does he ever think of me?'

Tiddles hissed and I wholeheartedly agreed. '*You* don't get to ask those questions.'

This time Ashina Barrow didn't say anything.

'There is a spriggan waiting at a nearby café. Once I give him the nod, he will come here and give you the box containing your wolf. We had a deal and I will keep my end of the bargain.'

I gazed at her. 'If you ever try and contact Thane, if anyone from the Barrow pack ever hurts him or attacks him, if I have the slightest suspicion that you've done anything against him, I will come back here,' I told her. 'And I will kill you. I'm capable of more than I appear.' Tiddles miaowed so I added an extra comment. 'So is the cat.'

She looked at me and I knew she got it. Then I turned and left with Tiddles at my heels.

# EPILOGUE

Four hours later, Thane and I were seated in my garden, sharing a bottle of wine. I'd left a spare glass out for Bin. Once he arose he might enjoy a drink before he returned home to Green Humbleton, and he certainly deserved one. I suspected he'd skedaddle as soon as he could, but I wanted to make sure he knew how grateful I was for his help. The trows had been invaluable in catching Jimmy Leighton.

Although it was too light yet for Bin, all the cats were with us. My motley crew were stretched out together in the day's last patch of warm sunshine, while Tiddles was on Thane's lap offering him the furry comfort he needed. I had spared him no details. He had listened but asked no questions. It was a lot to take in.

'We can tell the world, if you wish,' I said. 'We can set the record straight and clear your name.'

He shook his head. 'I know the truth now. That's enough.'

'Say the word and I'll kill her. And the entire Barrow pack alongside her.' I was only half-joking.

Thane smiled faintly. 'Nah. It's in the past now. We should let sleeping dogs lie.'

From her position on his lap, Tiddles looked up and narrowed her eyes. 'Sorry,' he murmured, scratching her ears. 'We don't need to put a cat among the pigeons. It's all done now. Thank you for finding out the truth, Kit. I don't need anything else. I don't *want* anything else.'

I raised my glass towards him. 'You're the boss.' Tiddles miaowed sharply. 'Stop that,' I told her. 'You're not in charge here, Tiddles, no matter what you might think.'

Naturally, she ignored me. She yawned, stretched out her front paws and miaowed again. I lowered my wine glass without taking a sip and gazed at her as she started to groom herself. She was looking very smug and self-satisfied.

'Are you sure?' I asked, my heart sinking.

Thane frowned. 'What?'

I didn't look at him: my attention was wholly on the ginger cat as I asked her, 'That's the name you choose for yourself?' Her whiskers quivered.

I glanced across the garden and saw that all five of my cats had abandoned their patch of sun. I caught a brief glimpse of She Who Loves Sunbeams vanishing inside where she'd be safely out of the way. I had never thought of my furry brood as cowards but there was a first time for everything.

I looked at Thane. 'What?' he demanded. 'What name has she chosen?'

I bit my lip. Perhaps I was a coward too.

'Kit! Tell me!'

I sighed. Then I gave in to the inevitable and told him.

# AFTERWORD

This is far from the end for Kit McCafferty. Her adventures will continue in 2026 and many more books are planned. The next instalment, Night Maze, will be released in May 2026. Before Kit's next novel, however, there will be a detour with some other Coldstream characters whose own stories demand some attention.

Squib, the first book in The Coldstream Chronicles will be released in January 2026: https://mybook.to/squib  It is available for pre-order now.

# ACKNOWLEDGMENTS

As always, there are many thanks to be made. First of all, to Karen Holmes for her continuing and superlative editing. Her enthusiasm for this series is a genuine thrill and she's a true joy to work with. Jay Villalobos created the cover design for both this book and the series as a whole and has captured both Kit's spirit and that of the cats' with such clarity that I can't wait to see what he comes up with next. I'm also particularly happy to be able to express my gratitude to @chrissyofthevale who has been working on some immense illustrations for The Cat Lady Chronicles and whose inspiring ideas and drawings amaze me every time.

I have a long running relationship with Kara Stebbins and the rest of the Tantor audio team who all deserve mention - and especially Ruth Urquhart who does such a sterling job with her narration and who is so wonderful and picking up loose typos and inconsistencies that have been missed. I'd also like to thank the lovely authors who I meet with online and who always inspire me to do and be better, especially Heather G Harris, Debra Dunbar, Lauretta Hignett, Annabel Chase and Deborah Wilde.

Last, but certainly not least, a special thank you to Scout, Mavis and Lara. Your furry company is always welcome, even when you fall asleep on top of my keyboard.

# ABOUT THE AUTHOR

After teaching English literature in the UK, Japan and Malaysia, Helen Harper left behind the world of education following the worldwide success of her Blood Destiny series of books. She is a professional member of the Alliance of Independent Authors and writes full time, thanking her lucky stars every day that's she lucky enough to do so!

Helen has always been a book lover, devouring science fiction and fantasy tales when she was a child growing up in Scotland.

She currently lives in Edinburgh in the UK with far too many cats (and dogs!) – not to mention the dragons, fairies, demons, wizards and vampires that seem to keep appearing from nowhere.

www.ingramcontent.com/pod-product-compliance
Lightning Source LLC
Chambersburg PA
CBHW050602190726
48283CB00007B/2245